KILLER DOLLS

KILLER DOLLS

NISA SANTIAGO

Killer Dolls. Copyright © 2016 by Melodrama Publishing. All rights reserved. No part of this book may be used or reproduced in any manner whatsoever without written permission except in the case of brief quotations embodied in critical articles or reviews. For information, please address Melodrama Publishing, info@melodramabooks.com.

www.melodramapublishing.com

Library of Congress Control Number: 2015912274
ISBN-13: 978-1620780886

First Edition: October 2015
Mass Market Edition: November 2017

Model Photo: Frank Antonio
Cover Model: Nefertiti

Printed in Canada

Falcon Trails on the Web

To learn more about Falcon or to get detailed information about our more than 10,000 published trails and routes, go to **www.falcontrails.com.**
While there, purchase custom topo maps, view real-time weather, post and review trail reports, and much more.

BOOKS BY NISA SANTIAGO

PROLOGUE

Winter

Aoki had underestimated the bitter temperature. As she bowed her head to her chest, the cold breeze blew right through her shearling coat. She cursed herself for not wearing additional layers of clothing, always opting to put fashion sense before common sense.

Aoki's hair fell loose about her face, tousled, as she walked briskly to her home. She dared to wear her extremely high heels in the winter, but she had to look cute 24-7.

"Ahhhhh!" she yelled out as she slipped and fell to her knees on black ice, scraping both her hands. "Fuck me!"

Part Jamaican, part Japanese, she was beautiful with a unique name, pronounced *A-O-KEE*. She was the perfect eye candy with dark chocolate skin, straight, long jet-black hair, and Asian, but very sad, eyes. She had a small face with delicate features like a baby doll. Her accent, intriguing to the guys, and the ladies too, was slightly Jamaican because of her father's heritage. Aoki was only sixteen years old and stood out like a black swan in a flock of white.

The frigid air quickly seeped up into the vulnerable areas of her winter coat, and soon her petite frame felt quite icy as she hurried home around midnight, after hanging out all night with her friends. She didn't have a curfew and wasn't worried about any punishment raining down on her. Her home was just a house to lay her head and get some sleep, her parents being drug addicts.

She stormed into the house trying to leave the cold outside, however her home didn't provide too much warmth. Once inside the living room, she locked eyes with her parents, Maxwell and Lucy. As usual, they were slouching on the living room couch sharing a crack pipe. Not once did they pay her any attention.

Aoki frowned. She didn't acknowledge them.

Her father had come straight off the boat from Kingston when he was just a boy, and her mother Lucy was from Chiba, a city in Japan. A long time ago, they'd both had prominent lives; now they were society's undesirables— falling deep between the cracks and getting lost in shame and addiction.

Maxwell was sixty-nine, and Lucy was thirty-six. For a drug addict, Maxwell didn't look a day over forty-five, though he was sixty-nine. The two met in Japan when Maxwell, an aging staff sergeant in the army, was stationed there. He had rented a house from her parents. They met and fell in love right away, subsequently marrying a month later. Many thought she married Maxwell as an escape. Lucy was seventeen at the time, and he was fifty. He brought her back to the States, where they had Aoki when Lucy was twenty.

Maxwell was able to pay the mortgage on the house with his disability checks and his police pension. It was purchased long ago when he was viable in society; before the drugs. He'd received an honorable discharge from the military and retired from the NYPD after giving them twenty years.

Lucy was a tiny woman who mostly took the brunt of his rage. For many years she had been contented with being a housewife to her husband, following his every lead. Lucy was Japanese, and culturally the women of Japan were unusually dedicated to their families, especially their husbands. Lucy was raised in a society where women did not seek personal fulfillment through a career. Instead, she got her satisfaction in helping other family members achieve success. She always put her husband first.

For a time, life was good for Aoki. She was living a normal childhood, growing up biracial and beautiful. Then came Maxwell's retirement from law enforcement, which led to his depression, anger, and rage. The drug use went from every so often, to frequently, and it didn't take long for her mother to become addicted as well.

The small three-bedroom house had a putrid smell. Every room was dirty, dishes a week old piled up in the sink, trash overflowed in the kitchen, and clothes, drug paraphernalia, and remnants of carryout were everywhere.

Aoki escaped into her bedroom—the only clean place in the entire house. She made sure of that. She closed her room door, locked it and sighed. Her parents needed rehab.

She found coziness in her little haven. She had a neatly made queen-size bed, one window curtained with a square of starched colorless cotton fabric that drew over the panes by means of a white cord that ran at the top, a tiny dresser, an old-fashioned gilt mirror, and frayed carpeting.

Aoki sat on her bed and started to undress. She was tired. She needed some sleep. Clad in her panties and bra, she climbed under her thin blanket, folded herself into the fetal position, and closed her eyes. For the moment, everything was still and quiet.

Not even a half hour went by before loud screaming awakened her. It was common in her household. Her father was prone to drug-fueled outbursts. She could hear his loud, raspy voice through her bedroom door. He was in a rage. She heard her mother screaming back—almost a shriek. Her high-pitched voice and thick Japanese accent pierced Aoki's ears.

Aoki frowned at their conflict. She shut her eyes and tried to ignore it, but they got louder. Then the shrill screech coming from her mother was like nothing Aoki had ever heard before.

She jumped out of her bed and snatched opened the bedroom door. She rushed into the living room and was horrified at what she saw. Wide-eyed and in shocked, she witnessed her father standing over her mother as he repeatedly stabbed the thin woman in the chest with a pocketknife. Blood was everywhere.

Maxwell went from stabbing his wife in the chest to stabbing her in the neck and face—almost a half dozen times. Right in front of Aoki, he was mutilating her mother.

Aoki stood frozen; she didn't know what to do. Her mother's eyes were lifeless as she lay dying.

Maxwell turned around bug-eyed. He dropped the knife and was transfixed by something. He turned his attention to Aoki, looking edgy, his eyes dancing around the room.

Out of the blue, he exclaimed to Aoki, "What's in ya damn pockets?"

Aoki stood tensely in front of him. The pocketknife was on the floor, near his foot. But her father was still a big man, and he was high and hallucinating.

He started to babble something loud and incoherent about voodoo, hexes, and witches. Maxwell would suddenly start talking out loud as if he was in the middle of a conversation and would carry on with his insane script.

"She really wasn't ya mudda, Aoki, she wasn't," he exclaimed. "She wasn't ya mudda. She was some demon. I saw it. She wanted to hurt us, Aoki. I saw it. I fuckin' saw it!"

Aoki stared down at her dead mother's body.

Her father started babbling something incoherent again. She knew it was time to leave the room.

His eyes glared at her again, and once again he shouted, "What's in ya damn pockets?"

Aoki slowly brought her hands up and showed her father that she wasn't a threat. She had no pockets. She was in her panties and bra. "Nothing," she replied.

Maxwell sat back down near his wife's dead body. He picked up the crack pipe he'd dropped and started smoking crack again.

Aoki snapped out of her daze. She calmly left the room and walked into the kitchen. Something needed to be done. She refused to live in fear in her own home. There was no trace of tears in her eyes. She had no time to weep over her mother's death. She pulled open the kitchen drawer, reached inside, and wrapped her hands around the handle of a serrated knife.

She marched back into the living room, gripping the knife, her eyes narrowed, rigid, cold, and hard. In that moment she knew what had to be done—for her safety, for her survival. The feelings of her heart went into her eyes.

Maxwell was still cradling his crack pipe, puffing every last bit of rock into his system, his wife's body slumped in the corner next to him.

Aoki approached and, without any hesitation, slammed the knife deeply into her father's chest. He jerked from the thrust of the blade sinking into him, and his eyes popped opened.

Aoki pulled out the blade and slammed it into him again. She figured twice would do the trick. She stood up with the knife still in her hand and stepped backwards, her eyes still on her father. She felt no remorse as his blood trickled from the blade. He deserved it.

Maxwell clutched his bloody chest, but surprisingly, he stood up.

Aoki was shocked to see him stand erect, his hand against his chest and his eyes on her like a zombie. She felt he could charge her way at any moment, so she readied herself.

But then Maxwell sat back down, his back against the wall, his knees propped upwards, and he picked up his crack pipe. He added the remaining crack into it, lit it up, and took a strong pull. It was going to be his last high.

What the fuck!

Aoki approached closer, the knife still clutched tightly. She sat across from him and simply watched him die. She began telling her father how he fucked up their lives and how he wasn't shit. She cursed him heatedly. She wanted him to listen as he fought to breathe. Still, there were no tears in her eyes, no remorse for what she had done.

He simply nodded as she confronted him with all of her anger from past years. But, right before the light drained from his eyes, he looked at Aoki. His last words to her were, "Ya ain't gon' be shit, eda."

Both her parents were dead now, and Aoki didn't know what was next.

ONE

The winter sun was shining directly in her face. It was a new day, but nothing felt new in Aoki's life. Last night felt like a nightmare. *Was it real? Did I dream something terrible happened?* The house was quiet.

Aoki stretched and yawned. She then stripped and hopped in the shower. She washed yesterday from her skin and lingered under the cascading warm water, trying to collect her thoughts. After toweling off, she went on her smartphone to answer some social media requests and flirt with a few online cuties before getting dressed.

Today, she decided to wear her high-heeled boots, tight jeans, and a Montclair Flat Goose coat. She was a tiny woman like her mother, standing five feet even. Aoki never wore sneakers or flat shoes. She always wore stilettos, heels, or high-heeled boots, never anything less than five inches. She was the only girl around her neighborhood to fight in heels and hold her own. She was a tough cookie and had a reputation for being violent and crazy.

Dressed in her finest, Aoki checked her mirror. She was definitely wearing what she had on.

She walked out her bedroom and went into the living room where her dead parents still lay, rotting away. She picked up both knives and cleaned them off with steaming hot water. Then she placed the serrated knife back into the kitchen drawer and placed her dad's pocketknife into her own pocket, for keeps. She looked around her home, and it was just a mess. Aoki felt she didn't have time to clean up. The mess could wait, and so could her parents. She had more important things to take care of.

It was cold outside; Brooklyn felt like it had repositioned on the continent of Antarctica. Aoki expected to see polar bears and penguins soon. She bundled up and walked away from her home and toward the Pink Houses projects, a thirty-minute walk, but she was used to it.

As she walked to meet up with friends, she thought about the tragedy back home. *What am I gon' do?* she asked herself. She had to figure out what to do with the bodies and how to clean up. Calling the police wasn't an option for her. She was only sixteen. She could spend the rest of her life in jail for murder.

It was still early, and the Pink Houses projects looked deserted. The hustlers and troublemakers were still sleeping. Brooklyn, in the winter, was desolate and almost gloomy. The days were too short, the trees stood stark like x-rays of their summer selves, and the streets were decorated with winter frosting.

Despite the gloomy weather, Aoki still ventured out into the cold to hang out with her friends. She was a busybody, constantly moving, doing something, or starting trouble. She walked into the lobby of the building on Loring Avenue, where the dark hallways lacked security cameras, and elevator service was spotty.

But the projects were home to Aoki. She felt safe and protected there, even though she didn't reside there. She had her crew. She had her reputation.

A few days earlier, a seventeen-year-old boy was shot and killed in one of the dimly lit stairways of the housing project. He wasn't a friend of Aoki, but she could feel his pain.

The seventh floor was her destination. She knocked on the brown door and heard hip-hop music blaring from the other end. She waited a moment and then knocked again. Either her peoples didn't hear her, or they were playing games. She wasn't in the mood for games.

Finally, the door opened, and Tisa, popping her bubble gum and smiling, stood in front of her. In tight jeans and a pair of UGGS, Tisa was a typical seventeen-year-old with long, black hair, loud earrings, and a feisty attitude. She liked boys and toys, skipped school often, and idolized thugs and the street life.

"Damn! What took ya so long ta open da door?" Aoki hollered, her Jamaican accent surfacing.

Tisa popped her gum. "Bitch, we ain't even hear you knockin'."

"Ya need a fuckin' doorbell."

"You need to call first."

"Since when?"

"Since we ain't hear you knockin'."

"Whateva!"

Aoki stepped into the apartment. The heat was on blast, and the living room windows were open.

Rihanna, Ri-Ri for short, was in the kitchen getting her hair done. Gena, her mother, had just finished weaving Tisa's hair with two bundles of sixteen inches of Brazilian locks.

Gena, cigarette in her mouth, was great at weaves. Thirty-two years old and a hood rat, she loved to talk shit. She had her daughters when she was in high school, which prompted her to immediately drop out. Gena wanted her daughters to make a come up with a hood-rich nigga, someone to take care of them and get them all out of the hood someday. More like a good friend than their mother, she constantly tried to school them on how to get and keep a man, but they barely listened.

"You know how y'all bitches can get and keep a man, first, by keeping them pussies tight and clean. You think a nigga want a bitch wit' a stink pussy?" Gena took a pull from her Newport.

She continued doing Rihanna's hair, styling it into a long and fabulous weave for her to show off.

"You get a nigga to trick on you gradually. You give him enough to come back for more, but not too much, cuz you don't want to spoil him. Give him that nice, wet pussy; make the sex unforgettable for him. And y'all bitches gotta learn how to suck a nigga's dick. Shit, you make a nigga come real hard, and he'll give you the shirt off his mommas back," Gena chuckled at her dry humor. "Beat that bitch down to give it to you, then break into Fort Knox to get you some gold bars."

"Um, fuck Fort Knox! Cuz ain't no bitch tryin' to walk around the hood wit' some heavy gold bars. I'll take a nice ride, some spending money, clothes, and some diamonds," Tisa joked.

The girls laughed, but Gena didn't. She was serious about finding a hustler to spoil her with the finer things in life. She spat at Tisa, "See, that's what's wrong wit' y'all young bitches today—y'all not educated."

Gena thought she knew it all, and was always plotting, scheming, and backstabbing. She was willing to do whatever it took to climb out of the crab barrel.

Gena fixated her eyes on Aoki, and they lingered on the biracial beauty. There was something about Aoki that Gena didn't like, but she tolerated the girl because she was a best friend to Rihanna and Tisa. Aoki was too pretty, too sexy, and she was still young and vibrant. To top it off, her slight Jamaican accent mixed with a twang of Japanese was appealing. Gena wished she could be her. The look in Aoki's eyes said that she was a go-getter and could effortlessly snatch up any baller to take care of her. She'd heard her daughters talk about how much the boys liked Aoki.

"Hey, Aoki," Gena greeted dryly.

"Hey, Gena. Ya think wen ya got de time, can you do my hair too?"

From everyone's point of view, Aoki's hair was flawless, but she always wanted it messed over by Gena.

"What you need done wit' it?"

"I just want ya to straighten my edges out."

"No problem. Just let me know when."

"I'm on ya time," Aoki said.

"Get at me tomorrow then."

"Okay."

The girls in the projects wished they had hair like Aoki; it was long, shiny and silky, and all hers, no weave, no extensions. If she wanted to, she could model for hair magazines and do hair shows. Aoki had so much potential, but she was wasting away her life by being a knucklehead— no guidance, no direction.

While the girls lingered in Gena's apartment, Tisa started to roll up a blunt. Smoking was their pastime. Weed made everything funny.

All the girls had mastered rolling up a blunt. Tisa was the best at it, though. She had all the material she needed all laid out on the coffee table in front of her—a cigar, the weed, a knife, grinder, and a lighter.

Aoki took a seat next to her friend. She needed to get high. She didn't want to think about her dead parents. She still needed to dispose of the bodies somehow and clean the house, but that could all wait; her folks weren't going anywhere.

For a long time, Aoki had been burdened with pain and sadness. She felt she was hardwired for trouble—like it was programmed into her mind like computer software. She couldn't escape her harsh memories or hide from them. She wished she could put them in the trashcan where they belonged and toss them away.

Tisa started licking the blunt until it was moist. She then took the blade and cut a line lengthwise from the butt to the tip, nodding to Beyoncé's "Drunk in Love" playing in the background. She used her thumb to slide the guts out then she cut off the rounded end of the blunt to decrease the chances of prematurely rolling the blunt shut. When she got a nice rectangular blunt wrap, she licked the edges to seal up any small tears. Then she took the wrap and folded it in the center.

They all eagerly watched, their anticipation to start smoking some purple haze building.

Tisa spread the weed evenly down the length of the blunt then, shaping the blunt by carefully folding and rolling upward, she spun the blunt, running the flame from the lighter up and down its length in order to bake it. Tisa knew that the perfect blunt would darken in color slightly and dry the wrap without catching afire. She held the flame to the tip of the blunt, spinning the blunt around to evenly distribute the heat and minimize the possibility of developing a run.

Aoki sat there looking aloof for a moment. She was quiet.

"You okay, girl?" Tisa asked.

"I'm fine."

At the moment Aoki felt away from everything. Sometimes she would shift into her mood swings, ready to flip on anyone she felt was disrespecting her, or she got really quiet and lost into her own thoughts. Today, she was lost in her own thoughts.

Tisa took a deep pull from the blunt and enjoyed the potent high. "You smokin', Aoki?"

※

Aoki ate with the sisters, laughed, and joked around all day. They talked about boys and teenage things. Aoki felt trust and love with her crew. It was her second home. Being there took her mind off everything.

That evening, the girls decided to take in a movie at the movie theater on Linden Boulevard, just up the street from their project buildings. The movie theater was packed; everybody was waiting in line to see the new sci-fi movie with Will Smith. The inside of the theater looked like a nightclub, and the girls ran into a few familiar faces.

"Damn! The movie don't start until another hour," Rihanna said.

"What y'all tryin' to do?" Tisa asked.

"Go back home," Rihanna said.

Aoki said, "Fuck, no!"

As if on cue, Aoki turned to her left and saw AZ and Heavy Pop walk into the theater. She smiled seeing AZ, the only guy in the hood she liked being around and could talk to.

"Look who done walked into de building," she said, pointing out AZ and Heavy Pop to her crew. They all went over to greet the guys.

AZ smiled when he saw Aoki and her friends approaching. He stood proud and tall around the other patrons inside the theater with his right-hand man and best friend, Heavy Pop, standing by his side. AZ was a handsome nineteen-year old, and was always well-dressed. He had attractive brown skin with a low Caesar haircut and sported a Yankees fitted tilted on top of his head. He had muscles under his shirt, but not the bulky kind men can get from years of weightlifting. He had lost the traces of boyhood and become a feared drug dealer.

AZ used to be a boxer. He was nice with his hands, skilled in knowing how to knock a man out. He'd attended several boxing camps as a child, and over the years he received a reputation for hitting muthafuckas with a mean left hook.

AZ and Aoki were best friends. Their relationship was strictly platonic.

"What ya doin' here, AZ?" Aoki asked, standing close to him.

"What? A nigga can't go to the movies too?"

"I thought ya didn't have time for such tings."

He chuckled. "We gotta take a break from the streets too."

"What y'all here to see?" Tisa asked.

Heavy Pop chimed, "That new Will Smith movie."

"We are too," Tisa said.

"You know that's my boo," Rihanna said.

"Like Will Smith would give you a second look," Tisa said.

"What? You think a bitch like me can't bag Will Smith?"

"He lookin' at you, then he lookin' at me too—I got the bigger bootie."

"And? Will Smith likes his women petite and pretty. He fucks wit' Jada Pinkett, right?" Aoki added.

"That's Jada Pinkett," Tisa said. "She got class."

Rihanna shot back, "Bitch, I got more class than you."

"The only class you ever saw was walking in the hallways at school."

"Fuck you, Tisa!" Rihanna retorted faintly.

AZ and Heavy Pop shook their heads at the sisters' minor quarrel. It was humorous to see them argue over frivolous shit. But it was common between them.

AZ then looked at Aoki and said, "Hey, can I talk to you privately?"

She nodded.

The two walked away from their friends.

AZ left Heavy Pop to entertain the two knuckleheads, as Heavy Pop liked to call them. Heavy Pop was wide and tall and had always been big for his age. He stood six feet tall and weighed over 260 pounds, and his legs were as big as an adult's waist. Heavy Pop was a solid dude, but also a dangerous man to mess with. He and AZ were both street brawlers, good with their hands. He was well known for knocking niggas out with one punch, like Iron Mike Tyson in his heyday.

While Heavy Pop kept the girls company, AZ looked at Aoki and said, "I know you heard."

"Heard what?" Aoki asked with a raised eyebrow.

"You don't know?"

"Know what, AZ?"

"I got Lisa pregnant," he blurted out.

"What? Ya ah serious? How did ya get her bumbaclaat pregnant?"

"I fucked up," he said with his head down.

"Yeah, ya fucked up. Why ya ain't bag up ya dick fo' that nasty pum-pum?"

"I can't even argue wit' you, Aoki. I slipped up. It just happened." AZ shook his head, looking somewhat stressed.

Lisa was a light-skinned chickenhead from Cypress Hills projects with no future, and was known to be a grimy chick with a ton of drama.

"Listen, AZ, ya my friend, and I got ya back. And ya know if that bitch get outta line, I'll cut her ass."

AZ smiled. "I know, Aoki. You don't play, wit' ya crazy ass."

"Yes, ya know me crazy. Ya my best friend, though."

AZ had to tell his friend before the streets twisted the story about him and Lisa. He wasn't in a relationship with her; it was a one-night stand. He wanted to clear that up with Aoki. The two talked for a moment and then joined the group.

"So, what's the secret he had to tell you?" Tisa asked.

"It's none of ya business, Tisa. Why? Ya jealous?"

"Y'all two just need to fuck once and get it out the way," Rihanna joked.

Aoki sucked her teeth and flipped her friend the bird. Everyone always thought she and AZ were more than just friends. In reality, AZ was the older brother that she never had, and she didn't want to trade their friendship for anything.

TWO

Whenever AZ was around Aoki, he became a generous person. He went into his pocket and pulled out a wad of hundred-dollar bills. Aoki wasn't too impressed; AZ always had money and bought her things. They stood on line together at the concession stand. It was quite a wait. They talked and laughed. The night was young, and things were going good. She wasn't thinking about her dead parents.

From the other side of the movie theater Aoki heard the commotion and loud arguing. She craned her neck and noticed Tisa arguing with some girls from Queens. If her friend was beefing, then it became her beef. Aoki marched toward the commotion, with AZ right behind her. She was ready to attack. She slowly pulled her blade from her jeans pocket, her eyes fixated on the bitch in Tisa's face.

"Fuck you, bitch!" Tisa shouted.

"Stupid bitch!" the girl shouted. "What?"

Aoki hurried over, but before she could intervene, security stepped in and quickly defused the situation.

"Tisa, who dem bitches?" Aoki asked.

"Stupid bitch talkin' shit," Tisa replied. "That's all."

Aoki frowned. She eyed every last one of those Queens bitches, ready to spark some serious drama with them. Aoki was a volcano ready to erupt. She was ready to make her own action movie in the lobby. Once she got started, it was hard to calm her down.

Fortunately, AZ was able to talk to her and calm her. "Chill, Aoki. Everything cool, right?"

"I'm cool," she replied, aloof.

The theater was packed, and everybody was into the new Will Smith movie. Aoki and her crew sat in the back of the theater, two rows behind the Queens girls. While there was action and adventure happening on the big screen, Aoki glared down at the bitches that tried to fight with her friend. She took a handful of popcorn and decided to throw it at them. Childish act, but whatever.

The girls turned around, but they didn't say a word at first.

Tisa laughed, saying to Aoki, "You crazy, girl."

"Fuck dem hoes."

The Queens girls didn't want any trouble. The argument between one of them and Tisa was a simple misunderstanding that escalated out of control. But when Aoki started throwing popcorn at them, taunting them, they felt that they were being disrespected. Aoki hardly looked intimidating with her petite size and baby doll features. She continued throwing more and more popcorn at them, giggling while doing so.

Finally, one of the girls stood up and spun around. "Y'all bitches got a problem?" she yelled, and tossed a large Coke at Aoki. She got drenched in the brown, syrupy liquid.

Aoki leaped up and went charging, climbing over the seats like a bull seeing red. Even the folks in the row between the two clashing groups intervened. There were no holds barred when Aoki went in for the attack. She pushed the girl and punched her so hard, the girl stumbled, almost falling flat on her face.

Several pairs of hands attacked Aoki, and Tisa and Rihanna joined the fray.

Aoki was pulling out hair by the handful, scratching, biting, kicking, and even head-butting. She was a beast. The action in the theater was now in 3D—up close and personal for the moviegoers to touch and feel.

Punches were being thrown everywhere, and people were screaming. The lights in the theater came on, and people started to scatter.

Aoki reached into her pocket and pulled out her dad's pocketknife. She was attacked from behind. She spun around and started stabbing one of the girls with the knife. The poor girl screamed. Her shirt was stained with blood in several places.

Security came storming into the theater, and several security guards tried to break up the melee. Cops were on the way.

AZ grabbed Aoki from behind. "Aoki, we gotta go!"

Aoki was stubborn. She wanted to finish what she had started. She wanted to smash the girl's face permanently into the floor. The other friend was stabbed repeatedly and bleeding, but she was still alive.

By the time the cops hurried into the theater, Tisa and everyone else were already fleeing. AZ was trying to get Aoki to leave, but she looked like she was possessed, eyes wild and crazed.

Cops were coming her way. The looky-loos who remained behind to take in the action all pointed to Aoki as the instigator.

"Ms., come here!" one of the officers yelled.

Aoki backpedaled and then took off running the opposite way, and the officer gave chase. Aoki bolted through the exit doors in her high heels like she had on a pair of sneakers. Her heart was beating fast, and her adrenaline was pumping.

The cold, winter air attacked her as she punched away into the darkness, heading for the project buildings ahead. She ran without looking behind her, not knowing whether or not the cop was still chasing her.

She dipped into the lobby of one of the project buildings and slid into the dim stairwell. She took a seat on the concrete stairs and tried to catch her breath. She realized she didn't have her cell phone or her coat. She decided to linger in the stairwell for a moment, hide out, and be cautious until the danger was gone.

The smell of death permeated the living room. It was the most disturbing scent. Aoki's parents were rotting away, their bodies in rigor mortis, their limbs stiffening in the almost-dried pool of blood. She walked around the house contemplating what to do with them and the scene.

Hours had passed since the fight at the movie theater. She'd changed clothes and made herself comfortable. She was snacking on chips, staring at her parents. Her behavior wasn't normal; it was insane.

Just as she was pacing around, thinking and thinking, she heard someone at her front door. She looked to see who it was. It was Tisa.

Aoki opened the door slightly, refusing to allow her inside. "Wah ya want, Tisa?"

"I was worried about you. I tried to call your phone, but it's not on."

"I lost it during de fight."

"You okay?"

"Yeah, I'm okay. My parents, dey trippin' right now, especially me fada."

"So, you cool, right?"

"I'm okay, Tisa. Just need to 'andle some tings and I'll call ya in the mornin'."

"Okay."

Aoki shut the door. She still wasn't going to call the police about her parents. Perhaps it would have been easier to lie to them and say her father had gone into a violent rage, killed her mother and tried to kill her, but that would have been too much explaining.

Her second problem was that she was only sixteen. If she did beat the charges, the state was definitely going to place her in a foster or group home. She had no relatives on her father's side, and her mother's relatives all lived in Japan. They had disowned her mother and her years ago.

It took her all day and almost all night, and frequent trips to Home Depot via cab service for cleaning supplies, but she cleaned up the crime scene. She'd pushed the bodies onto two separate tarps and scrubbed the bloodstained floors, bleached out the blood, and tossed any bloody fabric into a black trash bag to be thrown away. She had cleaned the kitchen and gotten rid of the knife that she killed her father with. She opened all the windows in the house to free the smell of death and allow some fresh air in.

It was freezing in the house, but Aoki didn't feel a thing because she was too busy cleaning up, trying not to go to jail for a very long time. The house hadn't been that clean in years.

Aoki's next move was their bedroom. She went into closets and dresser drawers and started tossing all their belongings into trash bags—clothes, shoes, it was all junk. When she was done attacking the entire house, it was just furniture and lots of trash bags occupying the living room, along with her parents' bodies. It took her two whole days to do everything, all while ignoring her friends. The last thing she needed to do was dig two holes in the backyard and bury her parents.

Aoki tried to dig, but there was a problem; the ground was too frozen. The cold made the soil feel like thick ice. No matter how hard she tried, she couldn't break open the soil. It was almost impossible. Panic started to set in. The bodies were starting to stink even stronger.

Reluctantly, she made a phone call. Tisa, Rihanna, and AZ rushed over when Aoki cried out for their help. They were her only friends; she felt she could trust them.

Aoki was a little bit hesitant in answering the door. The house was immaculate, but her parents were fouling up the place. She opened the door.

AZ was the first to step inside. "Aoki, you okay?" he asked.

Tisa and Rihanna walked in behind him.

Aoki looked at them and said, "Can ya keep a secret?"

"Yeah, you know we can," AZ said.

"What's wrong, girl?" Tisa asked. "You in trouble?"

Rihanna made a sour face. "What's that smell?"

Aoki took a deep breath. "Follow me." She walked away. Her friends followed behind her. She led them into the living room, where her parents' bodies were on the two separate tarps.

Rihanna became wide-eyed. "Ohmygod! Aoki, what happened?"

"Are they dead!" Tisa cried out, trying not to panic. "What the fuck happened? What did you do?"

"Why are you blaming me?!" Aoki became defensive.

"Well who else did this?" Tisa was definitely shaken up.

Aoki thought about telling a long, elaborate lie that involved masked men, guns, and crackheads. But what would that prove? How would it help?

"Look, there has to be some kind of explanation here, right, Aoki. What happened? You can talk to us," AZ said, staring at his best friend for answers. He was shaken up too, but he refused to show it. He had never seen a dead body up close and personal.

"He went into ah violent rage, he killed me mother, he den came after me, so I had ta kill him. I didn't wanna hurt 'em."

Her friends knew about her father's violent past.

"How long have they been dead?" he asked.

"Two or three days."

Rihanna covered her nose, "I know, I can smell them."

"I tried ta bury dem, but the ground too frozen."

"Why didn't you just call the police?" Tisa asked.

"I can't call da police."

"She's right, she can't," AZ said.

"Why not? It was self-defense, Aoki, right?"

AZ said, "Think about it, Tisa—self-defense or not, cops will come and tear this place apart. And Aoki's sixteen. What you think they'll do to her when they find both her parents dead? They're goin' to take her away from here, put her in jail, a group home, or deport her or something."

"She's American, Einstein. They can't deport her!" Tisa wasn't listening to their logic. Not with two dead adults on the living room floor.

"So what we gonna do?" Rihanna asked.

"What else? Be a friend and help her out."

Aoki smiled. "Thank you, AZ."

"You know we got ya back, Aoki. You our peoples."

"Dis between us, right?" Aoki needed to hear all of them swear to secrecy.

"Aoki, you don't have to worry about us." AZ stared at Tisa and Rihanna.

Rihanna said, "Yeah, he's right, Aoki. You're our friend, and you don't have to worry about us. We're not gonna tell a soul about this. Promise."

Tisa hesitated, and then reluctantly said, "I promise too."

"Now, let's get rid of these bodies," AZ said.

It was late, the cold and wind was kicking everyone's ass outside. AZ felt he could break the ground in the backyard. He felt that he was strong enough. He picked up the shovel and marched outside. He tried to dig and dig, but to no avail. He might as well have been trying to break through steel.

After several attempts, winded and cold, he said, "Yo, this shit is fuckin' impossible."

Everyone was frustrated. If AZ couldn't do it, Tisa and Rihanna knew it was gonna be too difficult for them too. Why try? They all went back inside to come up with plan B.

"Yo, why don't we just burn the bodies?" Tisa asked.

"With what?" AZ shook his head. "That's gonna attract too much attention with the smoke, and it's too cold."

"Then let's try and chop them up, like in the movies," Rihanna suggested, "like the mafia."

Tisa looked at Rihanna like she done lost her mind. "So, you gonna be the first volunteer to go Tony Soprano on one of the bodies?"

"No," Rihanna said quickly.

"I didn't think so."

The girls were becoming annoyed. They tried to come up with solution after solution, but AZ would reject them.

The sisters wanted to go home. It was too much to deal with. Aoki was their friend, but they didn't ask to be put in her mess. She was making them all an accomplice to murder.

Tisa caught the attitude first, sucking her teeth and frowning.

Aoki picked up on the vibe. She looked at Tisa. "Ya got a problem wit' me, Tisa?"

"Yeah, I got a problem wit' you, Aoki."

"So, speak ya mind."

"This is fuckin' dumb! You're putting us all at risk here, Aoki. You should have just called the cops and came to live wit' us. I don't wanna go to jail over this shit."

"We're not goin' to jail, Tisa," AZ said.

"How you know that? We can't even come up with a solution to get rid of the bodies. It's cold outside, and I don't feel comfortable with your parents' bodies in the next room. I mean, damn, Aoki! Are you that fucked-up?"

"Ya know what, Tisa," Aoki hollered back, "if ya me friend, then be a friend and stop being a bitch!"

"I am your friend, but this is crazy."

"Look, both y'all just chill," AZ said. "I have an idea. We just need to keep cool and hang tight." AZ wasn't about to let his friend go down for anything. He hated her father, knowing the nigga was a prick and a bully, and most likely deserved to go to an early grave.

Aoki was desperate to know what he was thinking. "What's ya idea?"

"Listen, we can't dispose of the bodies right now because it's too cold, but what we can do is hide them."

"Hide them?" Tisa questioned.

"Yes, for the time being. I'll go to Home Depot and purchase two tin barrels and some quicklime, to keep the smell under control, along with the cold weather. We leave the bodies inside the barrels until the ground softens, and then when it's convenient, we bury them."

Aoki thought it was a genius plan. She was ready to implement it.

AZ smiled at her. "You know I gotta always come through for you."

"I guess that's a plan," Tisa said dryly.

Rihanna thought it was perfect.

The next day AZ went to Home Depot as planned and purchased two large tin barrels using cash. He then purchased the quicklime from a separate store, trying not to arouse suspicion. They then dumped Aoki's parents into the barrels and placed them in the backyard, away from prying eyes.

Aoki knew that her parents weren't going to be missed. They were junkies. They didn't have a nine-to-five, friends, or coworkers. Her father didn't have any family, and her mother's family was estranged and thousands of miles away in Japan. Most likely, no one was going to come around snooping.

THREE

Spring - A couple years later

The handcuffs were tight and digging into Aoki's slim wrists as she sat in the backseat of a police car. They were purposely put on that way. She was arrested for fighting again, but this time the charges were a lot more serious. Aoki had a feeling she was going to jail for a long time. She had also assaulted the female police officer trying to arrest her. The lady cop was familiar with Aoki's history.

"You are out of control," the lady cop said. "They need to lock you up for a very long time. You're a true menace to society, Aoki!"

Aoki frowned. "I'm nah scared of jail. Fuck you!"

"You need to be scared of something," the cop retorted.

With brute force, Aoki repeatedly kicked the back of the officer's seat.

The cop turned around and sprayed mace in Aoki's face.

She screamed, "Ahhhhhhhhh! Fuck you, cop! Fuck you! Me 'ate you!" Her Jamaican accent was becoming more prominent now.

"Calm down, little girl," the female cop ordered. "I hope the judge gives you a lot of time. You don't deserve to be free."

"Suck me pussy out!" Aoki screamed out.

Aoki was now eighteen, and her violent behavior was growing worse. She was a nightmare in the neighborhood. Many started to fear her. She was unpredictable. She and her crew were nothing to play with. She had a long rap sheet, from assaults, carrying a deadly weapon, to petty drug dealing. Aoki was a high-school dropout with anger issues.

Aoki stared out the police car window while being driven to the local precinct. The mace in her eyes still burned a little, but it was wearing off. It calmed her down, though. The arresting officer had promised to spray her again if she didn't shut up and relax. Aoki didn't want another round of that stuff, so she relaxed and frowned heavily.

At the precinct, Aoki was handcuffed to a bench and virtually ignored for hours. She was used to the routine, being one of the regulars. As she sat, pouting and angry, she reflected on the fight earlier. She and her crew had exploded on rival bitches over a rumor in the hood. She, Tisa, and Rihanna had gotten into a full-on brawl with Stephanie, Kim, Lady, and Penny over a rumor about Rihanna getting fucked on the rooftop by Monty, a local hood nigga. Supposedly, he took Rihanna to a McDonald's drive-thru for a date afterward. It was an ugly, untrue rumor, and Aoki and her crew weren't going to stand for it.

Aoki and her crew fought hard and viciously, even though they were outnumbered. It took police sirens blaring for the fight to break up. But Aoki was always the last one standing. She went straight for her rivals—pummeling, hitting, kicking, and biting. When the police arrived, Aoki had Penny balled up, almost unconscious, and bloody on the ground while she repeatedly bashed a large rock against her face. Penny was the alpha of her crew, and the two had hated each other since grade school.

Aoki was about to reach into her pocket and pull out her pocketknife, but Officer Winslow had quickly intervened, snatching her off the girl. Aoki turned on the female officer. She swung at the cop, but was overpowered and subdued by her partner. Aoki fought hard to prevent the handcuffs from clamping around her wrists, but to no avail.

She was the only girl arrested. While she was fighting with the cops, everyone else had run away.

Aoki had stabbed plenty of girls in different areas throughout East New York, Brownsville, Bed-Stuy, and Bushwick. But no one snitched on her. They refused to talk to the cops and give her up, keeping true to the code of the streets.

As Aoki sat frowning and handcuffed, Sergeant Snashall noticed her sitting in his precinct once again. He sighed heavily and shook his head. He eyed the beautiful, young teenager. He hated to see her locked up.

Sergeant Snashall, a burly Irishman, had been at the same precinct for three decades now. In his late fifties, he wasn't jaded from being a cop. Every now and again he saw something in the perps that ended up in his precinct, and he wanted to mentor them with a good lecture into changing their lives. Aoki was one of his projects. He felt sorry for the girl he'd met when she was eight years old, after she'd run away from home. He knew both her parents were strung out on heroin and crack cocaine and were unfit to raise a child. ACS had been called to their household numerous times by the neighbors and school officials, but somehow her case would always slide through the cracks, leaving Aoki a child in danger.

Aoki would go to school hungry and smelling, and the kids would tease her mercilessly about her appearance and her Jamaican accent and Japanese heritage. They picked on her constantly, giving her wretched names like "Chinky Stinky" and "Mixed Bitch."

In the beginning, she would cry. Then she hardened herself and kept quiet, and would try to ignore the name-calling and teasing. But it all finally progressed to her full-on rage and anger. Aoki would fight her classmates so intensely, it was hard for anyone to break up the fight and pull her off the student she was beating on. She felt vindicated when she fought her teasers. She would punish them severely with bloody noses and black eyes. She even broke a boy's nose and had been suspended from school.

Sergeant Snashall walked over and took a seat next to her.

She wanted to ignore him. He was always preaching, and she didn't want to listen.

He looked at her and asked sternly, "What is wrong with you, Aoki? Aren't you tired of this back-and-forth shit? I'm tired of seeing you here in handcuffs."

She turned her attention away from him. She grimaced. She had no choice but to listen because of her restraints. Snashall was going to school her, whether she liked it or not.

"You're smart and beautiful, and you deserve so much more, Aoki. I know you lived a hard life, with your parents being on drugs, the kids teasing you, but that's still no reason to fuck everything up for yourself. Do you wanna go to jail? Huh? Is that what you're looking for?"

She didn't respond to him. She sat slouching and frowning.

"You're a tough girl, huh, kid? That's what you want to be all your life? You want to fight everybody and everything? You wanna be angry at the world? You want to turn away and ignore the people that want to help you?"

Aoki's silence didn't deter Sergeant Snashall from talking to her. He was used to kids trying to ignore him, not wanting to listen to what he had to say. He was persistent, though. He believed he could make a change.

"Why don't you go back to school and get your education? I know you can do it. I know behind all that anger, violence, and frustration, you want something better for yourself."

Aoki growled, "How do you know what the fuck I want? Nigga, you don't fuckin' know me."

"I don't think you know yourself, Aoki." His eyes were sincere. He really did care.

"Don't you want out of your situation? Out of the ghetto? Isn't it tiresome to you?"

"It's fine to me," she replied with attitude.

"What are your future plans, Aoki?"

Aoki was only trying to survive one day at a time and was tired of people like Sergeant Snashall trying to change her, trying to tell her what was best.

"Where are your parents?" he asked. "I haven't seen them around lately."

Aoki sucked her teeth and gave the sergeant the same lie she gave everybody else. Her father was still strung out, in the streets, and her mother had moved back to Japan. She was alone. She was eighteen now. She was officially an adult. So she didn't have to worry about any group homes or foster care. The state couldn't touch her. She felt proud about that.

Snashall stood up. He looked down at her. He sighed heavily. "This is going to be the last time, Aoki. I'm going to help you out, but I can't continue giving you these breaks, especially if you're not willing to help yourself. You should be on your way to Rikers Island for assaulting a police officer. But I'm gonna have them let you go. But I want more from you. Promise me, Aoki, that this will be the very last time I see you in this precinct."

"Why do you care so much? Why would you let me go again? I don't want your pity, Sergeant Snashall."

"I only care because I know you don't. But I know if you grew up under a different set of circumstances, if life had dealt you a different hand, then you would be reaching your great potential instead of blowing your future running the streets. I've been a cop for many years, Aoki. I've seen kids like you come and go. The streets chew them up, then swallow them up. They don't spit you back out. Out there don't give a fuck about you, you hear me? Out there, those streets, it's a selfish world."

Aoki looked at him. She didn't care for his long-winded speech. She wanted to go home, and he was the way out. So she had to put on a front and lie. She looked him straight in the eyes and told him what he needed to hear, but Snashall knew it was bullshit.

"I see you in here again, Aoki, and I don't know you. I'm not helping you out."

Aoki nodded. She understood.

The female arresting officer was highly irritated by his decision. She believed that Aoki should've been booked, arraigned, and sent to Rikers Island.

AZ pulled up to the precinct in his used gray Yukon. He'd heard about Aoki's arrest and came prepared to bail her out, again. He had five thousand dollars on him, and wanted to know her arraignment date. He was hoping her bail wasn't too high. He killed the engine to his truck, and the minute he climbed out of his vehicle, Aoki was prancing out of the precinct.

AZ was taken aback to see her exiting the building. *What miracle did she perform now?* A huge grin spread across his face. He tapped his horn, catching her attention.

Aoki smiled and walked toward the Yukon. They hugged each other tightly, grateful to see each other. From a distance, anyone looking at them would think they were a couple.

"Yo, how did you get out?"

"A friend."

"Tisa called me and told me what happened."

"I just wan' to go." She climbed into his Yukon and sat back.

AZ started the vehicle and drove off. While driving her home, he asked, "What happened?"

Aoki didn't want to talk about it, but she decided to tell him the details. She told him how the fight started over a rumor being spread about Rihanna.

AZ laughed. "But it's true."

"What's true?"

"Monty's my dude, and he did fuck Rihanna on the rooftop. That nigga ain't got no reason to lie, especially on his dick."

"Bullshit! I don't believe it."

"I know she's a friend, Aoki, but your girl gets down like that. And you got arrested over that bullshit? That's crazy. You need to chill out."

Aoki sucked her teeth. "Me ain't like dem bitches anyway; dem deserve what they get."

AZ shook his head. He stared at her while idling at the red light. He said to her, "You know, you're too beautiful to be out here wilding out like this, especially over some rumor."

"Listen, no bitch gon' disrespect me and my friends, ya hear?"

"Even when there's some truth to the rumor, you still gonna wild out, huh? Damn! You love to fight until somebody beats ya lil' ass out here."

Aoki sucked her teeth. "Ne-ver. Ya hear me? Never happen pon me."

Aoki knew he was telling the truth. She loved violence, and felt she'd inherited that from her father. In the service Maxwell was a coldblooded killer, a combat soldier, going from one theater to the next. During his stint in the NYPD, her father was an asshole on the streets. Nobody liked him.

Before AZ drove off, he asked playfully, "So, when you gonna let me eat out that pussy?"

Aoki laughed. "Ya so silly, AZ. Ya can't handle dis pum-pum."

"Your pum-pum needs to get service. And you don't know what I can't handle."

"Me pum-pum is just fine; me can service myself."

"Self-service, huh? I know that can get boring."

"Ya a damn fool, AZ," she replied.

They looked at each other and then broke out laughing. They both never took each other seriously. They greatly loved each other.

Aoki knew she would never take it there with AZ. She didn't want to ruin what they shared. AZ was more like a brother, like family to her than anything else.

It was an amusing ride with AZ, like always. AZ was like her guardian angel. Whenever she was in trouble, he came running, with a fist full of cash or his pistol to help bail her out.

AZ sat idling in front of her home. The block was quiet. It'd been two years now, and so far Aoki's secret had been kept quiet. Like they predicted, no one came around asking for her parents' whereabouts. They weren't missed at all.

"How you holdin' up?" AZ asked.

"I'm fine."

"You need some company, or you wanna be alone?"

"I'm fine, AZ. Ya don't need to fret 'bout me."

"A'ight. But do me a favor."

"What dat?"

"Stay the fuck outta jail," he joked, "cuz your bail can get pretty expensive." Then he got serious. "But real talk, just keep your cool, Aoki, and don't let these muthafuckas get to you. You ain't gotta fight everybody. You're my best girl, and you know if you need anything—to talk, extra cash, anything—you can come to me, right?"

She nodded.

"I love you, girl."

"I love ya too."

They hugged each other, and then she climbed out of his Yukon and walked toward her front door. AZ watched her until she was inside, and then he drove away.

In order to cover the mortgage, Aoki had been endorsing and depositing her father's checks. What was left, she used to pay for small repairs and household expenses. She made a few small upgrades, but that was it. Aoki wanted to do a full renovation, but that required a large sum of cash.

For additional income, Aoki, along with Tisa and Rihanna, worked as a drug mule for AZ. It helped her do small renovations on her home. Working for AZ helped her become more independent. The trio traveled the five boroughs on NYC transit, and sometimes to Philadelphia.

Aoki undressed and went into the backyard. She looked at the two tin barrels still hidden away on the side of the dilapidated shed. Her parents' bodies were still rotting inside. But every month, late in the night, she would go out and cover the bodies with quicklime to keep the smell contained and help preserve the remains. Aoki never got around to burying her parents. She was contented with having both of them still around, their flesh rotting away slowly but surely. It was a reminder to her how fucked-up they were and what she did not want to become.

FOUR

AZ parked on the tranquil Brooklyn Street in Canarsie. It was late in the night, and he was exhausted. He climbed out of his Yukon, pushed the alarm, and then climbed the steps to his two-bedroom home on 91st Street. For AZ, it was the perfect area to live in. It was away from East New York and the grimy streets. Canarsie was a middle-class neighborhood—blue-collar and hard-working.

AZ walked into his home, placed his gun on the table, and got relaxed. There was no place like home. He turned on his television, rolled up a blunt, and got high in his living room while watching ESPN. He learned his Knicks lost again, adding to their losing streak, making this one of their worst seasons ever. Once again, Carmelo Anthony was out for a few games due to an injury. He cursed the Knicks' wretched season. AZ was tired of losing money on them.

"What is this nigga made of? Glass?" he said to himself. He shook his head at another losing NBA season and downed his beer. He decided to change the channel.

AZ tried to keep his life simple, though he was a drug dealer on the come-up. He'd dropped out of high school a while ago not because he couldn't handle the work, but because of peer pressure. He always needed to fit in. All of his friends cut class until they eventually dropped out, so AZ had to do it as well. Only, he did it first. He didn't want to look like a follower. He wanted to think of himself as a leader. He was fifteen when he dropped out of school, and then he secretly took the GED exam at sixteen and passed it with flying colors. AZ was smart, but, in his world, being a book smart thug could cost him his life, so he hid that side of himself from everyone, even his best friend, Heavy Pop.

AZ had a ten-year plan, which was to make as much money as he could in the drug game and then invest his money in affordable housing. He was aware that real estate was where it's at.

His mind was on business—not street business but legit business. Maybe one day he'd have his own legitimate empire to be proud of.

The flat-screen was on CNBC, and AZ was watching The Profit, a reality show starring Camping World CEO Marcus Lemonis. AZ had become a fan of the show a few months earlier. Every week, AZ was intrigued by watching this multimillionaire invest around two million dollars of his own funds into struggling companies in exchange for a percentage of the business' profit. If selling drugs was a legit business, AZ felt he would be on his way to making the cover of Fortune magazine and probably have his own reality show. He was coming up fast in the drug game and making a name for himself.

Real estate, yes, that's where the money was at. It was

going to be the key to his success. America was always building somewhere, and people needed a place to live and feel comfortable. Having land was valuable. AZ felt the more land and property he owned, the more blessed his future was going to be. The city was always purchasing land and developing something. He wanted to make legit money and didn't want to always have to watch his back.

AZ was gradually learning the market. A good real estate investor knows the locations and the history of the land and area. They also must know what new developments are being planned. They know everything about the area where they invest. A good businessman knows it all. AZ wanted to become a good businessman; he was surely a good hustler.

He was also minimalist by nature. For a drug dealer, he wasn't flashy. He didn't overindulge in jewelry, cars, sneakers, or other frivolous items that drugs dealers bought. His way of thinking was different from everyone else. He felt that a person could live in 250-350 sq. ft. He'd already hired an architect to design plans for a building he planned on erecting throughout the world, with high-end finishes. His buildings would be ideal for college students and young professional adults entering the work force. Once he got enough drug money saved up, he would purchase the land and begin construction. He was extremely passionate about his future but kept his plans to himself.

AZ had a one-year-old daughter to help raise and a crazy, jealous baby momma from a one-night stand. Lisa wanted to be in his life, but he was against it. Dealing with her was a mistake, but his daughter wasn't. He loved his little girl and tried to see her whenever it was possible, whenever Lisa didn't make things a headache.

The night went on with him watching one show after another. He thought about Aoki and hoped she was okay. He thought about the day they'd first met in the schoolyard. She was the cutest thing he had even seen.

❧

Aoki was ten, and he was thirteen. Aoki was trying to fight a bigger, older boy. The boy was definitely stronger and manhandling Aoki like she was a rag doll.

AZ came around, didn't like what he saw, and quickly intervened, making it his fight. He beat the bully down and sent him running away with a bloody nose and black eye. Then he tried to help Aoki off the ground.

She pushed his hand away. "Me didn't call 'pon ya help."

"I don't like bullies."

"And me don't know ya. Me can 'andle 'em."

AZ smiled. She was feisty and rough. He liked her already. He was intrigued by her accent and her looks. At the time, Aoki sported two long pigtails, and her clothes were of the Goodwill variety. She was skinny and short, but her eyes were filled with sadness and pain, and she rarely smiled.

"I was just trying to help."

"Leave me."

"What's your name?"

Aoki stared him down and walked away without giving him her name or thanking him.

❧

A week later, they met each other again. Aoki had gotten into another skirmish with some kids. They were teasing her. She fought back. AZ came around and helped her with her battle. It became like that. The two would see each other around the neighborhood constantly and developed a strange friendship, and they had that unspoken respect for each other. It was friendship from a distance.

Both of them had come from rough homes. AZ lived with his single mother and was the only child. His mother's boyfriends were all abusive and violent, and most nights would use AZ as a punching bag when they became agitated. His mother didn't do a thing to protect him. AZ felt vulnerable and abused. She loved a man more than her own son. His uncle got him into boxing and would send AZ to boxing camps when he could afford it. AZ fell in love with it. He had to protect himself.

One night, AZ left home with a black eye, a bloody lip, and nowhere to go. It was cold and late. He had gotten in to it with Tony, his mother's new man. He ran into Aoki at the playground. She saw his pain. They talked. She offered him a place to stay at her house. He accepted it.

Both her parents were junkies, and she was an only child too. It wasn't going to be hard to sneak him into the house. Either her parents weren't home, or they were too high to care. That night, AZ slept on the floor at the foot of her bed. From there on, the two had each other's back.

After AZ hit the streets selling drugs, trying to become a man, whenever Aoki needed cash or food, he provided it. Whenever she had beef, he was there to aid her with his boxing skills. Whenever he needed a place to stay, her bedroom became his bedroom. As the years passed, they became inseparable, like brother and sister.

❦

AZ fell asleep on the couch with the TV still playing. He woke up at one in the morning to his cell phone ringing. He looked at the caller ID. Aoki was calling.

He figured she had a reason to be calling so late. "Yo, everything okay?" he asked nervously.

"Yes, everything is okay. I just called to say gudnite."

He smiled. "Gudnite," he replied, imitating her accent. "Tomorrow then," he said.

"Tomorrow." She hung up.

AZ sat up from his comfortable sleeping position and turned off the television. He wasn't tired anymore. He was awake and wanted to get his workout on.

He removed himself from the couch and went into the second bedroom, where he had a weight bench and a few dumbbells arranged nicely on the floor. His favorite piece of equipment was the punching bag hanging from the ceiling. He'd installed it himself. It was his stress reliever.

He peeled off his shirt and eyed himself in the mirror. His body was drool-worthy. He had a chiseled chest, and his skin glowed healthily. His abdominals were sculptured to perfection as his six-packs popped, instantly giving off the impression that he came out of a Calvin Klein shoot. The ladies loved him.

AZ put on his boxing gloves and pounded a few hard

and rapid hits into the punching bag. His technique was nice. He continued punching the bag for a half hour, breaking into a healthy sweat. When he was done, he downed bottled water, took a shower, and then jumped into his bed.

Tomorrow was another day, another hustle, and maybe a day closer to achieving his dreams.

FIVE

Aoki woke up to incessant knocking at her front door, the doorbell ringing, and her cell phone ringing. She became agitated by the noise. She climbed out of bed naked and donned a long T-shirt. She hurried toward the door and saw Tisa and Rihanna standing outside her home. She opened the door and allowed them inside.

Tisa threw her arms around Aoki, hugged her, pulled away from her and then said, "Girl, how did you get out already? You snitchin'?"

Aoki knew her friend was joking, but she didn't like the word "snitching." She spat back, "Ya know I'm nah ah snitch, Tisa. Don't even talk like dat ti me."

"I know, Aoki. I was just playing."

"A snitch ain't nuthin' to joke 'bout."

Rihanna hugged her friend too. They were both happy to see that Aoki was home.

"It was crazy, yo," Rihanna said. "They said you beat up a cop."

"I didn't touch no cop. I just didn't want ta get arrested."

The girls laughed. Still, they were curious to know how she got out of jail after being involved in a beatdown like that and resisting arrest without having to pay any bail.

Aoki told them about Sergeant Snashall.

"He just tryin' to fuck you; that's all," Rihanna said.

"Yeah, because all of the boys like Aoki," Tisa added, dryly.

"He's ah pain," Aoki said. "Dat's what him is."

"Girl, any cop that helps you out as much as that fool gonna want something in return," Tisa said. "The question is, when he comes ready to cash in, what you gonna give him?"

Rihanna nodded. "I know right? Cuz ain't no cop in the world that nice."

Aoki grimaced. "I'll give him me fist and ah bloody lip. Him keeps sayin' he wants to help because him cares. I'm like his pet project."

"Yup, he wants to pet something all right," Tisa joked. "And maybe his project is his hard and small dick he wants Aoki to suck and ride."

Rihanna added, "Maybe give the nigga a hand-job for a release."

"Both of y'all a fool."

"Anyway, what you doin' today?" Tisa said.

As Aoki was about to answer, AZ pulled up in his Yukon with Heavy Pop in the passenger seat. He stepped out into the beautiful day clad in a wife-beater, blue jeans, a pair of white-on-white Nikes, and his signature Yankees cap tilted on his head. AZ wasn't a jewelry person, but he loved to dress, always sharp, meticulous from head to toe. The girls eyed him and smiled. He was definitely eye candy, his lean, muscular physique rippling through his tank top.

Heavy Pop walked behind his friend, looking like a tall and giant wall, but dressed just as sharply. "Hey, knuckleheads," he said jokingly.

Tisa flipped him the bird. "You the knucklehead."

Heavy Pop asked, "Y'all knuckleheads behaving yourselves?"

"Are you?" Tisa quipped back.

AZ went straight toward Aoki and swept her up into a tight bear hug. He lifted her off her feet and then gently placed her back on the ground. "You looking good, ma."

"Me look terrible."

Tisa eyed the two of them with a deadpan stare. "Y'all sure y'all ain't fuckin'?"

"We just friends," Aoki repeated to them for the umpteenth time. "Why? Ya jealous?"

Tisa laughed her comment off, but in actuality, she was somewhat jealous of their relationship. She knew AZ probably liked Aoki as more than a friend. She was pretty. She was interesting. She was an engine of beauty and pain gliding on the train tracks, and all the niggas wanted to ride her.

Tisa wanted AZ for herself. He was fine, and he was making money. She made it her business to say something slick to him once in a while, so he would get the hint. She said to AZ, "Oh, only Aoki can get a hug? Or can I get a hug too? I thought we were all friends, AZ."

"Ah, Daddy needs to give his ladies a hug. You do look good in them jeans, Tisa. Got your bubble in the back showing. You ready to have it popped from the rear?

She smiled. "You know if you ask nicely, maybe you can have a piece of this."

He laughed.

Tisa decided to throw some shade at AZ. "You still fuckin' with that bird bitch, Candi?"

AZ smirked. "Yeah, that thot sucked my dick, but I ain't touch that nasty dirty bitch."

Everyone laughed.

Aoki did too. She's wasn't jealous of the women he'd been with. She could be protective of her friend, advising him, but he was a man with a dick, and niggas gonna be niggas. But, somehow, whenever someone mentioned another bitch that AZ had been with, they would look at her for a reaction. Aoki didn't give it the time of day. She was cool with his promiscuous ways, as long as he protected himself.

The group thought Tisa was playing herself by throwing herself at AZ when everyone knew he had eyes for Aoki. Tisa didn't give a fuck. She knew what she wanted, and that was a piece of AZ.

AZ said, "Yo, we gonna run, but I wanted to make sure y'all good over here. We still okay wit' that run to Queens today?"

"We ready to get that money," Tisa replied. Working for AZ was their bread and butter.

AZ smiled. "Money, money, money."

Heavy Pop handed the girls a book bag filled with a kilo of cocaine, worth $29,000. AZ knew his product was in good hands. Aoki wasn't going to allow anything to happen to it.

AZ and Heavy Pop got into the truck, and AZ drove off. Aoki went inside, and when the Yukon was out of sight, Rihanna looked at Tisa and said, "Tisa, why you keep playing yourself? You know he got eyes for Aoki."

"Well, maybe one day he'll have eyes for me. Shit, he seems to have eyes on everyone else and having babies wit' these thots. Besides, Aoki keeps sayin' they friends."

"What? You wanna be next on his list?"

Tisa smiled. "I'm tryin' to be first on his new list. What do Aoki got that I don't have?"

"Obviously, his undivided attention," Rihanna snapped. AZ was a catch, but she didn't want him. They had been friends for a long time, and she didn't want any problems with her friendship with Aoki. However, Tisa didn't care at all. She wanted him, even though he liked her friend.

Aoki came strutting outside wearing her high heels and tight jeans. Her hair and makeup were done up flawlessly. She smiled at her friends. "Ya ready to take dis trip?"

"We waiting on you, girl," Tisa said.

Aoki had the book bag slung over her shoulder, the ki of cocaine secured for delivery. She also carried her pocketknife.

They took the E train to Queens. For the duration of the ride, the girls talked loudly and joked around. It was early afternoon, so the subway car wasn't crowded with rush

hour hours away. Aoki felt comfortable holding the book
.bag. To everyone else they looked like three teenage girls on
their way home from school.

Tisa said, "Aoki, let's be for real wit' each other. Do you
have any sexual feelings at all for AZ?"

"Him just a friend, Tisa."

"Just a friend, huh? So you never thought about testing
the waters, dipping your feet into the pool? Or thought
about how big his dick is? I mean, did you see the dick?"

"Tisa, why you in her business?" Rihanna asked.

"I'm not in her business. We just havin' some girl talk.
That's all, right?"

"What, Tisa? Ya ready to spread ya pum-pum across
his dick and make boom-boom." Aoki stood up and did a
grinding motion, lowering herself to the ground and coming
back up, slowly.

Rihanna laughed. "Aoki, you crazy."

"I'm just curious, Aoki. That's all," Tisa replied.

"Why ya curious, though?"

"It's obvious the nigga wants more than a friendship
from you, but you being stingy wit' the pussy, playin' games
wit' him. Why let a good man like AZ go to waste?"

"Tisa, what I do wit' me pum-pum is my business. Ya
understand? And ya don't need to be too involved in me
friendship or me sex life. We have somethin' dat ya don't
understand, so me appreciate if ya shut de fuck up 'bout it."

Tisa didn't have a reply. She sat back quietly and folded
her arms across her chest, not wanting to push Aoki's
buttons.

Rihanna couldn't stop chuckling. She had that look on her face that said, *I told you.*

Tisa threw up her middle finger at her, while Aoki now sat quietly.

The train moved speedily through the dark tunnels of Manhattan into Queens, rattling every so often.

Rihanna couldn't stop taunting Tisa. It was all jokes and fun. That little sour situation between Tisa and Aoki didn't stop the party; it just made them seem normal while carrying drugs. They seemed regular.

The E train rumbled into the last stop on the subway line, Jamaica Center on Parsons and Archer. Everyone spilled off the train onto the platform. The girls walked behind the crowd and emerged onto the bustling street beneath a bright blue sky.

Aoki walked like a diva in her wedge heels and tight jeans that accentuated her lower figure. She turned heads and caught fleeting looks. Tisa and Rihanna were by her side looking like cute schoolgirls. All three jumped into an idling cab and drove to Jamaica Houses, AKA 40 Projects. The distance was only a few blocks, but Aoki and her girls were too cute to walk the short blocks to the projects, and the fare was only ten dollars.

The cab came to a stop on the corner of South Road and 160th Street. Aoki paid the driver, and they all climbed out. Half a block away a few neighborhood fellows were lingering, posted up against a black E-Class Benz that sat on 20-inch chrome rims, rap music blaring. They were drinking beer and smoking weed. The loud, intimidating group of men caused passersby to cross the street nervously.

Aoki strutted their way with no fret. When the girls got closer to the group, they caught the men's attention. Aoki walked pokerfaced, the book bag still slung over her shoulder. She was determined to deliver for AZ.

Tisa smiled their way. Rihanna was silent and cool.

One of the men looked strongly at Aoki and Tisa and removed himself from the hood of his car. He stood six two, and was tattooed heavily with a dark beard. He smiled at Aoki and the others and said, "Y'all a long way from home."

"And why you care, Rhino?" Tisa shot back. "You always think we here to see you."

"Why not? What? I'm not handsome enough for y'all bitches to come see a nigga? It ain't always gotta be business with Tiger."

"Then who you tryin' to do business wit'? Huh, Rhino?" Tisa flirted with him, smiling.

"You already know, ma, all work and no play … "

"No, I don't already know. Tell me somethin' good, because right now it's all work, if you can't afford to play."

"Where is Tiger? Him home?" Aoki asked, disrupting their little connection.

"Yeah, he home. What? Y'all got somethin' nice from the candy shop?" Rhino asked.

"We wouldn't com' dis way if we didn't," Aoki said.

Rhino took a quick pull from his cigarette and then flicked it away. He eyed Tisa with a slight smile; Tisa eyed him back. It was obvious there was some attraction between them.

"I'll call him and let him know he got company," Rhino said. He pulled out his cell phone and started calling the boss, who was also his friend. His goons flanked him, and they all stared at the beautiful trio, but they didn't disrespect the ladies.

"Yo, it's me. The girls are here," Rhino said into the phone. "A'ight . . . got you." Rhino hung up. "Go on up. He waitin' for y'all," he said to Aoki.

As the girls started to make their way toward the lobby, Rhino said, "What? All three of y'all need to go up? I'm sayin', let your girl hang out for a minute so we can politick."

Aoki looked at Tisa, who looked like she wanted to stay behind and continue flirting with Rhino.

"Ya cool?" Aoki asked her.

"Yeah, I'm cool."

Aoki nodded and continued walking, while Tisa stayed behind with Rhino and his boys. Tisa knew how to handle herself. She liked Rhino. The man was exactly her type—big and strong-looking, his thick beard trimmed and shaped, and he was a thug. Tisa loved the thugs.

Aoki and Rihanna walked into the project lobby and took the stairs to the third floor. They knocked on the apartment door, which opened immediately. One of Tiger's goons in a wife-beater with wide arms and a big gut was staring the ladies down.

Aoki glared back and quickly wisecracked, "What? Ya want ah fuckin' password?"

He stepped aside and allowed them to come in.

Tiger sat at a table playing dominos with his cronies. The apartment was well furnished with leather couches and armchairs. A 60-inch TV played highlights of the Knicks' loss against Miami the night before. Beer bottles, ashtrays, cash, and marijuana remnants, along with the dominos, littered the large Nyman table they were playing on.

Tiger stared at the girls entering the room. The game paused for a minute. Tiger looked at Aoki with no smiles, no hellos. He was a powerful-looking man—the alpha male— hefty with thick facial hair like Rhino. He was shirtless with a 18k solid gold chain draped around his neck, his large body wrapped with tattoos and war scars.

"Y'all got what I need, right?" he said to Aoki. "I assume."

"We wouldn't be 'ere if we didn't," Aoki replied.

Tiger took one last drag from the Newport in his hand and doused it out into the ashtray. He stood up and walked Aoki's way, his bald head gleaming, his eyes cold as ice.

Aoki removed the book bag from around her shoulder and handed it to Tiger, who took it from her and quickly unzipped it. He glanced inside.

"I told AZ three kilos. What the fuck is this?" he barked.

"Is what him gave me."

"I'll shit this in a few days. He don't think I can handle three? Yo, get that nigga on the phone right now, so we can talk."

Aoki frowned. She didn't like his attitude. She was only the messenger, or the delivery person. Whatever issues they had were between them, and she didn't want to get involved.

"Him pay me to deliver, not ta talk him business, ya 'ear me?" Aoki's accent was put on extra thick, something she did when she was in stressful situations.

"Aoki, I know that's your boy and all, but this shit ain't right. I wanted three bricks. Now either shit is missing, or AZ fuckin' up—which one?"

"What ya tryin' to say, huh? Ya sayin' me a t'ief?"

"I'm sayin' exactly what the fuck I said."

"Me no t'ief, Tiger!" she said loud and clear. "And my friends ain't either! Ya call him fi ya self and work it out. I'm nah ah part of his business."

Tiger scowled.

Aoki didn't flinch. She wasn't intimidated by his massive presence. Tiger had to respect her gangster.

Tiger turned to the table and said, "Mitch, toss me the fuckin' phone."

The cell phone was quickly tossed Tiger's way and he caught it. He dialed AZ while Aoki and Rihanna stood there wondering what would happen next. They were professional mules, and so far every delivery had gone smoothly. But somehow, there was a problem with this distribution. Rihanna kept calm. She felt that as long as she was with Aoki, and Aoki was handling things then everything was going to be okay. She trusted her friend. She felt that Aoki wouldn't let anything happen to her.

Tiger had the cell phone pressed to his ear, while staring intently at the girls. AZ answered, and Tiger immediately said, "AZ, we got a fuckin' problem here?"

"What problem?"

"My one instead of three."

"Three? Where you get three from, nigga, when you usually go one and a half?"

"Yo, you misheard me the other day. I said I wanted up."

"Okay, you want up then that ain't no problem, but that up cost, nigga, and you ain't paid that price. What? You wanted it on credit?"

"Nigga, you know I'm good for it. Hook a nigga up next time."

"A'ight. Give me two days and I'll have that for you."

"My nigga, and sorry about the misunderstanding."

"It's cool. Love is still love. Just make sure my girls get back home safely."

"Nigga, in my hood, they always protected," Tiger replied.

After the call ended, Tiger looked at Aoki and Rihanna. "We all good."

Aoki rolled her eyes; Rihanna did too.

Aoki didn't like to linger around in Queens. It was too far from her home, and the peoples weren't her peeps.

After they got everything squared away with Tiger, they left the apartment. Walking outside, they saw Tisa nestled in Rhino's arms, laughing and smiling. She'd shared a blunt with him and a 40 oz., and she looked like she was ready to have his baby.

"Ya ready?" Aoki asked her.

"Damn! Y'all finished already?"

"What ya think? We ain't come ta stay all day."

Tisa sucked her teeth and reluctantly pulled herself away from Rhino's strong arms.

Rhino didn't look too pleased. "Yo, why y'all gotta leave so soon? The party was just gettin' started."

"We got we own party ta gwon to," Aoki said.

Comp, one of Tiger's soldiers, eyed Aoki like she was a piece of candy to unwrap. "Yo, Aoki, I like the way you talk. That shit is sexy, ma."

Aoki paid him no never mind. She rolled her eyes and was ready to walk away.

Tisa hugged Rhino and said to him, "Call me, okay?"

"Yeah, we gonna link up, shorty, no doubt about that."

Tisa smiled.

"And tell your friend to loosen up somewhat and let that coochie breathe a little. Don't choke it to death, baby," he joked.

His boys laughed.

Aoki walked away from their party, but she slapped her ass while strutting away.

SIX

Cypress Hills Houses was full of life on this warm, sunny day. Euclid and Dumont Avenues were flooded with traffic and people, and the playground was swamped with children and adults enjoying the spring weather. Everything was blooming, from the trees to the plants on the ground.

Aoki and her crew were loitering on the weathered bench near the playground, smoking and talking loudly. They'd decided to walk to the Cypress Hills Houses from the Pink Houses to chill. It was one of their many stomping grounds.

Mostly everyone was talking about the recent fight they'd had with Penny and her crew. The girls laughed and continued to share war stories and talk about rich niggas, hot whips, and Instagram beef. Aoki stared at Penny's building and smirked. Her foe's bedroom window was right above the playground, so Penny could easily see Aoki and everyone else down below, laughing and hanging out. Aoki didn't give a fuck about anything. She was definitely a troublemaker; a troubled child who had turned into a troubled adult.

"Fuck dat bumbaclaat bitch Penny!" Aoki cursed at full volume, glaring.

KILLER DOLLS

Penny gazed out her bedroom window and watched Aoki, Tisa, and Rihanna sit on the bench discussing the brawl with some of her own peoples. She still had the bruises on her face from the fight. They were healing, but not fast enough. She tried to be as tough as Aoki, but there wasn't any comparison. Aoki was full-blown crazy. Penny felt that she and her girls were too cute to be out fighting every day; they had ambition. But Aoki and her crew were project hoochies and ghetto bitches from sunup to sundown and didn't have anything positive going on.

Penny was taught to never fight a bitch that was ugly, argue with fools, or steal from a thief. She was also taught to never go against a person who had nothing to lose because their only mission was to have you lose everything too. Misery loves company, and Penny knew Aoki was miserable and troubled.

Penny wanted to get out of the hood someday soon. Unlike Aoki, she'd graduated from high school and planned on going to community college in the fall to take up nursing.

She got dressed in a new outfit, new sneakers, and her hair redone and looking tight. Her lip gloss was popping, and she used concealer to cover her bruised eye. Penny wanted to end the beef with Aoki.

Penny saw something blank and distant in Aoki's eyes while they were fighting. Aoki was reaching for her knife, but the cops arrived just in time. Penny felt if she didn't end her war with Aoki, she might end up seriously hurt if not dead.

She swallowed her pride and headed downstairs to join in with the others and Aoki. It was going to be awkward, but she had planned to let Aoki and everyone else know that she had come in peace.

※

Aoki still clowned Penny, but there was no violence. Penny joined in on the laughs and shared a blunt with Rihanna and Tisa.

Aoki looked at Penny and uttered, "Bandulu-ass bitch," Jamaican slang for fake or trick.

Penny didn't take any offense. She kept quiet and continued to chill, ignoring Aoki's insults. They didn't like each other, but it was best for her to try to get along.

As everyone was chilling outside, the girls noticed a black-on-black Range Rover with black rims pull onto the block. The girls perked up, knowing who the occupant of the vehicle was. Their eyes were fixated on the lavish truck.

The doors opened up, and B Scientific stepped out, along with two of his goons. B Scientific was a drug dealer from Bed-Stuy. He was high-end, not low-level like AZ, and his name rang throughout Harlem, the Bronx, and Brooklyn.

B Scientific was an Adonis with street swag—handsome, dark skinned, bald-headed, with a dark goatee. He stood six feet tall with a lean, cut body, and had a narrow face, intense eyes, and a raspy voice, probably from smoking cigarettes.

He walked toward the girls, who were all transfixed by him, especially Penny and Tisa. The way they stood and gawked, it looked like their pussies were throbbing. Like almost every chick in Brooklyn, they wanted to be with him.

Aoki smoked her Newport and looked unconcerned about the man everyone else was drooling over. *What's so special about him?*

Word on the streets was that he already had a bitch in his life. Brandi from Harlem was a jealous and vindictive woman. She loved her dude deeply. But he was a ladies' man. He had groupies chasing him like a major rap star. It was no secret that B Scientific fucked other bitches, but Brandi had his heart.

As he walked toward the building, he stopped to chat with a few niggas lingering around on the benches in the projects. Penny, Tisa, and the others were just a few feet away, looking and admiring everything about him. Even his name stood out—B Scientific; it made him sound like a Five Percenter, like he was an intelligent guy, and he was. The guys dick-rode him like bitches, showing him mad respect.

For a moment, he looked the girls' way, observing Tisa, Rihanna, and a few others. They were all beneath him— chickenheads, hood rats, ghetto bitches he wouldn't give the time of day, except maybe to suck his dick. But when his eyes came across Aoki, his stare lingered longer. For a moment, they locked eyes.

Aoki turned her look away from his and frowned. She wasn't interested. She wasn't like everyone else sweating him, on his dick tight like a condom.

B Scientific had seen Aoki around in passing, but this was the first time he truly noticed her. He said good-bye to a few niggas and walked toward his grandmother's building. B Scientific loved his grandmother deeply. Every now and then, he stopped by to give her a few hundred dollars.

Rihanna said, "Damn! He was clockin' you for a minute, Aoki."

"Who de fuck ah him?"

Ginger, an associate of the crew, said, "Girl, a nigga like B Scientific can definitely give you the fuckin' world."

"Me don't need de world, me just want fi me respect."

"Shit, fuckin' with B Scientific can give you all the respect in the world," Tisa said.

"You buggin', Aoki," Ginger said. "I will suck that man's dick until my whole fuckin' mouth goes numb and I make his forehead cave in."

The girls laughed. Aoki didn't. She smoked her cigarette and sat perched on the bench like she was the queen of her domain.

B Scientific didn't catch her attention, but she had definitely caught his.

AZ drove his Yukon across the Verrazano Bridge and into Staten Island, moving through the costly tolls and merging onto I-278. The traffic was sparse and moving. Heavy Pop was in the passenger seat pulling on a cigarette and relaxing, enjoying the ride. Staten Island was peculiar grounds for them. Located in the southwest part of the city, it was called the forgotten borough for a reason; sometimes people forgot it was part of New York City. Crossing the Verrazano Bridge was the only way to enter Staten Island by car from the city. AZ drove north, toward Stapleton, Staten Island, a violent, crime-ridden area. They planned to meet with Peanut, a local drug dealer in his early twenties who was looking to buy some weight from them.

"This fuckin' Peanut, you know what he's about?" Heavy Pop asked his friend.

"We spoke briefly," AZ said. "He sounds legit."

"He *sounds* legit? Nigga, either he is or he isn't. I know we light on customers, but I ain't tryin' to rush into business wit' every dealer in the city, AZ. We ain't that thirsty. Besides, I fuckin' hate Staten Island, and I hate everything it comes wit'."

"Nigga, lighten up. We just gonna feel the nigga out and shit. What? You hate Wu-Tang too?"

"They the only fuckin' exception."

AZ laughed. He steered his truck north on Bay Street. The neighborhood they entered was filled with Spanish bodegas, graffiti-covered buildings, and a few liquor stores. It screamed "the hood" loud and clear.

AZ took out his cell phone and called Peanut. "We close," he said.

There was a short pause before AZ hung up.

"What he say?" Heavy Pop asked.

"He's waiting for us."

Peanut was a grimy dude. He had a host of soldiers under his wings, mostly teenagers from 14 to 17 years old—his corner boys, triggermen, and lieutenants. Peanut was copping half a ki and three pounds of weed from AZ. Peanut used to buy from a young fledgling hustler named Bird, a kid from Harlem. Well, Bird had given Peanut a ki on consignment. Peanut sold the ki, but refused to pay Bird his money. Tensions mounted, harsh words and threats were exchanged. Bird wanted his money; Peanut laughed at him. The two men were now at war with each other.

Peanut had heard about AZ. The two men met in a nightclub and talked. AZ needed to increase his clientele, and Peanut needed a new connect. It was the perfect formula, or so it seemed.

For now, Peanut was going to pay for the weight from AZ. He needed to test him and see how weak or strong the nigga from Brooklyn was. See, Brooklyn and other boroughs always shitted on Staten Island, put their borough last. They underestimated niggas from Staten Island. If Peanut felt AZ was weak, he planned on robbing him of more than half a ki. But, first, he needed to gain the man's trust.

AZ's Yukon pulled up to a local barbershop on Bay Street.

Peanut was inside, seated in one of the barber chairs. He had just finished getting a haircut.

When AZ walked in with Heavy Pop, Peanut removed himself from the chair, slipped his barber, an older man in his

60s, a twenty-dollar bill and was ready to conduct business with AZ. Peanut was short and a little stocky, a brutish person with notable power. He moved with confidence that bordered on arrogance, like he owned everything.

"Welcome to Shaolin, my niggas." Peanut gave AZ and Heavy Pop dap. "Y'all niggas need a haircut?"

"Nah, we good," AZ replied.

"Y'all sure? Slim is the best cutter on Staten Island."

"We'll take a rain check on that," Heavy Pop said.

"Cool."

The barbershop wasn't crowded at all; just a few locals waiting for a haircut. The TV was small and outdated, and tons of magazines were spread out for customers to read. Everything inside was retro.

AZ and Heavy Pop were both armed. They were in a different borough and a long way from home. Peanut indicated for them to follow him into one of the backrooms of the barbershop. The men walked into a makeshift bedroom.

Peanut shut the door and looked at AZ. "I'm glad y'all niggas could make it. So let's talk business. Where's the stuff?"

"It's close," AZ said.

"Close, huh? I see you tryin' to feel me out. I respect that."

"You watchin' your back, and we watchin' ours," Heavy Pop said.

Peanut chuckled. "Yeah, that's smart on both ends. Stupid people make stupid mistakes."

"Exactly," Heavy Pop replied.

Heavy Pop removed a sample from some tin foil for Peanut to check out. Word around the city was AZ had pure coke and quality weed. It was high quality that could be stepped on a bunch of times and still maintain its potency. AZ's connect was a mystery, and he was riding high with it.

Peanut sprinkled a little of the sample cocaine on the back of his hand and snorted it into his nose. It sparked him up. "Damn!" he uttered, satisfied with the blow.

"I don't lie about my shit," AZ said. "Now for the weed, my high quality goes for three hundred and forty an ounce. The coke twenty-nine thousand a kilo. You want half that, it's eighteen."

"Damn, you up there, huh?"

"You want the best, then you pay for the best," AZ replied.

"Oh, I'm willing to pay for the best."

Heavy Pop said, "For what we got, you can push an eight ball for two hundred and fifty or more."

"That's what we here for," Peanut said, "to make some fuckin' money, right?"

AZ nodded. "It makes the world go round."

"It damn sure do. 'C.R.E.A.M. Cash is all I need around me,'" Peanut said lightheartedly, messing up the lyrics. He said to the two men, "You show me yours, and I'll show you mine."

AZ nodded to Heavy Pop, who left the room to retrieve the goods.

The back of the barbershop was secure and very private. It was a well-known and a respected location. Slim was an old-school *G* and Peanut's uncle. He'd done his part in the game and done his stints in various prisons. Now he was trying to school his out-of-control nephew who, yearning for a quick come-up, refused to listen to any of his advice.

Peanut had a plastic bag filled with cash. It was money from doing stickups, drug deals, and robberies.

"Yo, let me take y'all niggas to get somethin' to eat after this," Peanut said.

"Nah, we good."

"You sure? Because I know this great place that makes the best burgers and fries around."

"Next time."

"You missin' out, my nigga."

"It's cool," AZ said dryly.

Heavy Pop walked back into the room with the goods and his .9mm concealed in his waistband.

Peanut nodded and smiled at the product—a ½ ki of cocaine and three pounds of weed, packaged nicely. He handed AZ the plastic bag filled with cash. It was disorganized and unprofessional. The money was crumpled and sloppy, but there was a lot of it.

AZ shook his head and said, "Really?"

"It's all there, my nigga, trust me."

AZ took the bag and handed it over to Heavy Pop, who didn't hesitate to count it. Heavy Pop wasn't leaving the room until he was certain all the cash was exact.

AZ thought, *Why the sloppy cash? Is it a trick to try and get us to stay longer? Is Peanut trying to short us or set us up to get murked?*

It didn't take Heavy Pop too long to count the money. It was all there—$34,320 for the half a ki and three pounds of that Sour Diesel. "We good," he said to AZ.

AZ and Heavy Pop finally exited the barbershop without any problems. The two left Staten Island feeling content that they had a new, legit client.

SEVEN

The aroma in the project apartment one Friday afternoon was coming from pork chops and fish dinners being made by Gena. The smell of soul food had everyone drooling. Gena could definitely burn. It was her forte.

Aoki, Tisa, and Rihanna were chilling inside the apartment, trying to help Gena out in the kitchen. Like always, on the 1st and the 15th of the month, Gena got her hustle on by selling dinners to put extra cash in her pockets. The ghetto always looked forward to Gena's cooking. She usually made around $300 to $400 and give the girls $20 each. They didn't do it for the money; they all liked hanging around Gena when she was in a good mood, giving them advice about niggas, sex, and getting money. But then there was a flip side.

Gena danced around her kitchen with the fish frying in the grill and the pork chops cooking in the pan. She had a special way of making her pork chops. She would heat the canola oil over medium to medium-high heat, and then add salted butter. The butter was the flavor, and when the butter melted, she would add the pork chops three at a time two to three minutes on the first side, and then flip them until cooked well with a golden brown look. Along with the fish and pork chops came the side dishes—baked macaroni and cheese, string beans, cornbread, and peas and rice.

Aoki and Rihanna helped out with the macaroni and cheese while Tisa tried making the cornbread.

"Tisa, don't put too much milk in that batter," Gena said, "And, Ri-Ri, put a little more milk into that macaroni."

While they cooked with R&B music playing, the people were knocking at her door already, ready to pay her ten bucks a plate.

Gena had on a pair of coochie-cutting shorts and a small shirt. She swore she was still the shit and teenage young and behaved half her age. Back in the day, she was considered a dime. She loved that the girls listened to her advice, but deep down, she was bitter that she'd never gotten out of the hood.

While Gena took care of the pork chops and fish, she turned around and looked at Aoki. The young, biracial girl was looking too cute in her short shorts. Gena was envious that Aoki could wear, strut, run, and dance in six-inch stilettos as if they were high-tops. Gena stood five-nine in bare feet, so six inches would giraffe her. And even though she was a grown ass woman, Gena would boil inside when people would tell Aoki that she resembled anyone famous, like Naomi Campbell or Jhene Aiko. Each time someone praised Aoki's looks it would thoroughly irk her nerves.

Gena continued looking at Aoki, and she couldn't help but to be jealous of the young bitch. Aoki was clearly prettier than her daughters. She was envious of Aoki's soft and long hair, her dark-chocolate flawless skin, and her toned, athletic body. She hated that Aoki lived in a house with two parents, even if they were strung-out drug addicts. Of course, she was unaware that they were dead.

Out of the blue, Gena said, "Who makes more money, a crack dealer or a prostitute?"

The girls waited for the punch line.

"A prostitute—she can always wash her crack and then sell it again!"

The girls laughed.

Aoki didn't laugh as hard. She knew the joke was about her mother. It was no secret that Aoki's mother used to sell her ass on the streets for drugs.

Gena continued joking with, "What do women addicted to crack got in common with ice hockey players? They both change clothes after three periods."

A few more laughs.

"I can't . . . I can't," Gena howled at her own joke. She continued with, "I got one more joke—How can you pick out the crack addict in the grocery store?"

Aoki stopped laughing. She was tired of Gena subtly trying to come at her. Aoki didn't want to disrespect her friends' mother in her own place, but there was so much she could take from the woman. Aoki shot Rihanna a stern look, who then told her mother to knock it off.

"What?" Gena said, feigning innocence. "What did I say?"

The apartment was jumping with company going in and out, buying dinners, and kicking it with the girls. Weed smoke was everywhere. Gena was also selling cups of Hennessy for five dollars a shot. It was like a nightclub lounge in the apartment. People were being fed, drinking and mingling.

Aoki smoked her cigarette by the window and gazed outside at two crackheads walking briskly on the sidewalk. They somewhat reminded her of her parents. A bit of sadness overcame her for a moment. She didn't want to drown in depression, so she removed herself from the window and joined Tisa on the couch. She didn't touch the Hennessy or weed. A cigarette was good enough for her.

A few niggas tried to flirt with her, but she shut them down like school on a snow day.

In the middle of a full house with money flowing, Gena slipped away from it all and locked herself inside the bathroom. Inside, she stripped away her clothing and turned on the shower. It was getting late, and she had someplace special to be. The water cascaded down on her naked frame. She made sure to wash all of her areas thoroughly and took her time cleaning her kitty kat.

An hour later, she came strutting out of her bedroom looking dolled up and sexy in an extra tight dress and high heels that made her legs stretch to the heavens. She immediately caught everyone's attention in the apartment. The men were wide-eyed.

"Shit!" a man uttered.

Gena smiled.

"Where are you going, ma?" Rihanna asked.

"I got a date tonight."

"A date?" Rihanna replied, shocked.

"What?" Gena said, hands on her hips. "You think a bitch don't practice what she preaches? You think I be talkin' 'bout sex and niggas for my health? Yes, I got a date wit' a fine-ass nigga tonight." Gena's wide smile meant he probably was a keeper. Gena ate up the attention that she was receiving in the room. For once, in a long time, she had all the boys— and even the girls—staring at her milkshake.

The girls were happy for her.

"Who's the lucky man?" Tisa asked.

"He's a secret."

"C'mon, Ma, who is he?" Rihanna asked. "Is he someone we know?"

"A woman never tells her business."

The girls continued to press Gena, but she refused to tell them who it was. The only thing she would say to them was, if she played her cards right with this one, he would be her ticket out of the hood. She also told the girls that he loved her matured pussy, and it was only a matter of time before he bought her a five-bedroom home on Long Island and showered her with gifts and cash.

"Damn. It's that serious that you can't tell us who, Gena?" Tisa said.

"In due time." Gena smiled and left out the door looking like a million-dollar whore.

Gena strutted out of her building on cloud nine. She walked up the block, away from prying eyes. The mystery man she was meeting didn't want to be seen picking her up in the neighborhood, so she had to either walk or take a cab to their get-together points. What she didn't mention to the girls was that her mystery man had threatened to kill her if she ever told a word about them messing around. His threat was real. He'd murdered before.

She walked toward the movie theater and went into the crammed parking lot, where she saw his truck idling from a distance. It was definitely him. The smile on her face was so wide, that it wet her ears. She hurried to his truck and climbed inside.

"Hey, you," she greeted cheerfully.

"What's good, ma? You look nice tonight," he said warmly.

"Thank you." Gena eyed him like he was a celebrity. She wanted to give him babies. "What we doin' tonight? Where we goin'?"

"To chill."

"I'm down."

"I know you are. But, first, you know what I like," he said, unzipping his pants and pulling out his thick, black dick. He was barefaced with her and didn't care at all.

"Yeah, I know what you like," she said, smiling, eager to please.

Gena had no shame in her game. Movie parking lot or not, she was willing to please him. She lowered her head into his lap, cupping his erection with her manicured hand, stroking the dick effortlessly, and then slowly wrapped her glossy, full lips around the mushroom tip. She slid her lips slowly down his large erection and sucked him off in the front seat while he moaned and closed his eyes, entangling her long weave in his hand.

"Deep-throat that dick, ma."

She did it with no hesitation or problems at all. It was all about him tonight. Her head bobbed rapidly, up and down on his dick with spit all over his shit.

He reclined back in his position and enjoyed the sexual favor. She was the best.

Whatever it takes, Gena said to herself. *Whatever it takes to get out of the hood.*

If her daughters ever found out whose dick she was sucking, they would both be envious and upset with her. But Gena didn't care; it was about survival. And may the best woman win.

EIGHT

The late hour was the best time to ride the 495 Expressway going toward Riverhead, Long Island. AZ didn't have to worry about rush-hour traffic. The expressway was moving like a gust of wind on a windy day, nothing stopping it. It was a little over an hour ride to Riverhead from Brooklyn.

AZ was truly excited about this drive. It had been a rough week, but a good week. He had Peanut, who lived in Staten Island, as a new client, and he seemed legit. With him, business was going to boost. Also, Aoki had been cool lately; no drama, no arrests and no fights. She and her crew had been on point with their deliveries. The minor incident with Tiger worked itself out. Now Tiger was buying more from him. Tiger was good peoples, and AZ didn't want to lose him as a client. AZ was lucky to connect with a high-ranking Colombian named Don Esposito from New Jersey by chance. It was the best move he'd made in his life.

It was two in the morning when AZ arrived in Riverhead. It was almost the end of land out east. It felt like the town would break away from the island and float out into the sea. AZ steered his truck deeper into the quiet neighborhood. The town looked small and felt like a place where neighbors knew neighbors for miles and miles. The streets were lined with mom-and-pop shops and family-owned businesses. Everything was closed for the night, and the entire area looked like a ghost town.

AZ stopped in front of a white house with a white picket fence. It was a quiet, tree-lined block with beautiful homes costing from three to five hundred thousand. He killed the engine and removed a half pound of weed from the backseat of his vehicle. He'd concealed the drugs in a small bag.

He took a deep breath and stepped out of the Yukon. The area was still and tranquil. There were no worries about stickup kids and harassing police in this part of town. He didn't need a pistol. He trusted the home and the area. Stapleton, Staten Island, and Riverhead were worlds apart. AZ walked the narrow paved walkway toward the back of the home and tapped lightly on the back door, the thick shrubberies giving him cover from any nosy neighbors.

AZ waited patiently. The homeowner expected his arrival. He looked around, taking in the spacious backyard and the freshly cut grass. There was an oak tree and an old half-built tree house.

"Who?" someone asked from the other side of the locked door.

"You know who. It's me. Open the door," AZ replied composedly.

The door opened and standing in front of AZ was a young man named Connor. Connor was thin and brown-skinned with snow-white teeth and curly black hair. He was eighteen and he was well put-together, always dressed trendily.

AZ held up the bag with the half-pound of weed.

Connor smiled and said, "Well, it's about time."

"You know it's a long drive from Brooklyn to here."

"As long as you came." He stepped aside and allowed AZ into the home.

The two went downstairs into the basement, which was Connor's bedroom. It was meticulously neat and furnished with all the latest amenities, including a flat-screen television, woven carpet, a queen-size bed, and a shelf filled with books.

Connor lived with his parents, who were sleeping upstairs. He'd just graduated from high school with honors and was on his way to Yale in the fall. He looked at AZ and excitedly said, "Give me, give me. I've been waiting all night for this," he said with his arms outstretched.

AZ walked toward him, and the two embraced intimately into each other's arms and then kissed passionately. Their kiss was affectionate and heated. AZ enjoyed his boyfriend's warm breath and tender touch. Their embrace was so lovingly entwined; they resembled a piece of erotic artwork.

Connor pulled his lips away from his lover. "I missed you."

"I missed you too."

"I hope you're not becoming too busy for your number-one guy."

"No, I'm not."

Connor smiled. He didn't want to free himself from AZ's manly arms. He loved him. He was openly gay, but

AZ was still in the closet, hiding his sexuality from an intolerant world. If the streets ever found out about AZ's homosexuality, they would burn him at the cross and watch him rot. Connor's parents didn't approve of his sexuality, but they were tolerant.

The two men kissed again. Their lips locked passionately, and their clothes started to peel away.

Connor kissed AZ all over and fondled him below. "I see you always come with treats," he said, referring to his erection and the weed.

Connor was well-spoken and educated. Both his parents were doctors. He was spoiled and had been sheltered his entire life. AZ was his bad-boy lover, his heartthrob and his heart. The two had met a year earlier at a gay club in Long Island. AZ sometimes frequented the club alone. It was his getaway from Brooklyn, where he could be himself. Connor and AZ locked eyes near the bar, and a conversation ensued between them.

"I love you," Connor said, touching his man passionately.

There was kissing, sucking and loving. Position after position, they enjoyed each other. Connor moaned from his lover's touch. His eyes closed from feeling the pleasures, and his toes curled up as AZ made him come.

"I love you, baby," Connor said, his sweet voice echoing off the walls.

They fucked and sucked some more.

An hour later, AZ held Connor in his arms as they lay naked on his queen-size bed. They had also finished smoking a blunt. AZ was having a post-coital moment. He lay there looking pensive, thinking about so many things.

After it was over, after the intense sex with Connor, AZ hated the feeling. He hated being gay. He hated being trapped in the closet. His friends wouldn't understand his homosexuality. He wanted to like girls only, but when intimate with them, it was difficult for him to get an erection. But with Connor, he always grew hard like a rock.

AZ had purposely gotten Lisa pregnant to hide the truth about himself. He felt like an outcast on both ends, pretending to like women all his life. Hiding and fighting his secret was becoming tiresome. He'd even kept it from Aoki, not knowing what her reaction would be.

"I gotta go," AZ said, removing himself from Connor's naked brown flesh.

"Go? Why, baby? Why are you leaving me so soon?" Connor asked, looking upset.

"It's a long ride back to Brooklyn, and I got a lot of things to take care of in the morning."

Connor released a frustrating sigh. "I thought you were going to spend the night with me. My parents won't mind."

AZ started to get dressed. Connor removed himself from his bed and tried to wrap his arms around him while he was getting dressed.

AZ pushed him off. "Look, I can't spend the night with you, okay?"

Connor folded his arms across his chest and pouted. "So it's like that, huh? You come over, get you some ass, and leave like a thief in the night. I thought I was more to you than just a booty call, AZ. I thought I was important. I thought you loved me."

AZ threw on his shirt and then turned around and looked at Connor, who was pouting heavily, looking like he had sucked on a sour lemon.

"Look, I do want to be with you, but I got a lot to take care of . . . and, it's complicated."

"Complicated? Baby, I just thought that maybe we wake up together, have some breakfast, and enjoy a day together, like a couple. Why are you so nervous about coming out, AZ? It's who you are; accept it."

"You just don't understand."

"Then explain it to me."

"Look, your world and mines are completely different."

"Different? We both like dick, and we like each other, so what's so different about us?"

AZ sighed.

Connor would never understand. He was safe, far away from any danger the streets could cause. Connor was insulated from the bullshit. AZ didn't have a hedge of protection. If he fell, he didn't have accepting parents to catch him. He didn't have a trust fund. He wasn't going to Yale. He didn't graduate from high school. He didn't live an hour and a half away from the street life. There were so many differences between him and Connor.

Connor gazed at AZ getting dressed. Teary-eyed, he asked, "Are you fucking someone else?"

"What? No!"

"Just be honest with me, AZ. If you are, I won't get

mad. I know about your daughter. I know your baby mother was before we met. I understand that. I'm with you, and I only want you. No other person has been invading your territory, baby, believe that. I just hope no one has been invading mines either."

AZ sighed. He had cheated on Connor numerous times. "Look, I'm good to you," he said brusquely. "That's all you need to know."

"Good to me? Being good to me is spending the night and taking me out occasionally. Being good to me is about spending some quality time in public. I want you to take me to Brooklyn someday. I want to see where you grew up at, meet your friends someday. It's been a damn year, AZ. I'm tired of these late-night rendezvouses. Do you fuckin' understand where I'm coming from?"

AZ saw the bitch in Connor spilling out. It was definitely time to leave. AZ shot back, "Yeah, it's time for me to go."

"Go then, motherfucker."

He started walking toward the exit. Connor followed behind him, still naked, dick hanging.

"So you really just going to walk out on me like that, AZ? You get your nut and leave. Fuck you, AZ!"

When AZ got to the back door, Connor pushed him. "I hate you! Don't fucking come back! I'm through with you, AZ. I swear, you won't be getting any more dick from this end. Go fucking be with your whores in Brooklyn."

It was the same song and dance with Connor. First there was the excitement and passion between them, the sex and lovemaking, then the weed smoking and nestling, followed by AZ's abrupt departure and Connor's nasty attitude. But then Connor was always forgiving right afterwards and blowing up AZ's phone, apologizing, and begging for him to come over.

"Yo, I'll call you," AZ said.

"No, nigga, don't call me. Don't you ever come back to get you some of this tasty, big dick." Connor grabbed his long, flaccid penis.

AZ continued walking away. He climbed into his truck and started the ignition. Before pulling away, he lingered behind the steering wheel and thought about his lifestyle. He shook his head. He wanted tonight to be his last night with Connor, but lust always pulled him back.

NINE

Aoki and her crew rode the subway train into Manhattan on their way to NYU with three pounds of weed and three ounces of cocaine for a student named Emilio. He was AZ's new client. It was a busy day with the girls running around town from Queens and Brooklyn in the beginning then Manhattan, and the Bronx their last stop.

The girls were dressed stylishly, Aoki in tight blue jeans, high heels, and a halter top from a bargain store that she put together well with her outfit. Aoki carried the book bag like always. The book bag had enough contraband to get her a lengthy sentence in an upstate women's facility, but she was always cool like a cucumber.

The girls stepped off the train, out of the subway, and into downtown Manhattan. It was a beautiful day. The city was bustling with traffic and walls of people cluttering the sidewalk. NYU's main campus was only a few blocks away in Greenwich Village. The girls strutted through the concrete jungle, staying focused and on a mission to drop off the product. It was one of the better neighborhoods for them; a bit less risky. They tried not to stand out in the city; almost everyone was able to fit in somehow.

NYU was a big university with a cluster of buildings thinning out for blocks, from MacDougal Street to Broadway, its purple-and-white flag with the burning torch marking its properties like gangs mark the walls and streets of their neighborhood.

Aoki led the way, and Tisa and Rihanna followed.

The area was swamped with college students in their NYU hoodies and T-shirts marching to and from classes. Some ladies sported their bohemian outfits, their hemp book bags slung over their shoulders.

Aoki found her way to one of the university's twenty-two residential buildings, a place called Goddard Hall, which was less than a five-minute walk to Washington Square Park. It was six stories and crowded the entire corner of Washington Square East.

"This ah de place," Aoki said, looking up at the building.

She didn't want to take any chances walking anywhere and looking suspicious with drugs on her. Security looked tight downstairs in the lobby, and all the students walked around with ID badges. She thought she might need an escort to enter the building. She got on her cell phone and made the phone call to Emilio. She listened to the cell phone ringing.

After the third ring, a male answered, "Yo, who this?"

"Ya expectin' us, right?" she said to him.

"Yeah, yeah. Where y'all at?"

"Downstairs."

"Okay, I'm coming down now." He hung up.

Aoki and the girls waited. They took in the area. Students and people were everywhere; the nice and warm day made Washington Square Park the perfect place to be.

"All these white people out here, looking cheery and shit. They couldn't last one day in our hood," Tisa said.

Aoki and Rihanna laughed.

"I know, right? They lookin' like they don't have a care in the world," Rihanna said.

"They probably don't," Tisa said. "Mommy and daddy take good care of them."

Emilio came down to greet the girls. He smiled, they didn't. He was what the girls predicted him to be—a clean-cut Hispanic from California attending NYU on a scholarship. Clad in a pair of beige cargo shorts, sandals, and a purple NYU T-shirt, he was extremely cute. However he had no fire to him, no edge whatsoever, from what the girls saw. Not even a piercing in his ear. He looked nothing like a drug dealer, but he sold drugs to sustain himself through college. New York was a very expensive place, and a scholarship could only carry you so far in the Big Apple.

"Hey, I'm Emilio. It's nice to meet you," he greeted, extending his hand for a handshake.

The girls looked dumbfounded by his hospitality.

Aoki shook his hand. She wanted to burst out in laughter, but she kept her composure. It was still hard to picture him being a drug dealer.

Emilio invited them up to his dorm room, which was neat and simple and shared by his roommate, who wasn't around. There were two twin beds on opposite sides of the room, matching desks near the window, and laptops on both of them. There was one decent-size flat-screen connected to various game consoles. Various posters from rock bands, movie posters, to hip-hop icons covered the walls. They also had a fine-looking view of the park from the sixth floor, the greenery of the park contrasting with the buildings around, and the people below scattered everywhere.

"Nice room," Rihanna said.

"It's home for now."

"Let's just get dis don' wit'," Aoki said.

Emilio gazed at Aoki. He said, "I love your accent."

"Thanks," she replied, being short.

"What part of Jamaica are you from?"

"Me born 'ere."

"Oh! Okay." Emilio wondered why her accent was so thick for an American-born Jamaican.

Aoki was there for business. She removed the product from her bag and placed it on his bed.

Emilio went into his drawer and pulled out a wad of cash. Tisa was immediately impressed.

"Shit!" she uttered.

Emilio smiled. "You gotta do what you gotta do to survive in this city."

"I see."

"Where's your roommate?" Rihanna asked.

"In class. Won't be back for another hour or so."

They started to do the exchange. Coke and weed was all he needed. Business was booming on campus.

"I didn't know college kids get high like that," Tisa said.

Emilio laughed. "Seriously?"

"Ain't all y'all some goody two-shoes?" Tisa said.

"You really don't get around much, I see," Emilio said.

"What you mean?"

"College kids, we get high all the time, we party all the time, and we fuck up all the time. I'm just cashing in on a good thing here—the right product, the right clientele—and it's a free-fall of cash. College kids have a lot on their minds, do a lot of studying, lots of late nights, and sometimes the right things keep us going, keep us moving."

"You ain't worried about getting robbed carrying around all that cash?" Rihanna asked.

"I move in silence, and I move smart. I keep a low profile and know who and when to sell. And I keep this for those just-in-case situations." Emilio removed a small revolver from his desk and showed it to the girls.

Aoki wasn't impressed by his speech. If he moved in silence and kept a low profile, why was he sharing so much information with them? He was going out of his way to impress at least one of them.

Emilio was a brilliant student. It showed. He had character and a slight edge to him. While Rihanna and Tisa continued to think he was corny because he was educated, Aoki saw a slight bad boy in the college nerd. Selling weed and cocaine on a college campus was definitely nothing to sneeze at. If he got caught, he was looking at expulsion from school and arrest—and probably hard time.

"Hey, what y'all doing after this?"

"We have more runs to make," Rihanna said.

"It's a nice day today. I figured we could go get something to eat, my treat," he offered. "This area has a lot of cool places to dine at."

Emilio stared directly at Aoki. It was his personal invitation. He locked eyes with her. Tisa and Rihanna picked up on it. They knew the deal. Aoki was used to men flirting with her, trying to be subtle with their approach.

"We all have to eat, right? And I'm paying," he continued.

"We down," Tisa said, speaking for all of them suddenly.

Now that Emilio liked Aoki, Tisa felt jealous, and she now wanted him. Emilio wasn't her type, but somehow she could make it work with him, if he gave her a chance. She wanted to take his attention away from Aoki, if it was possible.

They all walked across Washington Square Park with its large arch and wide fountain, the dominating icons in the open area. Students, street entertainment, and people were everywhere. They ended up at the Courtyard Café, its décor average and the occupants mostly students and locals.

Emilio continued talking to the girls, telling his story, especially to Aoki.

Tisa tried to get his attention, saying things out of the blue like, "You know, you are a cutie," but it wasn't working. Aoki had his attention.

Aoki chomped down on a turkey and cheese club sandwich, and Emilio tried getting her to try a latte. It was an unfamiliar drink to them. The girls tried it and liked it.

"See, don't knock it until you try it," Emilio said, looking at Aoki.

"Well, I would like to try a lot of new things," Tisa said.

"Like what, Tisa? Some different dick?"

"Oh, you funny, Ri-Ri. Just Kevin Hart funny and shit," Tisa spat back.

"And you just hot all year around."

"You talkin', huh? The pot tryin' to call the kettle black, after your late-night rendezvous with Monty in the hood. Ain't he ya boo thang now?"

"We're not a couple," Rihanna corrected.

Tisa chuckled and replied, "Says the rooftop—'Hope you didn't get too much gravel in your pussy while lying on your back.'"

"Ha! Ha! You so funny, Tisa," Rihanna replied dryly.

"*Def Comedy Jam*, bitch," Tisa quipped back.

Emilio couldn't believe what they were bickering about. He was waiting for one of the girls to drop some dirt on Aoki, but they didn't. He watched her as she sat, quietly, observing her friends make fools of themselves.

"So what about you?" he asked.

"What about me?" Aoki replied.

"What's your story?"

"Me have no story.'"

"Sure you do. Everyone does." He looked deeper. "Why are your eyes so sad? Start there."

Aoki was at a loss for words. What were her eyes telling people? Did Emilio see her dead parents behind her black pupils?

"One day, maybe me tell ya. But ya start first. Tell me 'bout you."

Within no time, Aoki found Emilio quite interesting. She wondered how AZ met him. Emilio wasn't his average clientele; he was a gentleman and was charming and ambitious. But AZ knew how to network with people and draw them in. The man had personality, and he was always thinking outside the box. So Aoki wasn't too surprised that he was in business with a college kid.

After the café, the girls said their good-byes to Emilio, but not before he and Aoki exchanged cell phone numbers.

"Call me," he said.

Tisa wasn't too happy about it, but she kept her mouth shut. She didn't want to be seen as a hater. The girls went into the subway and got on the uptown train to the Bronx to deliver three ounces of cocaine to a low-level dealer named Lamont.

While on the train, Aoki thought about Emilio.

Tisa said, "You really gonna call him? He ain't even ya type, Aoki."

TEN

Yo, I got three hundred, my nigga. Three hundred down. Roll them fuckin' dice and lose ya fuckin' money, nigga!" Greasy Dee hollered at AZ.

Greasy Dee was a grimy nigga from Brownsville. He was tall, black, and sloppy. He and his friend Polo had a reputation for everything—stickups, drug dealing, armed robbery, and even murder.

"Lose?" AZ laughed. "You talk a lot of shit, nigga. You ain't tired of losing money? I already got you for two hundred. Shit, ya money is better in my pocket anyway, nigga." AZ shook the dice, getting ready to roll.

"Nigga, I'm tired of ya fuckin' mouth. I'ma get my money back."

"Not tonight, nigga. Not tonight," AZ shot back.

The dice game was in full effect in the building lobby, which reeked of weed. The local goons crowded over the five hundred plus dollars on the floor, passing around blunts and guzzling forties.

The game had been going on for over an hour, with a lot of shit talking and cursing.

Heavy Pop stood in the background, watching his partner in crime work magic with the dice. Heavy wasn't a gambler; he was a hustler.

Everyone was betting against the shooter.

AZ rolled the dice, letting them free from his hand coolly and confidently. All eyes were watching intensely, anticipating the outcome.

When the dice hit the wall, bounced off, and stopped rolling, AZ cheered. "Yeah, nigga, give me my fuckin' money! How you gonna bet against the house? Nigga, don't you know the house always fuckin' win?" He snatched the loot off the ground and counted it openly, showing off.

Greasy Dee frowned. He was losing big in one night.

As AZ continued to clown him, Heavy Pop smiled and shook his head. "My nigga," he uttered.

"Yo, fuck it! Run it back," Greasy Dee said.

"Damn, nigga, you ain't sick yet? Shit, when I finish wit' you, ya mama gonna owe me her damn house."

Everyone laughed.

"Fuck you, faggot!"

"What, nigga? What the fuck you call me?" AZ exclaimed, puffing his chest out and tightening his face.

"You heard me, nigga—you a fuckin' faggot! What bitch you fuckin'? Huh, nigga? Walkin' around the block like you gangsta like that. You ain't shit, nigga. Fuckin' faggot! Booty-bandit nigga!"

Greasy Dee didn't know AZ was gay in real life. But AZ felt so embarrassed and guilty, he just reacted without thinking.

AZ clenched his fists and swung at Greasy Dee, striking him in the jaw. Greasy Dee stumbled backwards, confused, but he didn't go down. A fight ensued. Both men rumbled and tussled, throwing blow after blow.

AZ caught a few heavy licks to his face, but he wasn't made of glass. He was a boxer and put his hand skills to use, striking his foe with a hard right hook and then a left. He wanted to beat Greasy into the ground.

"Yo, let them fight! Let them fight!" someone shouted.

AZ quickly took the upper hand when he smashed a beer bottle over Greasy Dee's head, and Greasy Dee went down.

Polo, Greasy Dee's right-hand man, lunged forward, lifting his shirt to pull out his burner.

Heavy Pop was quickly on it, pulling out his own pistol and screaming, "Back the fuck up! Back the fuck up!"

The crowd froze up, including Polo and Greasy Dee. Everyone had their hands in surrender in the air.

Heavy Pop scowled. He pointed his burner like a madman at everyone, threatening to shoot.

"Yo, you got it, nigga," Greasy Dee said dryly, backing away from the threat. "You got it."

"Yeah, nigga, I know I got it," AZ said, now pointing his own pistol at Greasy Dee.

For both Brownsville men, it was a no-win situation. AZ and Heavy Pop had the upper hand. Heavy made Polo surrender his gun. Plus, they took him for his gold chain.

"Nigga, bounce, and be lucky y'all leavin' with y'all lives," AZ said, talking that shit.

Greasy Dee's frown was so intense, it looked like he was born like that. Both men reluctantly went to the exit, robbed and embarrassed.

One of the players looked at AZ and said, "Yo, you know it ain't over wit' them niggas. They some serious goons. Y'all should have bodied them Brownsville niggas cuz they ain't gonna let this shit slide."

AZ didn't respond to the comment. He stood there silent and pondering. He knew he'd made a grave mistake by pulling a gun on Greasy Dee and Polo. But it was too late, and he wasn't about to be humiliated and called a faggot in front of his own peoples.

There was another fact AZ kept hidden away from the streets—he wasn't a killer. He pretended to be, but his heart didn't run that cold. He was selling kilos but was grateful that the wolves didn't come lurking at his doorsteps to take a bite out of him. What AZ had a reputation for was his hand skills—knocking niggas out. So the streets automatically thought he would buss his gun too, him and Heavy Pop.

"Yo, we out," AZ said, almost a thousand dollars richer from the dice game.

The two men marched cautiously out the doors and toward the truck.

AZ had to cool his head. He lit a cigarette and sat behind the steering wheel. Heavy Pop was reclined in the passenger seat and chilling.

"You believe that shit? Nigga tryin' to disrespect me and call me a fuckin' faggot."

"I would beat a nigga down myself for sayin' that shit to me."

After about a minute, AZ started his Yukon and drove off. He wasn't tryin to fret about Greasy Dee and Polo. They were two clown-ass niggas living on borrowed time.

AZ had money to make. Business was good for them both. Peanut was trying to reach them for another sale; two kilos this time. The meeting was set.

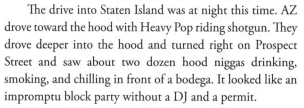

The drive into Staten Island was at night this time. AZ drove toward the hood with Heavy Pop riding shotgun. They drove deeper into the hood and turned right on Prospect Street and saw about two dozen hood niggas drinking, smoking, and chilling in front of a bodega. It looked like an impromptu block party without a DJ and a permit.

"Damn!" Heavy Pop said. "What? Is it a fuckin' carnival out this bitch?"

"I know. Shit is lookin' crazy out here."

AZ's eyes darted around for Peanut in the crowd of hoodlums. He didn't push his truck any farther down the block, but let it stay idling by the corner. He kept his gun close.

"Yo, call this dude because I'm not about to go out there and look for this nigga," Heavy Pop said.

AZ pulled out his cell phone and speed-dialed Peanut's number.

Peanut answered, and the first thing he said was, "Yo, that's you at the end of the block?"

"Yeah, it's us."

"Yo, park the truck and get out. Come have a drink wit' us and chill."

"Nah, we good," AZ said. "We would have you rather come to us."

"Oh, okay. I feel you. Too many niggas on the street for y'all."

AZ hung up. He looked ahead and noticed Peanut coming their way, a red plastic cup in his hand.

Peanut climbed into the backseat of the Yukon and greeted AZ and Heavy Pop with glad hands. "My niggas," he said, smiling.

"Y'all having a party or something?" Heavy Pop asked.

"Something like that. We havin' a little memorial for my nigga Raze; it was his funeral today."

"My condolences," AZ chimed.

"What happened? If you don't mind me asking?" Heavy Pop asked.

"I got a l'il beef wit' this Harlem nigga, but it's all good. Me and my goons gonna see that nigga real soon. Let the streets talk back wit' that big boom and let them Harlem cats know they can't sleep on Staten Island niggas. Y'all feel me? Niggas be thinkin' Staten Island is pussy out here, but we ain't. Our guns pop off too, y'all feel me?"

"Yeah, we feel you," AZ replied halfheartedly. He couldn't care less about Peanut's beef with a Harlem nigga.

"Yo, y'all can roll out fo' a minute so we can talk," Peanut said. "I don't want all these niggas in my business anyway."

AZ and Heavy Pop agreed. The Yukon was put into reverse, and they drove away from the busy area. They rode two blocks away and parked somewhere with less traffic and fewer people.

Peanut immediately went into negotiation mode. "Yo, I wanna cop two bricks from y'all, but I need that favor."

"Favor?" AZ responded with a raised eyebrow.

"Yeah, let me get them on consignment for now."

"What?" Heavy Pop uttered.

"I'm sayin', my niggas, the block is kinda hot right now wit' this war goin' on wit' this Harlem nigga. The paper has kinda slowed down a little, but I'm still grindin' out there. But you got my word, AZ—I'm gonna have ya money, no doubt. I just need these two bricks to keep the machine goin'. I'm a real dude, yo; you can trust me. I ain't gonna shit on you."

There was a pause and a little hesitation from AZ's end. He barely knew Peanut, but he did come through with his last sell. He looked at Heavy Pop for advice.

Heavy shrugged. "That's your call, my nigga."

AZ sighed. He turned around in his seat and stared at Peanut. Peanut was waiting for an answer.

"Look, I ain't comfortable wit' this consignment shit."

"Yeah, I know. But you know where I'm at every day. Y'all niggas can come see me anytime. I ain't goin' anywhere. I'm a local nigga, and I'm a real nigga."

"Here's what I can do for you—I'll give you one ki on consignment."

Peanut mulled it over and then said, "Yeah, that can work."

The two shook on it.

AZ wanted to continue his business relationship with Peanut. He'd worked hard at building his clientele and spreading his product from Queens to Staten Island.

AZ stopped at the corner of Bay and Prospect Streets. It looked like more and more niggas were converging on the street to join Raze's memorial.

"Y'all my niggas," Peanut said, giving the two men dap before climbing out of the truck.

AZ didn't drive away immediately once Peanut was out of his ride. He looked at the goons crowding the entire street and said to Heavy Pop, "Yo, you think we can trust him?"

"I don't trust anybody."

AZ sat for a moment and sighed. The one thing he didn't want to look like to his clientele was weak. He felt that he was doing too many negotiations with people and maybe it was time to slow that shit down. He wanted to make his peoples happy. He was a businessman, or he tried his best to be. He just hoped that no one forced his hand to react violently.

AZ drove away from the area trying to believe that he'd done the right thing. He lit a cigarette and tried to ease his mind. They crossed the Verrazano Bridge and were back in Brooklyn.

His cell phone rang. It was Aoki. She confirmed to him that all their deliveries had gone through smoothly. AZ was happy. He said, "That's my girl."

ELEVEN

The callous rain fell nonstop all afternoon, the steady downpour sounding like tap dancing shoes on hardwood floors. AZ was in a good mood. He and Heavy Pop were on their way into New Jersey to meet with a new connect named Oscar, a businessman and a drug dealer with connections to the Gulf Cartel. He was known in New Jersey as the Smiley man. The Smiley man was legit and cunning, and he only dealt with the heavyweights.

AZ needed a new connect. The Colombian he was dealing with had troubles in the legal department, and AZ felt it was best to cut ties with him for a moment. Oscar's name had been mentioned. Oscar was ready to link up with him and talk, after he had his people vet AZ. Oscar had the goods, and AZ had the cash. Oscar was also unequivocal that he didn't do business with anyone for anything less than five kilos.

Heavy Pop was driving, moving the Yukon through the streets of Brooklyn. AZ was on his cell phone conversing with a female.

"Oh, word? You tryin' to see me soon, huh?" AZ said, smiling. "And what you gonna do when I come over there?"

Her response made AZ laugh.

"I like the sound of that," he said.

Heavy Pop headed toward the Brooklyn Bridge. The streets were wet and tense. Sometimes the rain became so heavy that, even with the windshield wipers at full throttle, it was hard to see.

AZ continued talking *Love Jones* into his cell phone, pimping hard.

Heavy Pop smiled at his friend. "Yo, ask if she got a friend."

AZ grinned. "Yo, my dude wants to know if you got a friend for him."

Heavy Pop was waiting evenly for her reply.

AZ said, "Is he cute?—Yo, I don't judge niggas. That ain't my thing. She would have to see for herself . . . a'ight, that can definitely work . . . we can do that then." He ended his conversation with the female and said to Heavy Pop, "Yo, she's down."

"My nigga! I just hope she's cute."

"Pussy is pussy. Right, my nigga?"

"As long as she easy on the eyes—I ain't tryin' to put my dick in no gorilla-lookin' bitch."

AZ laughed.

As they continued driving, AZ's cell phone rang again. He looked at the caller ID. His mood changed to somber. He didn't answer the call. It was Connor calling him. It had been a week since their spat. AZ knew he was probably calling to apologize and ask to see him again. AZ definitely wasn't about to answer the call with Heavy Pop present. He allowed Connor's call to go to voice mail.

"Who that, my nigga?"

"Just some stupid bitch I ain't tryin' to see right now."

Right after AZ had Connor's call go to voice mail, a text chimed on his cell phone. AZ opened it. It was from Connor, saying:

BABY, PLS DN'T IG MY CALLS. I'M SORRY BOUT THE OTHER NIGHT, I KNOW I CAN GET EMOTIONAL SOMETIMES, BUT I LOVE U AND I MISS U. I WANT 2 C U, 2NITE IF POSSIBLE. CALL ME & I PROMISE I'LL GIVE U A SPECIAL TREAT 2NITE. ☺. XOXXOXOXOX

AZ missed him too, but he didn't want to be exposed. He kept a poker face while reading Connor's text repeatedly. Connor gave the best blowjobs ever. The way that nigga sucked dick was mind-blowing.

AZ deleted the text message. The last thing he needed was a stupid coincidence of that text message being seen. He sat back and said to Heavy, "Let's go make some money today."

The Yukon came to a stop at a red light on Eastern Parkway and Troy Avenue. The heavy rain made the streets empty. AZ's mind was in a different world. Why did Connor have to call him? He couldn't stop thinking about that man. It'd been a week too long. He wrestled with the idea of driving to Riverhead later that night to see him. The vehicle sat idling at the red light. Both men were quiet. It was a long trip to New Jersey, especially in the rain.

A black Denali pulled up next to their Yukon and sat idling at the red light too, windows tinted. Neither man paid any attention to the vehicle.

AZ removed a cigarette from his dwindling pack and lit it. Before he could take a decent drag from the cancer stick, gunshots cracked into the air all of a sudden, sounding loud like thunder and shattering the passenger window as bullets tore into their truck.

"Oh shit! Oh shit!" AZ hollered, ducking for cover from the gunfire as shards of glass rained down on him. "Drive, Heavy! Fuckin' drive!"

Heavy Pop ducked down in the driver's seat from the hail of gunfire and pressed down on the accelerator. He blew through the red light, barely missing a passing car. The car's horn sounded erratically.

The Denali blew through the red light too, chasing the Yukon. Gunshots continued ringing out. The occupants weren't cunning with their approach, but pure brutes in rage.

Heavy Pop had control of the truck as he sped down Eastern Parkway doing sixty.

AZ pulled out his pistol and fired wildly. He was scared! Bullets whizzed back and forth.

AZ knew it was Greasy Dee and Polo. "Crazy muthafuckas!" AZ shouted.

Bullets shattered the Yukon's back window, puncturing the rear of the truck.

Heavy Pop made a hard right turn toward the service road and blew through another red light, his pedal to the metal.

The Denali tried to follow but was cut off by a passing box truck.

By the time Greasy Dee and Polo came toward the intersection, AZ and Heavy Pop were long gone.

Heavy Pop continued to drive fast, cutting through block after block. When they were several blocks away, both men were able to relax and exhale.

Heavy Pop stopped the truck on Dean Street. Their truck was riddled with bullet holes, their back window and passenger window were gone, and rainwater was splashing into the vehicle. He exhaled noisily. He had his pistol in his hand and was watching out for the police and the niggas who'd shot at them. But everything seemed clear.

"Yo, what the fuck was that?" AZ said.

"Niggas tried to ambush us, yo."

AZ got out the truck, gun in hand, and looked around frantically. He didn't care about the rain drenching him. His only injuries were a few minor cuts on his face from the shattered glass. It took a moment for him to collect himself. He still had an important meeting with Oscar in New Jersey.

"Yo, let's go," he said to Heavy.

"You still headin' out that way?"

"Yo, ain't no life-or-death situation gonna stop the show and prevent us from gettin' this money." AZ was a little shaken, but he was still focused. He took a deep breath and jumped back into the truck. "Let's go park this shit and I'll borrow Lisa's hooptie to get us out there."

The meeting with Oscar was a game-changer for them both. AZ wasn't about to miss out on his opportunity.

An hour later they were in Union, New Jersey. The rain had stopped, but the sky was still cloudy and gray. They parked in front of two towering waterfront condos.

AZ stepped out. He took a deep breath as he gazed up at the buildings. "Nice," he uttered.

They walked inside, glided through the pristine lobby, and took the elevator to the 12th floor. Security answered the door and allowed the duo inside, but not before they were thoroughly checked for weapons.

"He'll be with you in a minute," the man said.

AZ and Heavy Pop lingered in the living room. They didn't look like they were just in a shootout. They were calm and ready to conduct business.

The glass balcony allowed an incredible view of New York City's skyline. They were so far up, it felt like they were standing on a giant's back.

"Gentlemen," Oscar greeted them from behind.

AZ and Heavy Pop turned around.

Oscar, dressed sharply in a three-piece suit, welcomed the men into his home with a formal handshake. He was handsome with a chiseled look about him, dark hair, and light caramel brown skin.

He gestured to the marble table and club chairs in the room. "Have a seat. Let's talk."

Oscar sat opposite of them, lit a cigar, and took a few puffs. He sat back in the club chair with his legs crossed. "I've heard some good things about you, AZ."

"I hope good enough to make us both happy today," AZ said.

"Let's talk business then. As you know, I don't do anything less than five ki's."

"I understand that, and I'm ready to make magic happen."

"Magic, huh?"

Heavy Pop, there for show and support, remained quiet in the room.

AZ leaned forward with his elbows in his lap and hands clasped together. He looked at Oscar and went to work on sealing a good deal with the man. He usually moved ten to twenty pounds of weed a month and three to six kilos. He needed to upgrade.

By the end of the meeting, they both agreed to ten kilos of cocaine and fifty pounds of weed, half of it on consignment. They shook on it.

With a new connection made and so much weight to distribute, AZ had to protect the empire he was trying to build, so he knew he had to deal with Greasy Dee and Polo real soon.

TWELVE

Word on the streets was that AZ and Heavy Pop ran like bitches after getting into a shootout with Greasy Dee and Polo. Greasy Dee was running his mouth, threatening AZ's life. It became the talk of the town. Greasy Dee made it known that he was looking for AZ and his friend. He continued to call AZ out, disrespecting him and slandering his name through Brooklyn and elsewhere, calling him a bitch and a faggot.

AZ quickly tried to tell his side of the story, telling anyone who was listening how he almost pushed Greasy Dee's wig back and wasn't afraid to buss his gun. But everyone knew that actions speak louder than words.

AZ had a serious problem on his hands. He understood that if he didn't do something immediately, maybe squash his beef with Greasy Dee, then he wouldn't be able to rise up and keep his respect. AZ felt like the streets were watching him closely and trying to pull his gangster card.

AZ smoked his thick blunt in Aoki's living room, exhaling the smoke and looking troubled about his beef with Greasy Dee. He told her about the shootout with Greasy Dee as he sat on her couch.

"It just happened, Aoki. We didn't even see it comin'. Niggas just rolled up on us on Eastern Parkway and opened fire. What was we supposed to do? I shot back, but they kept on coming, so we fuckin' got outta there."

Aoki sat next to him in a long T-shirt and tube socks, her hair wrapped up tightly underneath her night scarf. She looked plain and cute. It was late, and she was ready for bed. AZ had the right to come visit her at any hour, and she didn't care what she looked like in front of him. She'd heard about the incident through the grapevine, but now she was hearing the details from the horse's mouth.

She looked him square in the face. "Ya should 'ave killed dem in dat lobby. Now everybody's watchin' ya, an ya need ta react. Ya understand?"

AZ mulled it over. He sighed heavily and looked at her. "You think killin' someone is that easy?"

"It should be, especially in ya line of work."

"I'm many things, Aoki, but I don't think I'm that. I don't think I'm a killer," AZ admitted. She was the only person he could be honest with. Well, not completely.

Aoki didn't understand it or him at that moment.

"They respect me out here because of my hand skills, because I can box my ass off and knock niggas out. I was no joke growing up, made a lot of niggas scared of me. And I get money. But the game done changed, Aoki. I'm older, and these niggas out here are fiercer. They're killers."

"An wah are ya?"

"I'm scared."

"Scared? Wah make ya scared? Dat mon bleed just like you. Ya understand me, AZ?"

"I just didn't want to take it to this level."

"Well, it at dat level now." Aoki shook her head at her friend. She just didn't get it. Killing should be easy. She'd assumed that all drug dealers were coldblooded killers, but she had him all wrong.

"Me do it fah ya," she said, smiling.

"What?" AZ asked, confused.

"Me say, me do it fah ya," she repeated, but this time she wasn't smiling.

AZ didn't take her seriously at first, but the way Aoki looked at him, her eyes serious like cancer, he knew she wasn't joking with him. He sat up erect from the couch and looked at her.

"Can you really do it, for real?"

"Fah a small fee."

AZ sat quietly for a moment and thought about it. He nodded. He was more than cool with it. He looked at her and said, "If you can do this favor for me, I'll pay you five thousand dollars."

Aoki smiled. "Dat's cool. I'm ready."

Aoki didn't want to just get by on her father's checks. Besides, she wasn't sure how long the checks would last before the system caught on that he wasn't the one making the deposits and the withdrawals. She was also tired of being a drug mule for AZ. It was punk money to her.

AZ stood up and finished smoking his blunt. Once again, he asked, "You sure about this?"

With the coldness and gravity in her eyes showing, she responded, "Ya me bredren, AZ. Ya problem is my problem."

They hugged each other.

AZ was confident that Aoki would get the job done. He looked in her backyard and saw the two barrels still there, her dead parents still rotting away inside them.

AZ walked out of Aoki's home feeling a little of the weight lifted from his shoulders. He hoped that he wasn't putting his friend in any danger. Greasy Dee and Polo were two dangerous men, but Aoki was a force to be reckoned with. He saw it in her eyes. She was ready for this.

AZ climbed into his truck and drove away. He jumped on the Belt Parkway toward the Cross Island Parkway and then sped onto the L.I.E. and headed toward Riverhead. He was on his way to see Connor to spend some quality time with him. AZ had a lot of pent-up energy inside of him, and he was ready to let go and have some fun. He wanted to take his mind off the streets and his troubles.

THIRTEEN

Aoki sat for hours in her bedroom contemplating how to kill Greasy Dee and Polo. She remembered seeing them drive around in a black Denali, and those two meatheads weren't hard to miss. Aoki was ready to earn the five thousand AZ promised her. There was no way she was going to fail with the hit. So she thought hard and tried to come up with a foolproof way of slaughtering the two thugs without getting caught.

She would need help. And the only help she could think of was Tisa and Rihanna. Would they be down for the kill? Probably not.

She got on the phone with Tisa and Rihanna and invited them over.

The girls came over, and Aoki was all smiles and laughs. They ordered Chinese food and watched horror movies. Tisa and Rihanna smoked several blunts and drank. And they reminisced about the good times and the bad.

Tisa brought up AZ's beef with Greasy Dee. And then, in the middle of it all, Aoki brought up Brownsville, suggesting that they all go and chill in that neighborhood.

"Brownsville?" Tisa asked. "Why go there?"

"Because I want to," Aoki responded.

Aoki convinced them to go to Brownsville with her, claiming she wanted to see a friend in the Howard Housing project.

Tisa and Rihanna were cautious about trekking to that part of town. Brownsville was a rough neighborhood, its motto, *Brownsville, never ran and never will!* The streets and projects were more dilapidated than their own area, and the Pink Houses on Linden Boulevard was nothing compared to crime-ridden Van Dyke Houses or the Howard Houses.

It was late in the afternoon when Aoki and her friends got out of a gypsy cab on Pitkin Avenue, all three girls looking too cute. Rihanna and Tisa wore short shorts and close-fitting shirts highlighting their tits. Of course, Aoki wore a romper and her high heels, strutting on the Brooklyn sidewalk like she was on the catwalk at Fashion Week in the city.

They went in and out of the bodegas, buying snacks, catching the boys' attention. As they crossed the streets, car horns blew at them. They accepted the attention. Even a few bitches gave them hateful glances.

Aoki ate the attention up. It was what she was looking for. But she was looking for certain attention from certain people. It was the reason why she was in that hood and armed with her pocketknife.

The girls spent several hours in Brownsville after running into a few chicks they knew. Ultimately the trio ended up sharing a few blunts on the project bench with Sink, an associate of AZ who wanted to bag Rihanna.

Two days later, Aoki and her crew were back in Brownsville. She noticed Greasy Dee and Polo drive by them in their Denali. Greasy Dee looked her way, but he didn't stop. He kept it moving, like he had some important business to attend to. Aoki was patient.

Rihanna and Tisa had no idea why Brownsville had gotten Aoki's attention, but they were going with the flow. They loved the attention, especially Tisa. She collected numbers and flirted with all the hustlers that came her way.

For a week, Brownsville became the ladies' stomping grounds. Sometimes they went shopping for knickknacks, and sometimes they chilled with Sink and his peoples in the Howard Houses. Aoki was determined to get Greasy Dee's attention. Her outfits became sexier and sexier, and she was taking risks. Greasy Dee would drive by, but he didn't stop to holler at them.

On the seventh day, Aoki was coming out of the bodega on E. New York Avenue when she noticed Greasy Dee and Polo seated in their Denali on the corner and talking with a certain individual. Greasy Dee turned and looked Aoki's way. They locked eyes. Aoki remained deadpan.

Greasy Dee nodded and smiled, and then he called her over from the passenger seat. "Yo, ma, let me holla at you."

Bingo!

Aoki's white Seven jeans were extra tight and her silky long hair was shining. Rihanna and Tisa walked out of the store to see that Aoki had the attention of AZ's rival. All three of the girls soon had Greasy Dee and Polo's attention. Polo was seated behind the steering wheel, smoking a cigarette and looking extra shady.

The two men looked at Aoki and her friends like they were a juicy steak on a dinner plate. Aoki was exotic and beautiful—just his type. Aoki walked over with boldness and her eyes fixated on Greasy Dee. She was on a mission. Reluctantly, Tisa and Rihanna followed behind her.

Greasy Dee was transfixed by Aoki's beauty. Aoki walked toward the Denali and smiled. Greasy stepped out of the truck and went toward her, saying, "I've been seein' you around, ma, looking sexy and shit. What's ya name, ma?"

"Tina," Aoki lied. "An where ya go? Me gwon too."

Her Jamaican accent came out extra thick, making Greasy Dee's dick jump.

"Shit, you sexy wit' an accent like that, ma. Damn, you from Jamaica, right?"

She nodded.

"Tina, I like that," he said.

Rihanna and Tisa stood in the background and were taken aback by Aoki's sudden kindness to Greasy Dee. Both men were drooling, craving and lusting over the young girls. Tisa and Rihanna both rolled their eyes and were ready to go. They didn't want to be around the two ugly thugs. They also didn't like their grimy ways. Rihanna and Tisa were shocked that Aoki was engaging in a conversation with Greasy Dee. They both felt she was disrespecting AZ by talking to him and flirting with him.

"Yo, why ya friends so quiet?" Polo asked.

"Why don't ya ask dem yourself?"

"I'm sayin', we don't bite, right?" Polo said.

Rihanna sucked her teeth.

Polo looked at Rihanna and said, "I like ya friend." He was definitely feeling her look.

Aoki continued conversing with Greasy Dee. She put on an Oscar-winning performance by smiling in his face and being touchy-feely, touching his chest and his arms, and complimenting him on his manliness.

"Yo, ma, you and ya girls wanna go fo' a ride?" he asked.

"Me don't mind. Let's go," Aoki said quickly.

"What?" Rihanna said. "You serious?"

"Give me a minute." Aoki walked over to her friends and said, "Me know wah me doin'. Let's just go for de ride and chill. I got this."

"I hope so," Rihanna said back.

Grudgingly, the girls climbed into the Denali with the two men.

Greasy Dee and Polo were greatly pleased.

"Let's do this," Polo said.

Aoki got in the passenger seat, while Polo climbed into the backseat with the girls to keep them company.

Greasy Dee pulled away from the curb and shared a subtle look with Polo via the rearview mirror that said, *It's on!*

The guys drove into the city to midtown Manhattan where they had dinner at the Crab House on 43rd Street.

Once Tisa and Rihanna had a couple of cocktails in their system, they started to loosen up. They flirted back with the men, laughed and smiled in their faces.

Rihanna didn't mind that Polo had his hand on her thigh and tried to fondle her pussy underneath the table. Polo also held conversation with Tisa too, while Greasy Dee and Aoki seemed to be in their own little world, making what looked like the perfect connection. Also, Polo didn't know which one of the girls he liked more, so he was willing to take them both.

After dinner and many drinks, they drove back into Brooklyn, crossing over the Williamsburg Bridge. It was after midnight, and the traffic was light.

Aoki continued to flirt with Greasy Dee. She was all over him as he drove, kissing the side of his neck, groping his manhood, and stroking his ego to the point of no return. She had him so hard, it showed in his jeans.

Polo kept Rihanna and Tisa company in the backseat. He kissed them both and was ready to shed their clothing and ask for a blowjob.

"Baby, do me ah favor an' stop by me aunt's place," Aoki said out of the blue.

Tisa and Rihanna were bugging.

Tisa blurted out, "What aunt are you talkin' about?"

Aoki shot Tisa a sharp look, and she and Rihanna quickly began to play along.

"Oh, you talkin' 'bout ya aunt Shug. How she doing anyway?" Tisa said.

"She's been sick. Since we in de neighborhood, me just wan' to say 'ello to her."

Greasy Dee didn't have a problem with the plan. Whatever it took to make her happy.

Aoki directed him to the location in Brooklyn. They continued to converse, and she continued to stroke his ego and build his erection.

Polo was in heaven, sandwiched between Tisa and Rihanna in the backseat.

"Turn right," Aoki directed him.

She continued directing him until they parked on a residential block with a grade school and park down the street. They were across the street from a vacant lot. The block was quiet, the bodega closed, and nobody was around.

"I'll be right back." Aoki leaned over and gave Greasy Dee a kiss on his lips and caressed his private area; she had him extremely excited and hard. "Me won't be long."

While Greasy Dee was distracted by Aoki's seductive touch, she subtly removed her pocketknife from her back pocket and gripped it in her fist. She kept it concealed and ready. Her friends had Polo distracted too; he was almost in an alcoholic and weed stupor, his eyelids sagging.

Tisa and Rihanna were ready to go with Aoki, but she instructed them to stay put, she wasn't going to be long. "Dis won't take long," she said.

They wondered what she was up to. She didn't have an aunt living in the area—she didn't have any family here at all. They kept their suspicion to themselves and kept Polo entertained with kisses, touches, and smiles.

While Aoki fondled Greasy Dee in the front seat, he closed his eyes. He unzipped his jeans and whispered, "Before you go see ya aunt, ma, let me get a treat real quick."

"Oh, ya want ah treat from me, huh?"

"Yeah, kiss my dick." Greasy Dee had his dick in his hand, exposed.

Aoki stroked it.

"Oh yeah, do that shit, Tina."

As she seduced him, she thrust the pocketknife into his neck and twisted it, instantly striking his carotid artery.

"Dis ah fah me friend!" she shouted.

"What the fuck, bitch!" he screamed out, wide-eyed and twitching from the blade plunged into his flesh.

He tried to react, reaching for his gun tucked in his waistband, but Aoki reached for it too, and a violent tussle ensued in the front seat of the Denali, with Greasy Dee's blood squirting everywhere.

While the chaos was happening in the front seat, Polo snapped out of his drunken stupor. He screamed, "You fuckin' bitches!"

Tisa and Rihanna were shocked at what had just happened. They sat looking frozen, mouths gapping open, and couldn't believe it.

As Greasy Dee was bleeding out, Polo reached for his gun. He tried to point the weapon at Aoki, ready to blow her fucking head off. Polo was going crazy, screaming, "I'm gonna kill y'all bitches!"

"Grab him!" Aoki shouted. "Grab him!"

Tisa desperately grabbed Polo's wrist, trying to steer the barrel of the 9mm away from Aoki's face.

Greasy Dee was dying, and Aoki was still wrestling with him fiercely, enmeshed in blood. Greasy Dee wasn't about to die so fast. He was fighting with the pocketknife in his neck.

Aoki couldn't control them both at the same time. She needed help.

Polo was trying to shoot her in the face at point-blank range. He was heavily resisting Tisa's feeble attempt to stop him. "I'm gonna kill y'all bitches!" he shouted.

Tisa bit Polo on his neck so hard, it caused him to flinch and drop the gun. Rihanna went reaching for it.

Polo was drunk, so he wasn't his strongest or most accurate. He fought with Tisa, throwing his weight into her, making her unbalanced and then punching her in the face repeatedly.

Then he tried to strangle her, wrapping his powerful hands around her neck and squeezing tight, his face flaring with rage and anger, becoming rigid with his jaw clamped tight, his eyes bright red and his teeth grinding.

"You fuckin' bitch!" he shouted.

Tisa gasped for air. She tried to fight him off of her, but to no avail. Her eyes pleaded Rihanna's way for help. She was dying.

Aoki still had Greasy Dee to deal with. The man wasn't going out without a fight. His blood was everywhere.

Bak! Bak!

Abrupt gunfire burst out.

Two quick gunshots suddenly exploded inside the truck, throwing everyone off.

Polo freed his hands from around Tisa's neck and slumped forward from the bullets that tore into him.

Rihanna had shot him twice in the side.

Tisa coughed and gasped. She was in tears. She was

shocked and scared. Everything happened so suddenly.

Greasy Dee stopped moving, finally succumbing to his wound.

Aoki was in the front seat, breathless and looking disheveled. She looked back at Tisa and Rihanna. Both ladies were in tears and didn't know what to do. They stared at Aoki and wanted to run away.

Rihanna went to open the back door, ready to flee the crime scene, but Aoki screamed, "No! Not yet!"

"What? We gotta get outta here!" Rihanna cried out.

"No, Ri-Ri, wait!" Aoki said. "Just don't move, not yet anyway."

They both thought Aoki was crazy. There were two dead men in the vehicle with blood everywhere. Why linger and get caught?

Rihanna looked like she was hyperventilating, wheezing heavily like she had asthma.

The gunshots were loud, and were most likely heard by the residents. Aoki peered up at the windows to the tenement buildings and saw a few lights turn on. Aoki figured the neighbors would be looking for some kind of movement, maybe a dead body on the street. But they saw nothing but a few cars, including the Denali parked on their street with the lights off.

Aoki didn't want any witnesses to see three females fleeing from the Denali. So she told everyone to stay put and keep their cool. Moments later, the tenements lights shut off and curtains closed, meaning no more eyes on the block.

"Okay, we good," Aoki said.

"We good? Are you fuckin' serious, Aoki? We are not good! We are so far from it!" Rihanna exclaimed, teary-eyed.

"Please . . . help me."

The girls jumped, startled by Polo's words.

"Help me. T-take me to the hospital. I-I don't w-wanna die," he stammered.

Aoki decided to finish him off. She took her pocketknife and stabbed him in the chest twice, and he stopped moving.

Tisa and Rihanna had seen enough. They wanted to go home.

Aoki ordered her shell-shocked friends to grab the gun, Polo's wallet, and his jewelry. Reluctantly, they did so. Rihanna and Tisa's hands were trembling as they stole from the dead man.

Aoki took from Greasy Dee. Then she took the red bandana he kept in his pocket to wipe off her fingerprints from the door, the dashboard to the steering wheel, and clean off the blood on her. It was messy and she did the best she could.

"Let's go," she said to her friends.

No one was around when all three girls slowly exited the vehicle. It was late and quiet, making it the perfect moment to make their escape without being seen. They left the vehicle with both bodies slumped inside. They hastily and nervously walked block after block in silence, looking over their shoulders and being paranoid.

Rihanna and Tisa feared that the cops were coming to arrest them. Aoki was expressionless and cautious all the way.

They got on the subway and took the C train to East New York. They arrived home around five a.m.

Rihanna and Tisa went to Aoki's place. Inside her home, one by one they took a long shower, washing off any blood on them and any DNA evidence. Tisa and Rihanna were still shocked about the night's horrific episode. They wished it was a nightmare they could wake up from. They were still quiet and almost in a trance.

Aoki cleaned the bathroom with bleach and Pine-Sol until the whole house was permeated with the clean scent. She then gathered everyone's clothing and placed them in the trash. And after that, all three of them squeezed into Aoki's queen-sized bed and went to sleep. Even though there were two other bedrooms in the house, the girls refused to sleep in any one of them, especially Aoki's dead parents' bedroom. Aoki's home felt creepy to them, so they stayed near each other, still never uttering a word to each other about what had happened and why.

FOURTEEN

It was early morning and the vibrant sunrays percolated through the bedroom window to start another warm day in Brooklyn. Aoki was the first one to wake up and remove herself from the bed.

Aoki donned a long T-shirt and peered out the window, the events of the previous night still in her head. She couldn't believe she'd actually pulled off the hit. It seemed like they had gotten away with murder. Greasy Dee and Polo weren't well liked in the neighborhood to begin with, and had a long list of enemies. Aoki felt that she'd cleaned up the inside of the Denali good enough to not leave any trace evidence behind.

In a chain reaction, Tisa woke up next and then Rihanna. Aoki, still standing by the window, smiled at them, but they didn't smile back. They hadn't forgotten. It was still heavy on their minds. Both girls were still shocked and quiet.

Rihanna spoke first. She was still spooked and upset. "What the fuck did you do, Aoki? Why?"

"It was ah favor."

"A fuckin' favor? For who? You got us involved in a fuckin' homicide! What the fuck!"

"Ri-Ri, just chill."

"No, I can't chill. I killed a man last night."

Tisa was still shaken up too. She started to cry, thinking that they were all going to get caught and go to jail. "This is gonna come back on us," Tisa said reflectively.

"It's nah gon' come back on us, ya hear? It's taken care of." Aoki tried to assure them, but she wasn't convincing.

Tisa and Rihanna were overwhelmed with worries and concerns.

"Who was the favor for?" Rihanna asked.

"It was fah AZ. Him needed me help."

"He couldn't do the shit himself!" Tisa screamed.

"Him could, but him was willing to pay us fah it," Aoki told them.

"Pay?" Rihanna uttered, looking perturbed by her answer. "How much was he paying?"

"It's good money. I'm guh split it wit' ya."

The girls couldn't believe what bullshit Aoki was telling them. They could be going to jail for life.

Rihanna exclaimed, "You should have told us, Aoki!"

"Me should, but would ya agree?"

"You know we wouldn't," Rihanna replied.

Aoki knew there was no way she could do it alone. Their help was critical to her executing the hit. She was good with a knife, but Rihanna looked like a natural when she pulled the trigger on the gun and shot Polo.

"Y'all don't need ta fret. We covered our tracks."

"You believe that?" Tisa said.

Aoki nodded.

Tisa and Rihanna couldn't relax at all. Paranoia still showed on their faces. They didn't want to leave the bedroom, scared of arrest or retaliation from Greasy Dee's people. What did Aoki get them into?

"I need my fuckin' blunt," Tisa said.

"Me make breakfast then." Aoki left the bedroom and went downstairs.

Tisa shut the bedroom door. She gazed at Rihanna with heavy concern in her eyes. Rihanna was quiet, looking pensive, as she sat at the foot of the bed.

Tisa went to Aoki's dresser and removed the pre-rolled blunt that she had pulled from her jacket pocket before she was ordered to throw her clothes away. It was still intact after her scuffle with Polo. She meant to smoke it, but after being thrust into chaos and the murders, she had forgotten about it. She lit the blunt and took a much-needed pull, allowing the potent Kush to take control of her nervousness. She needed to get her mind right.

Tisa shared the blunt with Rihanna.

Tisa's eyes rested on the two, huge tin barrels in the backyard as she stared out the bedroom window. She knew what was inside those barrels. It'd been two summers already and they were still around, not buried into the ground like they were supposed to be. Tisa asked herself why Aoki's parents were still in the backyard, still exposed for anyone to see. It was foolish. It was evidence for the police.

"She's losing it, Ri-Ri," Tisa said.

Rihanna took a few pulls from the blunt and passed it back to her sister. She nodded at what Tisa said, agreeing wholeheartedly.

"This bitch done pulled us into another murder rap. This is the second time, Ri-Ri. What is goin' on wit' her?"

"She's crazy."

"I know."

"What we gonna do?"

"You know what I think. I think that Aoki probably killed both her parents. I think she went loco that night and snapped. I mean, how we know she's tellin' the truth? It's easy to blame her father for her mother's murder. What the fuck! How she gonna just kill people like that?"

"I'm still scared, Tisa. I just don't wanna get caught."

"Me either." Tisa almost teared up. "What we gonna do?"

Rihanna shrugged. "I don't wanna do anything right now. My head hurts."

"We gotta do somethin'."

"Like what?" Rihanna asked. "Go to the cops?"

"Maybe."

"You know we can't snitch. Besides, we'd go down too."

"This bitch got our backs up against the wall." Tisa found yet another reason to resent Aoki. Each time they got into trouble, from elementary school moving forward, it was always because of Aoki.

"How much you think AZ is paying her?" Rihanna asked.

"It better be worth it. We talkin' about our freedom here."

Kush smoke filled the bedroom room as both girls sat on the bed talking and letting their high take them away from their worries. Rihanna and Tisa felt stuck in Aoki's world now. They couldn't go to the police, and they couldn't tell anyone else about the murders.

Aoki walked into the bedroom carrying a tray filled with scrambled eggs and buttered toast, along with waffles and orange juice. It was the least she could do for their help. She owed them big time. They barely ate, though. Rihanna and Tisa were depressed.

Aoki tried to lighten their mood, but to no avail. They simply went back to sleep while Aoki got on her cell phone and called AZ. He answered, and Aoki simply said to him, "It's done! Come now."

AZ drove toward Aoki's home doing seventy on the Long Island Expressway and thinking about her phone call. He couldn't believe it. Were Greasy Dee and Polo really dead? Was Aoki crazy enough to pull off a hit like that? He smiled at the thought of it. "Wow!" he uttered to himself.

He was coming from Connor's place. AZ had needed the time away to relax and be himself. Connor was able to take his mind off the streets and his beef. Last night was amazing. They both had multiple ejaculations. Connor didn't get emotional this time, and he did tricks to AZ's body that would make a magician crave for his secrets.

He merged onto the Cross Island Parkway with the morning traffic. AZ sighed with relief thinking about Aoki.

There was a part of him that felt guilty. What if she had been killed while implementing the hit? How would he have forgiven himself?

As he drove, his cell phone chimed in the passenger seat next to him. He scooped up his phone and saw that it was Heavy Pop calling. He answered right away. "Yo, what's good?"

"You heard?" Heavy Pop said.

"Heard what?"

"Greasy Dee and Polo were gunned down last night."

"Shit! Fo' real? Damn!"

"Yeah, it's all over the hood. The streets are talking."

AZ smiled. He wanted to tell Heavy Pop that he was behind the murders, but he didn't want to talk over the phone. There was no telling who was listening. He had to be careful.

"Where you at?" Heavy Pop asked.

"I'm comin' from this bitch's house. Why you ask?"

"We need to talk."

"A'ight, I'll be around your way in about an hour. I gotta stop by and see Aoki first."

"Okay, get at me. One!"

"One, my nigga!" AZ hung up.

AZ still needed to wrap his head around the reality that Aoki was a hardcore killer and not just a girl caught in a violent situation like with her parents. He didn't push her to kill for him; she'd volunteered.

As he got closer to Brooklyn, his cell phone rang again. It was one of his associates calling. The man informed AZ about Greasy Dee's and Polo's sudden demise. Just like that, all types of unbelievable stories started to surface about how the two thugs were murdered. Everyone assumed AZ had murdered them, or had them murdered, blowing up his street credibility. That incident alone, those two murders, suddenly made him more feared than ever.

AZ pulled up in front of Aoki's place. He picked up his cell phone and dialed. She answered.

"I'm downstairs," he told her.

"I'll be down in ah minute."

"Okay."

He hung up and waited. He lit a cigarette and listened to the Hot 97 morning show with Rosenberg and Ebro. He sat back and listened to their musical guest, T.I., talk about his new movie, his reality show, his relationship with Tiny, and his life in ATL. He sat for a minute or two until Aoki knocked on the window. He gestured for her to get in on the passenger side.

When she was seated in the truck, he gave her a big squeeze and a quick peck on her lips. "I love you, girl!"

It was a long, sensual hug and a sudden kiss that she didn't expect. He never kissed her on the lips. It was strange. It made Aoki think that he wanted her for more than a friend. Or maybe he was just really happy that she'd come through for him. Either way, AZ was in a very good mood.

He handed Aoki an envelope containing five thousand dollars cash.

"It was ah easy hit," she started to say. "We caught dem attention, and—"

"Aoki, chill. I don't wanna know the details. It's done, and that's the only thing I care about."

"Ya sure?"

"I'm sure."

Aoki shrugged.

"That's the five grand I promised you."

Aoki opened the envelope and saw it was filled with cash, mostly hundreds and fifties. It was a lot of money for her. She needed the cash. She smiled. "Dis money, it made fi me day."

AZ saw that she was totally fine with taking someone's life, and that is what prompted him to make the next proposition.

"Well, how would you like to make some more of that?"

"What ya mean?"

He took a deep breath and gazed at her. She was a Barbie doll, but the coldness in her eyes made her the femme fatale.

"I want you to continue to kill for me."

"Ya have beef, AZ? Wit' who?"

"Nah, you took care of my immediate threat. I'm talking about in the future, when a situation like that comes up again. I need someone to rely on, who won't flinch when taking someone's life. In this game, the Greasy Dees and Polos are inevitable; they're gonna always be around, and I need the protection. Think about it. My enemies would never expect a woman like you; they wouldn't even see it coming."

She was down for the job, but, she wasn't too sure about her two friends.

"Me is down wit' the plan, AZ, but Ri-Ri and Tisa, I'm nah suh sure of. Dem ah still spooked."

"Well, make them un-spooked and have them get down wit' the program. I'm willing to pay y'all handsomely. I need this. I can see y'all doing well with what I have planned. Besides, what else do them two knuckleheads got going for themselves?"

Aoki unexpectedly received a text message that made her smile. She quickly responded.

AZ looked at her and asked, "Who that?"

"Ah friend," she simply replied.

"A friend, huh? That friend definitely got you smiling hard."

Aoki continued to text. Unbeknownst to AZ and everyone else in her circle, Aoki and Emilio had started talking on the low. She didn't expect to talk to him. She didn't expect to like him. It just happened.

"Why don't you stop texting your friend and talk to me?"

"Me talk to ya."

"No. I mean, become my girl."

Aoki turned his way and smirked. "Me know ya jokin'."

Yes, he had to be joking. They'd been friends for too many years to jump into a relationship. She loved AZ like family, but how could they mesh as a couple? Could he make her sad eyes smile?

As she pondered all these questions, AZ turned to her and said, "Aoki, I need to tell you something. It's important."

"Ah wah?"

He locked eyes with her and took a deep breath. He then said, "I've been keeping this a secret for a long time now, but I just need to tell you this." He paused for a moment and quickly announced, "I'm gay!"

She laughed. "What?"

"I'm gay, Aoki."

The seriousness in AZ's voice said that he was serious. Aoki was in disbelief. The shock of his words silenced her. She was taken aback. He couldn't be gay. It didn't make any sense to her. "Ya gay?" she said in an incredulous tone.

"I'm gay or bi. I mean, I like pussy too, maybe, but I get really aroused for men. It's just confusing."

"What 'bout Lisa an' de baby? Ya can't be a batty bwoy!"

"But I am. And I'm telling you this because I trust you, Aoki. I'm begging you to keep this a secret. I just needed to come out wit' it to someone." AZ exhaled and turned his attention away from her. Then he added, "Lisa and the baby was a front. I'm a front, Aoki. This is me—a fuckin' faggot."

"Me still can't believe it."

"Yeah, I know it's a hard thing to swallow." Another hard sigh escaped AZ's lips and then he asked, "Can you do me a favor, Aoki?"

"What ya need?"

"I need a cover."

"Ah cover?"

"I got dreams, Aoki. I mean, I feel I'm so much more than the streets. I wanna be somebody other than a hustler, maybe invest in real estate, become a businessman. But I gotta live long enough to get out the game. I can't have anyone second-guessing me, second-guessing my sexuality. I need a cover, and you can be that cover."

Aoki had a dumbfounded look on her face.

"I know you're confused. It's simple—I want you to be my girl, my ride-or-die chick. No sex, just us lookin' the part."

"Me ready fi ya ride-or-die chick," Aoki said with a smile. "Whateva ya need."

AZ smiled. It was what he wanted and needed to hear. "What would I do without you?"

"Probably die," she joked.

AZ chuckled. He was grateful that she wasn't disappointed with him. AZ leaned closer to Aoki's luscious lips and kissed them so gently and lovingly, it almost took Aoki's breath away. He then pulled away and said, "Thank you."

She was the perfect beard. Everyone already thought they were fucking or had fucked already.

"Me have ya back. Always!"

"And I got yours."

"So now that you're my girl, first thing we gotta do is take you shopping."

"Me ready."

"I'll hit you up."

She exited his vehicle and went back inside with the five grand, still taken aback by AZ's sudden confession. How could he be gay? His name rang out in the streets, he was a great hustler, and a baby father, so it didn't make any sense to her that her best friend liked dick. It was mind-blowing.

Usually, Aoki would shun a nigga like that, but AZ was her brother, her best friend, a mentor, and someone who had helped her out plenty of times. She would do anything for him. Aoki had a deep throat and had made a promise to keep his secret. The cash was also able to make things a little bit simpler for her and hopefully her friends.

She walked into her bedroom where Rihanna and Tisa were awake, dressed, and still looking upset.

"That was AZ outside?" Rihanna asked.

"Yeah."

"Why didn't he come inside? I mean, the least he could do is come inside and say 'hello, how y'all bitches doin', thank you.' Especially after we done killed for him," Rihanna said.

"He got a whole heap to do today," Aoki explained, "Besides, him already showed his gratitude."

"His gratitude?" Tisa asked.

Aoki tossed the envelope filled with cash on the bed, where her friends sat. They looked at it.

Aoki said, "Five thousand dollars cash right there."

Tisa and Rihanna were dumbfounded. It was a lot more money than they made being drug mules for him.

"Plus, we got dem cash and jewels from de licks."

Aoki dumped the stolen contents from the dead men onto their bed also and said, "We paid, ya hear?"

The cash from the niggas' wallets totaled close to six grand, and with the 5k from AZ, the girls were looking at over ten thousand to divide between them. Plus, there was the jewelry to think of. It was expensive stuff.

Aoki smiled. "Ya nah happy?"

Tisa said, "It's just everything is comin' so unexpectedly, Aoki. I mean, what are we, assassins now?"

"We tryin' to make money, ya hear?"

"This though, it's blood money," Tisa griped.

"Me can split it fairly, fi ya both, four thousand apiece and me take the almost three thousand, and wit' de jewelry pawned, it will bring more."

Rihanna was silent, staring at the money and contemplating something in her mind. It was the quickest four thousand she'd ever made. It was like they'd hit the jackpot. Rihanna had never seen that much money all at once in her life. All of a sudden, Rihanna didn't feel too upset or guilty about last night.

"Ri-Ri, you agree with me?" Tisa asked.

Rihanna eyed the money like it was calling her name.

"Ri-Ri!" Tisa called out.

"What?"

"I know you can't do this. This is wrong."

"And what is wrong about it, Tisa?" Rihanna said, suddenly having a change of heart.

"What we did and then taking the money. What do that make us?"

"Caught up," Rihanna replied.

"And there can be a whole heap mo' where dat came from," Aoki said.

"What you mean?" Tisa asked.

"Him give we ah job."

"A job?" Rihanna said.

She nodded.

"What kind of job?" Tisa asked.

"To be his protection."

"What! We bodyguards now?" Tisa uttered, continuing to be sarcastic.

"We employed," Aoki said.

Tisa chuckled and shook her head. "Y'all can't be serious." Tisa felt they were about to get into something that was way over their heads.

Aoki thought differently. She looked at the employment opportunity as a come-up, a well-paying job. She wanted to shine, and this was her way to do it.

Tisa looked like she was definitely against the idea, but Rihanna was still open to it. Aoki looked at her and said, "Ri-Ri, what ah fi ya answer?"

"What do I have to lose? I'm down."

Aoki smiled.

Tisa was shocked to hear Rihanna join in on the delusional plan.

Rihanna and Aoki stared at Tisa, waiting for an answer from her. She felt pressure against her. Two against one were not very favorable odds.

"I need time to think about it," she told them both.

"Don't think 'bout it too long," Aoki said.

"I won't."

With that, the girls divided the cash and went to a pawnshop in Queens to fence the jewelry, knowing that pawning Greasy D's and Polo's jewelry in Brooklyn was just too risky.

Aoki was confident that she could do any job, no matter what. The only thing AZ had to do was point, and she would execute. She also didn't tell her friends AZ's secret. She was prepared to take it to her grave.

FIFTEEN

A Z, are you fuckin' listening to me?" Lisa shouted, snapping him out of his short-term trance. "What? Me and ya fuckin' daughter ain't that important anymore? I said, I need more money fo' her. Do you fuckin' understand that? She needs her hair done and some new shoes. She's growin' up fast, nigga!"

Clad in a skimpy pink T-shirt and panties, showing off her curvy body and phatty, trying to look enticing to her baby's father, Lisa stood in front of AZ clutching his daughter to her hip. She eyed AZ like he was her own personal ATM. She was unemployed and lazy. And she was also known to be a sharp-tongued.

"What do you want from me, Lisa?"

"I want you to take your daughter sometimes. Why you always gotta be so busy for her? She's yours too. I didn't come in myself and get myself pregnant, nigga. Take care of your fuckin' responsibilities."

"I am. Don't I give you money every month and pay ya fuckin' rent, and helped furnish this place from room to room?"

Lisa had nice furniture, electronics, designer clothes, and all the latest amenities in her tenth-floor apartment in one of the high-rises on Sutter and Lincoln Avenues.

"Yeah, you do."

"So why the fuck are you complaining? Huh?"

"I'm complaining cuz I don't fuckin' see you often, AZ. It's just me and Alice, sometimes sitting in this hot apartment lookin' crazy."

"I thought it was more money you wanted."

"It's both, muthafucka! I want to see you too. I want some dick! You ain't fucked me in forever, and I miss it."

"Look, you already knew what it was when we got together. Don't go lookin' for anything to change between us, because it ain't. We got a kid together, and I'm there for her. But you and me, it will never happen. So you might as well go and put some damn clothes on, because I'm not fuckin' you, Lisa."

Lisa frowned. She continued holding her sleeping daughter in her arms and had no problems cursing and ranting while she was around. It was routine. She sucked her teeth loudly and rolled her eyes. She put Alice on the couch and then turned toward AZ.

"So, you see all this ass and tits and you don't wanna fuck me? What the fuck is wrong wit' you, muthafucka? I'm sayin, I know you ain't fuckin' wit' no new bitch! What? You don't like this pussy no more?"

AZ had to keep his composure. Lisa was pushing his buttons, and she knew it too. He scowled her way and had the urge to throw her out the tenth-floor window.

What the fuck was I thinking? He loved his daughter, but hated the relationship with Lisa.

"I don't like you, Lisa! I never did. You're loud, ignorant, and a fuckin' bitch." AZ was heated that he continually had to go through the same shenanigans with her. "I wanna see Alice, but you fuckin' make anything so simple almost impossible. I didn't come by to please you, so get us fucking or getting together out of your ignorant mind. It's about Alice and only about her!"

Lisa matched his hard scowl. She threw her right hand in the air toward his face and spat, "You a fuckin' trip, nigga! Look at all this good pussy and you ready to turn it down. What's wrong wit' you, AZ? I got plenty of niggas ready to fuck me."

"So go fuck 'em—I don't give a fuck what you do. Just take care of my daughter and stay out my fuckin' business."

As they argued, AZ's cell phone buzzed against his hip. He practically rushed to answer the call to keep from arguing with his baby mama. "Hello."

Lisa said, "You see that shit—always on ya fuckin' phone and not caring about us."

AZ shot her a murderous look.

Lisa knew it was safer to hush up, but her attitude still remained. She snatched her daughter off the couch and marched into the bedroom, slamming the door behind her.

"This bitch," he uttered faintly and then focused back on his phone call. "What's good, Heavy Pop?"

"Yo, you ain't heard?"

"Heard what?"

"Word on the streets is that Polo is still alive."

"What? You jokin', right?"

"Nah, I wish I was. The nigga is still alive, in critical condition or somethin'."

AZ couldn't believe it. "What hospital?" he asked.

"Kings County. But it ain't no use. He's under heavy police protection. We both need to watch our backs; this might come back on us, AZ."

"Yo, for what? Heavy, we ain't had shit to do wit' that, right?"

"I know, but everyone knows we had an issue with him and Greasy D and if niggas think Polo gonna make a full recovery, they might want to get at us to get on his good side, you feel me."

"We had an issue; that's all it was," AZ said, knowing he was talking on his cell phone. "Yo, I'll call you later."

"One, my nigga."

"One." AZ hung up.

All of a sudden, AZ's world became a lot heavier. Without saying good-bye to his baby mother or his daughter, he marched out of the apartment, his cell phone to his ear, calling Aoki.

"Hey," Aoki answered.

"We got a fuckin' problem."

"Ah what problem?"

"Not over the phone. I'll meet you," he said, and hung up.

The two met at Canarsie Pier on a sunny day. They walked side by side and talked to each other quietly. The pier wasn't too crowded with folks, only a few men fishing, sprinkled with a few couples slowly walking hand in hand, gazing out at the horizon, and a few young teens sitting on the benches, talking and having some fun.

AZ and Aoki were far away from prying ears, but no one paid them any attention. They looked like a couple walking and enjoying the day.

"Ya ah worried, so me can take care of it," Aoki told AZ. "Me know it's a problem, but don't fret until someone comes ah knocking."

"I can't believe this muthafucka is still alive, Aoki."

"Don't know how. Him was shot and stabbed dead."

"Apparently not," AZ replied, dryly.

"Me tink him nah gon' snitch. How would him look in de hood? Three girls did dat to dem. Him would be embarrassed."

"Even so, he's gonna come lookin' for us, looking for revenge."

"No time soon. Him really fucked up. But me can give ya half de money back, AZ. It's my fault."

"Nah, no need. I just want you to finish the job, Aoki. I want you to make sure Polo won't be a threat once he leaves the hospital."

"Him won't."

SIXTEEN

Polo lay in the hospital recuperating from two gunshot wounds and being stabbed twice in the chest. The shooting and stabbings took a lot out of him. He was lucky to be alive. He had flat-lined twice, once in the ambulance, and then again on the operating table.

Two weeks earlier, when he was in ICU, he was immediately hooked up to a respirator. The trauma team had to keep suctioning blood that repeatedly accumulated in his mouth. Polo looked like an extra from *The Matrix*, with all sorts of lines and wires for monitors, tubes for IVs and other machines. Polo seemed lifeless, but then he came through like a miracle. He was too tough to die so soon.

Now he was awake, but still in bad shape, and on his mind was revenge. Greasy Dee was gone. He still couldn't wrap his head around it. One moment he's having a good time, thinking he's gonna get some pussy, and the next, there's an ambush.

He remembered the sexy bitch in the front seat with Greasy Dee just suddenly went berserk and plunged that knife into his friend's neck with no hesitation at all.

Three bitches had outsmarted Polo. He had no clue that everything was connected to AZ. He didn't think it was a hit; it was just too sloppy in his eyes. He figured Greasy Dee had triggered that bitch somehow, made her upset. The way the other two girls were screaming, and the biting on his neck didn't smell like a hit. Assassins wouldn't handle business like that. But none of them were about to get a pass. Bitches or not, they were all dead.

Polo didn't remember much about them, but what he did remember was that one of them had a slight Jamaican accent and her eyes were unforgettable. He also heard the name Rihanna, and she was the one who'd shot him twice in his side.

As Polo started to recuperate, his hospital room became busier, first with detectives coming to question him. One was black and older, and the second detective was white and a little younger. They were both clad in dark suits and ties.

"I'm Detective Williams, and this is my partner, Detective Surdak. Do you remember anything about that night?" Detective Williams asked.

Polo frowned. He hated police. He wasn't a snitch, and he wasn't about to have the NYPD handle his business. "Nah, I don't remember shit!"

"You sure about that, Polo?" Detective Surdak chimed, intentionally calling him by his street name. "Whoever it was, they did y'all in good. Your friend is dead, and you're lucky to be alive."

"It happened so fast, detectives. I don't remember shit."

Both detectives sighed.

"Do you have any idea who might want you dead?" Detective Williams asked.

"Nah."

"Well," Surdak interjected, "we hear you have a beef with someone named AZ."

"Who? I don't even know that name."

"You sure? Because when they find out you're alive, what do you think is going to happen, Polo? Huh? I tell you what's going to happen—they'll come back to finish the job. And the condition that you're in, Polo, I don't think you can withstand another assault. We can protect you. We can help you," Detective Surdak said.

"Like I said, detectives, I don't know shit, and I don't know a nigga named AZ. Is that all?"

Detective Surdak scowled at Polo. "You sure about that?"

"Yeah, I'm sure," Polo growled his way.

"It's your funeral," Surdak replied.

"If you change your mind, here's my card," Detective Williams said, tossing his card on Polo's bed.

There was no way Polo was cooperating with the police. He didn't want anything to do with them. He watched both men exit his room, took Williams' card into his hands, and tore it up.

Later that day, Domino and Lavell, two of Polo's homies, came through to visit him. Both men were notorious gangsters and close with Polo and Greasy Dee.

Lavell said to Polo, "Yo, talk to me my nigga—who did this shit?"

Domino closed the door to give them some privacy.

"I ain't sure, but it was three bitches involved."

"Bitches?" Domino said.

"Yeah, they fuckin' set us up."

Domino continued, "It wasn't that nigga, AZ?"

Polo smirked. "That bitch-ass nigga ain't got the heart or manpower to come at us like that. Like I said, it was three bitches."

"So the three bitches had some niggas ambush y'all?" Domino was still confused.

Polo was highly aggravated by his line of questioning. It hurt to raise his voice, but he had no choice. "Bitches! Damn, nigga. Just bitches!" Polo coughed a few times and clutched his side. He was in great pain.

Lavell said, "Well, we 'bout to put word on the streets and hunt these bitches down. You know names, locations, what these bitches look like?"

"I've seen them around the 'Ville," Polo said, "mostly fuckin' wit' that nigga Sink. And one bitch name is Rihanna."

"Sink, a'ight. We on it, my nigga. Best believe that shit."

"I want them bitches dead, yo," Polo said in a hard whisper.

"They already living on borrowed time, my nigga," Lavell said. "Them bitches 'bout to be six feet deep."

Domino and Lavell left, leaving Polo to rest.

SEVENTEEN

Aoki was comfortable in the passenger seat of AZ's Yukon as he drove down 5th Avenue on a beautiful spring day. She gawked at the high-end shops and couldn't help but to smile. AZ had promised to take her shopping, and he was fulfilling his promise. Aoki stared at the stores— Louis Vuitton, Chanel, Armani, Fendi, Versace, Hermes, Cartier, and more. The traffic, the skyscrapers, and the crowds of people swamping the sidewalks was typical midtown Manhattan, but to her it felt new.

She deserves a day like this, AZ thought. Whatever she wanted, it was hers.

The hood started believing they were a couple. AZ and Aoki, the "It" couple in Brooklyn. It seemed real. With Aoki under his arm, no one suspected he was gay.

The first store they went into was Saks. AZ accompanied Aoki around the store. "Whatever you want, I got you."

Aoki smiled. She was like a kid in a candy store. She immediately went for the priciest clothing and accessories.

AZ sat and watched her try on outfit after outfit in the store. Piece by piece, he was marveled at how beautiful and sexy she was. Every article of clothing looked extraordinary on her. That day, no one could tell she was from the streets, or that she was crazy.

She twirled for AZ and smiled.

"You're beautiful," he said.

She continued smiling.

From Saks, they went into Fendi, then Chanel, Louis Vuitton, and Versace. AZ bought his friend nothing but the best. The bill totaled over ten grand.

Aoki looked like a whole new woman. She climbed back into his Yukon and couldn't wait to show off her new wardrobe in the projects. No other bitch would be able to fuck with her shoe game and new gear.

It may have been blood money, but after a while they didn't care. With four thousand apiece, plus the cash from the pawn shop, Tisa and Rihanna were living the life, and it felt like they had money to burn. They quickly went on a shopping spree from Pitkin Avenue to Jamaica Avenue then Kings Plaza Mall and Fulton Street. Every store was their target. They bought clothes and shoes, jewelry and smartphones, and new weaves, doing it big at the beautician's. Rihanna and Tisa strutted around their hood like two divas. The attention came to them like magnets to metal.

After two weeks, the money started to dwindle. They were styling in their newest outfits, but their pockets were low, and they were two broke bitches again. They both were like sharks tasting blood in the water and searching for a meal.

Tisa smoked her cigarette in Rihanna's bedroom and gazed out the window, mulling over her new employment opportunity. The money was good. Going on crazy shopping sprees in different stores was an exhilarating feeling. She now had fifty dollars to her name and was rocking a three-hundred-dollar outfit. While Tisa was still hesitant about the job, Rihanna felt she was ready.

"You okay, Tisa?"

"It doesn't bother you?"

"What are you talkin' about?"

"Pulling the trigger and—"

"Tisa, we don't need to talk about that right now. Just let it be. I try not to think about it, and you shouldn't either. We came out of it alive and well paid. Besides, if I didn't, then he would have killed you."

"I know."

Rihanna tried to block the events from that night out of her mind as best as she could. "You have to admit, the world we live in ain't no joke. It's either us or them."

"I can't lie, this shit Aoki got us into, it scares me. Murder . . . this is something serious."

"What else we got goin' on, Tisa? I mean, how else we gonna make money like this? I'm tired of being a mule for AZ. We get knocked carryin' those ki's we gonna do hard time anyways. Ten, twenty years, maybe even life for that coke. Even if we snitched—"

"We ain't snitches!"

"I know we ain't," Rihanna stated. However, they both knew deep down inside that if the shit hit the fan and they got jammed up, they *both* would snitch out AZ and Heavy Pop in a heartbeat. "But even if we did snitch, we'd still do a lot of jail time; the same time a murder rap could carry."

Tisa agreed.

"I want more, and I'm gonna get more. And it probably won't be that bad. It's been weeks now, and so far no cops or anyone else been sniffing around and suspecting us. We can do this," Rihanna proclaimed, hyping herself up too.

Tisa took a long drag from her Newport and exhaled. Her eyes still showed some concern, but the Christian Louboutin shoes on her feet, making her the envy of the projects, had her swaying to the job.

Rihanna continued to coax her into doing something horrendous. Rihanna knew she couldn't do it without Tisa on their team. She was the final piece to the puzzle, connecting the dots to the end game.

Rihanna said, "We just gotta be careful and think about it. Who we gonna kill—only bad guys, people that deserve it, like Greasy Dee and Polo."

Hearing Polo's name made Tisa shudder. "They say he's alive."

"I heard the same thing too. Aoki is gonna take care of it, though."

"You need to call her," Tisa said.

"I will."

Rihanna continued trying on new clothes and styling in front of the long mirror hanging on the back of her closet door. Her bedroom looked like three clothing stores exploded.

"I'm definitely wearing this tonight," she said to Tisa.

Knocking at Rihanna's door curtailed their conversation.

Gena walked in. All she saw was clothes and shoes on her daughter's bed. "I know some of this shit is for me. Damn! Y'all bitches musta hit the jackpot and snatched y'all a rich fuckin' dude to have him buy y'all all this nice shit." She picked up a few items from the bed. "Or either y'all stole this shit. Which is it?"

"What you want, ma?"

"This skirt would look so cute on me," Gena said, making herself very comfortable in her daughter's room.

"It's yours," Rihanna said. "You can have it."

"Can I get these shoes to match with it too?" she said, removing a pair of red bottoms from the dresser.

Rihanna sighed. "Of course." She wanted her mother to leave her bedroom, so she and Tisa could continue talking. The red bottoms Gena wanted cost $680. Unfortunately for Rihanna, she and her mother were the same exact size, from the hips down to their footwear.

"Take 'em," she said quickly.

"Girl, you are my favorite," Gena said with a wide grin. "Anyway, who you fuckin'?"

"Ma, we're having a very important conversation here," Rihanna said.

"Oh, y'all are, huh?"

"Yes!"

"Well, I'm gonna let y'all bitches be. But I'm so proud

of my babies. I taught you well. He's gotta be a keeper; I want to meet him." She moved toward the door and then wanted to know, "Tisa, what you got for your momma?"

Tisa rolled her eyes. She wasn't nearly as generous as her sister.

"Cheap bitch," Gena replied dryly.

Gena walked out of the room with over nine hundred dollars' worth of stuff.

Rihanna slammed the door and looked at Tisa. "I'm broke already."

"I am too."

"So think about it. With that type of money, we can do anything we want. I mean, we ain't gotta do it forever, just get our money up and make somethin' happen wit' it. Niggas do this every day in the hood. They plot on murkin' niggas for their shit. Two out of five big money niggas get murdered in the hood each year, and nobody cares. It goes with the territory."

Tisa joined in. "True. Like everyone knows Hassan killed Knowledge last summer for his Rolex watch."

"Exactly. And what about Puerto Rican Jose? We all saw him blast off and put those hot slugs into Pappy with our own eyes. And what was that about?" She didn't wait for her sister to answer. "Money."

"Yup! And ain't none of those niggas doin' a day in jail."

Rihanna became more confident. "Now let's politick about Black Wise."

Tisa nodded because she knew what her sister was about to say.

"Those alphabet boys bagged his whole team. They all doin' life in the fed pen and for what? Not murder." Rihanna shook her head frantically. "Drugs!"

"We know so many niggas doin' football numbers for moving weight, but how many niggas we know got convicted for murder?"

Rihanna hesitated trying to come up with a real number. "Maybe…two."

"We know at least ten, twenty niggas doin' drug bids."

"That settles it, Tisa. We the smart ones. We get in this murder game, maybe do two or three more hits. We save up our money and when we make, let's say, twenty-five thousand each we quit. Deal?"

"Deal."

Rihanna's cell phone rang. It was Aoki. "What up?"

"Where ya at?"

"In my bedroom. Why?"

"Me soon come," Aoki said.

"You alone?"

"Nuh. I'm wit' AZ."

"Okay, we need to talk."

"Den let's talk," Aoki replied coolly and hung up.

Rihanna took a deep breath. She was ready to jump into the mix of murder for hire. She stared at Tisa and watched her light another cigarette and gaze out the window. "I think you need to spark up something stronger."

Rihanna wondered, *Am I a cold-blooded killer?* She'd pulled the trigger to save her sister's life, but could she pull the trigger purely for profit?

Aoki stepped out of the Yukon looking flawless in a pair of distressed jeggings that hugged her curves in all the right places and a Chanel crop top with a zip-up front. She strutted against the project pavement in her brand-new canary yellow red bottoms, her long hair flowing naturally, her Gucci shades covering her cold eyes. Her Louis Vuitton Damier Duomo handbag was the icing on the cake.

To sell their relationship, she kissed AZ good-bye, and he drove off. All eyes were on Aoki. She walked toward the project building with no fret, and the gossip and whispers spread from corner to corner. She was AZ's main bitch.

Aoki walked into the lobby and took the elevator to her friends' floor and moved composedly toward the apartment and knocked twice.

Gena opened the door and quickly eyed Aoki up and down. "Well, excuse me. I didn't know Beyoncé was in town."

Aoki chuckled. "Ya like?" she said, twirling around for Gena to see.

"Who dick did you suck?"

Aoki didn't like her comment, but she kept her composure. "Me just tryin' to get mines, Gena."

"You and me both, girl. You know I was just playin' wit' you."

Aoki could see the green-eyed monster in Gena. They were cool, but not that cool. "Ri-Ri and Tisa home?"

"They in the room." Gena stepped aside, almost with an attitude, and allowed Aoki into her home.

Aoki walked toward the bedroom and entered without knocking.

Tisa and Rihanna were lingering inside the room, smoking and putting away clothes. Immediately, they too were blown over by Aoki's new look.

"Damn, girl! You lookin' like a diva wit' the capital *D*," Rihanna said.

"New man, new tings, new bitch!" Aoki uttered.

"I feel you. So any new jobs yet?" Rihanna asked.

Aoki was somewhat shocked that she was asking for another job to do. She looked Tisa's way, and she was quiet, smoking a blunt.

"Ya sure y'all ready?"

"What else we gonna do, Aoki?" Rihanna said. "We as ready as we ever gonna be, right?"

Aoki couldn't see herself doing it without them. But she told them that the next job would come only if AZ's life was in danger. Despite Polo still living, AZ was okay.

"What about Polo?" Rihanna asked. "I heard he's still alive."

"But him no threat right now."

"I'm still uncomfortable wit' him living, Aoki," Rihanna said. "He knows our faces."

"And him will be dealt wit'. Trus' me."

Rihanna wasn't shy about expressing her concerns and readiness. Their cash was low, and she wanted another come-up. That last cash flow was so sweet, it was almost better than some good dick. She was a little sour, though, thinking that Aoki was good either way. Working or not working, she'd be good since she and AZ were an item and she was riding around in style in his truck. Her clothes were a lot more expensive than hers and Tisa's put together. Rihanna wanted a piece of that.

"I don't wanna go broke again," Rihanna said.

Tisa nodded, agreeing with her sister. She whispered, "We've been politicking about this shit all day. And we ready to put in work. We ready to become assassins."

Aoki burst out into laughter. "Assassins? Ya watchin' too much TV."

Rihanna and Tisa were baffled at Aoki's response.

Rihanna spoke first. "What the fuck you laughin' about? I thought you promised us steady money."

"Me not make any promises." Aoki quickly became irritated. "And we not assassins; we triggermen. Or trigger wo-men."

"And, um, what's the fuckin' difference? People are gonna die, right?"

Aoki sucked her teeth. It was like schooling first graders.

"We down wit' AZ. He's my man, and we're his shottas. All drug crews have 'em and don't run round calling demselves 'assassins'. We protect the boss and collect our share of de profit."

Tisa and Rihanna looked Aoki up and down and scowled.

"You right," Rihanna said dryly. Neither sister wanted to argue with the crazy, bipolar bitch. "We just need to get our hands dirty one or two more times, save that money, and then quit."

Hearing the sisters beg had Aoki thinking, *What if AZ's life is never in danger again?* But that was almost impossible. Rising in the game, a hustler always would have enemies. But enemies could be sparse. That meant their quick cash could dry up. Everyone knew that, to net four thousand dollars working full-time at minimum wage, it would take at least three months, and they made that kind of money in a day.

"Lemme think of someting," Aoki said.

Aoki had an idea. Maybe she could approach AZ to get his friends to hire them, but first, they would have to prove themselves. After all, Polo was still alive.

When Aoki left Rihanna asked, "Is it me or does that bitch think she's cute now?"

"She always thought she was cute. I don't know where the fuck you been."

EIGHTEEN

AZ walked into Club Luv in Flatbush Brooklyn with Aoki under his arm and a huge smile on his face. He was looking great and feeling great. He and Aoki were the Beyoncé and Jay Z of Brooklyn. They both strutted into the club looking like superstars. Aoki was dressed sexily in a neon pink and white Brooklyn T-shirt and coochie cutter shorts, her long legs gleaming in a pair of pricey stilettos. Her hair was wild and curly.

AZ was dressed sharply in a dark gray YSL suit and sporting a pair of handmade David Chu bespoke Italian wing tips. He wanted to stand out from everyone else in the club wearing urban attire and gaudy jewelry.

Club Luv was one of the most popular clubs in Brooklyn, a place where all the hustlers and shot-callers came to show off their lifestyle, network, and have a good time without any hassle. It was a place where some of the finest ladies in the city frequented, coming dressed in their best and sexiest outfits and looking for a come-up nigga to splurge on them.

The club owner, Mink, was an ex-kingpin and ruthless heavyweight who had put in time on the streets and fifteen years in the prisons back in the day. He now just wanted to live comfortably and run his club in peace.

Inside, the music was blaring, and it was crowded from wall to wall. People were crammed on the dance floor. The place was ultra modern and boasted state-of-the art technology with TVs positioned around the club, and a full bar. The VIP suites were perched over the dance floor, giving its occupants a full sweeping view of the club and the revelers below. You had to be somebody or know somebody to get the VIP treatment. If you were a nobody in the game, then Luv wasn't the place for you.

Once inside the club, AZ and Aoki were escorted to one of the VIP sections, where they were treated like royalty. AZ was making money hand over fist with his connect, Oscar, and rising to the next level. His street credibility was fiercer now, because of the shooting incident a few weeks earlier.

After the two of them got comfortable in VIP, two bottles of Cristal were placed in front of them. AZ sat with his arm around Aoki, looking like the don of all dons in his suit. He nodded his head to the R&B playing.

"This is what's up!"

AZ was moving roughly fifteen kilos a month for Oscar, and he had the baddest bitch on his arm. Nobody could fuck with him.

"You okay, baby?" he asked her.

"I'm fine."

Aoki was enjoying the life too. Aoki had been a diamond in the rough, and too many niggas done slept on her back then. With her new position as AZ's girl, along with her new wardrobe, niggas started to take notice of her.

When the DJ started to play some Shabba Ranks, Aoki couldn't help herself. She stood up and started dancing to the throwback Jamaican music. First, she started to sway from side to side, bobbing her head up and down. Then she leaned from side to side, turning her shoulders and gradually showing her audience what she was made of. Then she started wining, feeling the groove in the music. The way she moved her hips and dropped down to the floor, her legs spread-eagle, her pink panties showing a little, was almost hypnotic and left everyone wide-eyed. People couldn't help staring at her.

The rest of the night, it was just AZ and Aoki drinking champagne and enjoying each other's company. He was showing her off, trying to make a statement.

Aoki also caught the attention of another major hustler inside the club. The man watched her movements from a short distance and was fixated by her beauty, her style, and her dance moves. He had seen her around, but tonight, she was looking extra special.

B Scientific made his way toward AZ and Aoki. He was alone, leaving his crew in the neighboring VIP section. He eyed AZ and smiled at the man. They knew about each other because they both got money in the streets. B Scientific was recognizing that AZ was coming up, but he wasn't touching B Scientific's net worth or his street credibility.

"AZ, that's you?" B Scientific asked respectfully.

AZ grinned like a Cheshire cat. "Yeah."

"Nice."

B Scientific was also dressed sharply in Tom Ford jeans, a white V-neck Ralph Lauren shirt, and a Hermes leather belt. He wore gold sunglasses and a diamond pinky ring, oozing power.

A small voice in AZ's head wanted to tell B Scientific the truth about their relationship, thinking B Scientific and Aoki would be a nice fit together, but common sense made him snap back to reality. There was too much at stake, so he had to stake his claim over Aoki, though it was obvious that B Scientific was interested in getting to know her better.

B Scientific extended his hand out to Aoki. "My name is B Scientific."

"Me know who ya are," she said to him.

"Of course you do. But I don't know who you are other than my man's better half."

"Aoki."

"A-o-kee? That's a nice name."

"Thanks," she replied.

B Scientific wanted to respect AZ, but he couldn't take his eyes off Aoki. She was extraordinary, and her accent was a turn-on. He had a beautiful woman at home, but Aoki was exotic and just too stunning. Her dark skin, slanted eyes, long, silky hair, and her high cheekbones—shit, she was perfect.

"Well, I'll see y'all around," he said, looking at Aoki. B Scientific thought he'd go after Aoki when she was alone.

"Okay," she replied, smiling. She clearly noticed how he looked at her. Inwardly, Aoki was amused by it.

B Scientific made his exit, and AZ felt like the man of the year.

⁂

"You think they're ready?" AZ asked Aoki.

"Dem ah ready, AZ; we need the cash."

"Shit is quiet right now in the streets, though. I mean, ain't nobody fuckin' wit' me right now, Aoki, and that's a good thing."

AZ navigated his Yukon across the Verrazano Bridge, on his way to meet Peanut and collect what was owed to him. As he approached the toll booths, he turned to Aoki. "Since Greasy Dee, my respect is on a whole new level."

It was news Aoki didn't want to hear. She was eager to get her homegirls some work. Rihanna and Tisa were acting desperate. They no longer wanted to be drug mules. Each time Aoki brought it up expressing that's how they could make money, they both refused to listen. Aoki had sparked something in them that she couldn't undue.

"What 'bout Polo?"

"What about him? From my understanding, the nigga is still laid up in the hospital, almost crippled and shit. He ain't in any position to come after me."

"And his peoples? Ya not concerned?"

"Not really. You chop off the head, and the body will drop."

Aoki pouted. It'd been several weeks, and AZ had the girls doing nothing, not even deliveries. The beef in the streets was as slow as a virgin's pussy. There wasn't anything happening. Aoki just played her part, pretending to be his woman.

In public, they put on a nice show, but in private, it was all the same. Aoki had been talking and texting Emilio. It wasn't anything serious. Emilio was becoming a good friend to talk to. Aoki also didn't broach the subject with AZ about being gay. She locked it away in the depths of her closet and wasn't trying to touch it. He liked dick, she liked dick; it was just something they had in common.

Lately, she had been accompanying him everywhere. She smoked her Newport and gazed out the passenger window, her eyes on the traffic at the toll booth. She didn't mind the ride. It was cool to escape from Brooklyn once in a while and enjoy seeing a different borough.

AZ was determined to collect the money Peanut owed him. He told Aoki that Peanut had been avoiding his calls.

"Ya tink him tryin' to stick ya?" she asked.

"I don't think so. I hope not. Nah, he seems cool."

"Tink the worst . . . hope for de best," Aoki said.

Her words had AZ thinking. He didn't know the nigga like that. He felt that Peanut was a good dude, talkative and a go-getter, but so far he'd never had any problems with him.

AZ steered his truck toward Peanut's hood. Like usual, the block was flooded with niggas doing their customary rituals of drinking forties, smoking weed, and rolling dice. And Peanut was in the mix of it all.

He slowed his truck toward the corner and gazed at Peanut, whose back was turned to the street as he focused on the dice game.

Peanut's friend, Nippy, tapped him on the shoulder and said, "Yo, Peanut, you got company."

Peanut turned and stared at AZ and Aoki in the Yukon. His face twisted into a scowl, and he locked his attention on AZ. "Yo, what up, nigga?" Peanut hollered sharply at AZ.

"What up?" AZ hollered back.

"You came lookin' fo' somethin', nigga?"

"Yo, what's up wit' this dude?" he said to Aoki. He then glared at Peanut and shouted, "Yeah, I came lookin' for that paper you owe me."

"What money, nigga?" Peanut hollered back. "You know me, muthafucka!"

"Peanut, don't play stupid. I want my fuckin' money."

"Yo, fuck ya money, nigga! You know where you at?"

The tension suddenly grew thick between them. Peanut's goons were watching and lurking. AZ didn't know what had gone wrong so suddenly. It looked like Peanut transformed and became this bipolar asshole. This wasn't the same man from before.

Aoki glared at Peanut also. She was ready to react.

But they were up against Goliath without their trusted slingshot. Peanut was daring them to do something stupid.

"So, it's like that, Peanut?" AZ said. "You know who you fuckin' wit'?"

"You know what, nigga?" Peanut suddenly turned his back to the truck, giving AZ his ass to kiss. Then he spun back around with his arm outstretched and gripping a 9mm, and didn't hesitate to shoot. *Bak! Bak! Bak! Bak!*

Aoki and AZ ducked so fast, they almost got whiplash.

"Pull off! Drive!" Aoki screamed. "Drive!"

AZ was able to put his vehicle in drive, dodging bullets and shattering glass, and speed away from the chaos.

Peanut wasn't done yet. "Yo, get the car, nigga!" he shouted to one of his cronies. "Get the fuckin' car!"

Peanut and his goons quickly jumped into several rides and gave chase, bullets flying and tires screeching.

AZ floored the pedal and hit the street corner doing sixty. He barely avoided slamming into a parked car. He couldn't believe he was in almost the same predicament with Greasy Dee and Polo.

He became a racecar and stuntman all at once, careening from corner to corner and fishtailing, avoiding obstacles and other cars, then zigzagging through traffic, blowing his horn repeatedly.

AZ sped down Targee Street and blew through a red light. He continued speeding away from the threat, and after several blocks, he realized that he'd lost them or they'd just stopped chasing.

AZ was furious. He cursed and threatened to kill Peanut.

Aoki smiled inwardly. It was payday. It was another job.

On the drive back to Brooklyn, AZ put the contract out on Peanut's life. He gave it to Aoki, like she expected.

"We gon' need some guns," Aoki said.

"Don't worry. I'll handle that. I can get you a couple of thirty-eights and some three eighties. But I want that muthafucka dead!" he said heatedly and repeatedly. "Dead!"

Aoki was so ready to execute the hit. This wasn't just business, but it was personal. She could have been killed. She was super-pissed that they wanted to murder AZ over his product and take her out as a casualty.

"Oh, and Aoki, if you kill some of his goons too, that's just fine with me. I'll pay extra," AZ added with a tight frown. "A grand per body count."

"Me on it, AZ. Me on it."

Immediately Aoki contacted her crew and told them the good news. Rihanna and Tisa felt they were ready to step up to the plate.

The girls were desperate to get their own place, an apartment together away from Gena, and maybe purchase themselves a car this time around. Rihanna's cell phone was on the verge of being disconnected. She'd splurged on clothes and things, but forgot to pay her bill. Tisa wanted to keep upgrading herself. However, she felt somewhat ambivalent about the job.

"Who and where?" Rihanna asked Aoki.

"Dis damn fool named Peanut."

Aoki gave them the rundown and told her crew what had happened. They were shocked. Aoki looked both her friends in the eyes and said, "Dis time, we do it right and no fuckups."

"I agree," Rihanna said.

It was on!

NINETEEN

Lavell wheeled a frail, crackhead-thin Polo away from his hospital room and toward the elevator ready to take his friend home. Domino walked behind them, his pistol concealed in his waistband. Polo was finally being discharged after spending weeks in the hospital. He sat in the wheelchair almost looking like the Crypt Keeper. He'd lost so much weight, he was almost unrecognizable to his friends. His doctors reiterated to him how lucky he was to survive.

The cops had finally stopped hounding him on who shot him and murdered Greasy Dee. There was no way he was talking to any pigs. He didn't need their help. He was utterly repulsed that they had to be in the same room with him and breathe the same air as he did. But the NYPD finally got the hint—he wasn't saying shit and didn't plan to.

Polo grimaced while being pushed into the elevator. He had a lot on his mind. He still couldn't forget it. He thought about that night over and over again; his mind was on repeat with the pain and loss of his good friend.

The elevator doors closed, and they were alone inside.

As they started to descend, Polo asked, "Any word on them bitches yet?"

"We still on it, Polo. I got my peoples lookin' for them everywhere," Lavell said.

"I can't believe these bitches are still breathing."

"We ain't gonna rest until we find them," Domino said. "For you and our nigga Greasy Dee. We gonna shoot their pussies out."

The elevator came to a stop on the first floor, and the doors opened. Lavell pushed his friend out.

It was the first taste of outside for Polo in weeks. He soaked in the summer weather as Lavell continued pushing him toward the minivan parked across the street.

"My nigga, you home now, and we got bitches and weed waiting for you back at the spot," Lavell said, trying to cheer his friend up.

Polo couldn't think about bitches and weed. He felt guilty about Greasy Dee's murder that he wasn't quick enough or didn't see the setup coming. Sweet revenge was the only thing that mattered to him. He was on a mission to get well and find all three of them. No matter what it took or what the cost was, Greasy Dee's death was going to be avenged.

TWENTY

Aoki got her friend Matt to hot-wire an old car for them, and they were all ready to take care of business. Aoki drove the Nissan Maxima, Rihanna rode shotgun, and Tisa sat in the backseat, where there were a couple of different colored wigs and the guns Aoki had asked for.

As they crossed the bridge, there was silence, their adrenaline pumping. They were approaching ground zero. This was an important job for AZ. It had to be executed just right. No fucking up. Peanut had disrespected her employer, and that came with a punishment of death.

The night was still young and balmy. Aoki and the girls were dressed down in jeans and sneakers, but Aoki wore her heels, as usual. They also carried knapsacks and looked like normal teenage girls. No one would suspect they were armed and dangerous.

The run-in with Peanut was forty-eight hours earlier, so Aoki easily remembered the location. They were only a few blocks away from Peanut's stomping grounds.

As they drove the wigs came on. Aoki donned the blonde one and dark shades. Rihanna and Tisa both wore brown. Aoki stuffed the .380 into her small handbag and was ready to pull off the murder contract.

Like Aoki expected, Peanut was a creature of habit, in the same place, at around the same time, doing the same shit. They circled the block and observed the target and his cronies. The car they were in was nondescript and didn't draw any attention, making it the perfect vehicle to commit their crime with.

"Ya ready?" Aoki asked her crew.

Rihanna nodded. Tisa did too, but she still looked unsure.

Aoki parked the Maxima a block away from the activity on Prospect Avenue, where there were goons playing dice, drinking forties, and smoking weed. Peanut, being the alpha male, was in the mix, wearing his red Yankees fitted and a red bandana dangling from his back pocket, indicating his affiliation with the Bloods gang. Peanut was loud, and his mouth was legendary.

Over a thousand dollars was up for grabs on the ground. The dice were shaking and moving. The men were loud, with a lot of shit-talking and cursing. The drug activity was hot on the block. It was an open-air drug market with fiends buying crack left and right. Either the police didn't patrol the area regularly, or they were paid to stay away. Aoki was observing it all with a keen eye, thinking all that money belonged to AZ. She wanted to take it all.

Aoki, Rihanna, and Tisa approached Peanut and his gang like soldiers, their faces deadpan, their movement subtle. It didn't take long for them to capture everyone's attention—three pretty females on the block were like rain in the desert. The catcalls came instantly. Peanut was still engrossed in the dice game.

Aoki decided to wing it, saying to the group of goons, "Y'all know a Marie?" It was just a random name that came to her mind.

Her accent caught everyone's attention, even Peanut's. He turned around and looked at all three girls. Aoki knew he didn't recognize her. She looked completely different.

"You mean Puerto Rican Maria?" Peanut asked.

"Ya."

"She just left wit' her moms, but I'm sayin' y'all can stay and chill."

Aoki smiled in his face, but being that close to him, knowing that he tried to take her and AZ's life the other day, she wanted to chop his head off.

"Yo, stop being distracted by pussy, Peanut, and roll the fuckin' dice," someone exclaimed.

"Nigga, hold da fuck up! I'm talking!" Peanut shouted.

Aoki pretended to be upset about Maria leaving, like she knew the bitch.

Peanut turned his attention away from the girls and focused back on the dice game.

"Can I get in dis?" Aoki asked, referring to the dice game.

The group was shocked that she asked.

One goon said, "Oh, word, shorty? You tryin' to play wit' the big boys? You know you need that serious paper to play."

"Yeah, you can play if you stand here and give me good luck," Peanut said.

"Me can hold fi me own, and me got de money." Aoki pulled out a nice chunk of cash from her handbag.

"Damn, ma! What you do—rob a fuckin' bank?"

"No mon," Aoki said. "Me wanna play, though."

"Let's play then," Peanut said, welcoming the girls into their circle.

Rihanna and Tisa played the background. Aoki did most of the talking. They were watching and being cautious. They didn't know anything about the neighborhood, but they kept their cool and tried to fit in. Inside, Tisa was trembling. She was so scared she wanted to run out of there as quickly as her legs took her. This wasn't like the car incident where things progressed rapidly and without much thought. This here, what Aoki was doing, had her nerves popping.

With Aoki leading the charge, it didn't take long for the girls to become one of the guys. While gambling, it gave them time to fully scope things out. Four goons plus Peanut, most likely they all were packing heat. They had to be fast and accurate. One mistake and Staten Island would be the borough they would die in.

Aoki was up five hundred dollars, proving she could hold her own. A half-hour passed, and it was all love and fun. Aoki even laughed with Peanut.

As Peanut was all smiles and jokes, winning money, losing money, Aoki looked at her crew, and her eyes said it was time to implement the contract.

"Peanut, we goin' to de store," she said.

"Yo, bring me back a few forties and a pack of cigarettes."
He went into his pocket, slightly exposing the 9mm tucked
in his waistband, and pulled out a wad of cash. He removed
three twenty-dollar bills and handed it to Aoki. "Keep the
change." Peanut acted like he gave her six grand.

Cheap bastard! Aoki thought.

The girls walked toward the corner store while Peanut
and his gang went back to gambling. Thankfully, Aoki
didn't notice any cops patrolling the area. She walked into
the corner bodega and purchased a few beers and a pack of
cigarettes.

"Ya ready to do dis?"

They nodded.

Tisa took a deep breath.

Aoki locked eyes with her and said, "We too deep now,
Tisa."

"I know."

Each girl grabbed a brown paper bag with a forty inside.
The girls exited the store coolly and strutted toward the dice
game. While walking, they hid their guns in the shopping
bags and cleverly kept them out of sight.

Peanut noticed the girls coming back and he smiled.

Aoki and her crew strategically positioned themselves
around the group, encasing themselves cleverly around the
game, making it difficult for anyone to escape. Most of the
men had their backs turned to the girls as they continued
to gamble.

"Yo, you got what I asked for?" Peanut asked.

"Yeah, we did," Aoki said.

She smirked, and then swiftly snatched her pistol from out the bag, and Rihanna and Tisa did the same and opened fire with steady hands.

Bak! Bak! Bak! Bak! Bak!

Peanut caught it first, two shots into his stomach, making him collapse to the ground.

Bak! Bak! Bak! Bak!

Pop!

Aoki and Rihanna got busy, but Tisa fired one wild shot, got spooked and retreated. She hurried back to the car, leaving her friends behind to do the slaughtering. They lit up the block like it was the 4th of July.

After the smoke cleared, five men were slumped on the concrete bleeding profusely and suffering from multiple gunshot wounds, including Peanut. Surprisingly, he was still alive, attempting to crawl away to safety.

Aoki walked his way, frowning. She aimed her gun and shot the man in his ass, toying with him. "Ya bitch-ass nigga! Ya should have paid fi ya debt!"

"Fuck you bitches!" he shouted.

Aoki wasn't done with him yet. Rihanna was ready to leave, but Aoki wasn't about to make the same mistake twice. She stood over a badly injured and dying Peanut, pulled out her pocketknife, crouched near him and placed it to his throat. He tried to struggle, but he was too weak.

Aoki quickly slashed his throat from ear to ear, killing him instantly.

He started to bleed like a stuck pig, his blood staining the sidewalk.

AZ was going to be pleased.

"Let's go! Let's go!" Rihanna screamed.

Aoki snatched the money off the ground, and she and Rihanna took off running.

Tisa was already seated in the car, looking like she was about to have a panic attack. Aoki jumped into the driver's seat, took a deep breath, and slowly drove away from the scene of her last crime.

Rihanna was extremely upset with Tisa. "You coward bitch! We coulda died because of you," she screamed.

"Fuck you, Ri-Ri!"

"You ran like a bitch, Tisa! What the fuck is wrong wit' you?" Rihanna was up in Tisa's face, flaring like a lit firecracker.

"Get the fuck out my face, Ri-Ri! I ain't the one," Tisa said through clenched teeth.

"Or what? Now you wanna get tough, huh? What the fuck you gonna do? Shoot me?"

For the moment, Aoki tuned out the heated argument in the room between Rihanna and Tisa. They were back in Brooklyn, in her living room, and she couldn't wait until payday. The loot they took from the dice game was rewarding too; it totaled fifteen hundred, an easy five hundred apiece.

Aoki sat in the corner reliving the moment when she put her knife to Peanut's throat and cut it, opening his flesh like a zipper. It felt good. AZ was going to be so proud of them. She took the risk, and it paid off.

"I thought you was down to do this, Tisa. Why the fuck you lying for?"

"I *am* down."

"What? You got cold feet, leaving Aoki and me to do the dirty work," Rihanna shouted.

Aoki lit a cigarette and exhaled. She'd heard some news about Polo being released from the hospital. She was sure he would come after her and her crew. It was only a matter of time. Polo wasn't the type of man to turn the other cheek. He had a reason to hunt Aoki, so she had to be ready. Her crew had to be ready.

Smoking her Newport, she turned her attention to Tisa and Rihanna. She stood up and shouted, "Would y'all two just fuckin' chill out!"

"But, Aoki, Tisa froze up, and we could have died out there."

"But we didn't, Ri-Ri. Ya hear? We didn't. Tisa just ain't ready."

Rihanna frowned. She didn't understand how Aoki could be so cool and not upset.

Aoki looked at Tisa and said, "Ya need training, and me gon' help ya kill smoothly."

Rihanna sighed and sat on the couch. She wasn't as forgiving. They'd only survived due to the element of surprise. Nothing more, nothing less.

※

The following day AZ arrived with the payment. When he heard about the murders, five dead, he was pleased.

This time, there were no survivors. Peanut got the message, permanently.

He greeted Aoki in the foyer with a hug and a kiss. Like before, he didn't want to hear the details. The job was done, and he was there to pay for their services. He pulled out a nice-sized envelope filled with cash and handed it to Aoki.

"That's nine grand, five for Peanut and a grand for each goon y'all put down," he said. "Impressive."

Aoki smiled. "Anything fah ya, AZ."

"Y'all do good work."

"Thanks."

AZ stood in the doorway. His Yukon was idling outside.

"Ya not staying?" she asked.

"Nah, I gotta make moves, you know."

"Yeah, me know."

They hugged each other, and he walked away. Aoki watched him get into his ride and drive away. She looked at the cash in her hand, and it felt so good. She'd earned it. Her girls had earned it, and she was ready to make a lot more of it.

She split the pay three ways with her crew, but Rihanna was upset, feeling Tisa didn't deserve her cut. But Aoki was more forgiving; they were all equal, no matter what. In due time, she felt Tisa would come around and become just like them.

TWENTY-ONE

AZ walked around the car lot in Bay Ridge, Brooklyn, his eyes set on a sleek Mercedes-Benz, the C63 AMG, black and fully loaded. He circled the car, running his hand across the hood.

"You're a Benz man, huh? You have good taste, my friend," the dealer said to him. "We can't keep these on the lot for long. They're selling fast."

"She's a beauty."

"She definitely is. Underneath the hood is a 6.2L V8, 451 to 510 horsepower, and the stereo system sounds like you are in the front row of a rap concert at the Garden. I can see you in this."

"I'm just lookin' for an upgrade."

"There's nothing wrong with that. What fun is life if we keep hanging on to the same old things, right?"

"Yeah, right," AZ replied dryly.

AZ fixed his eyes on every detail about the car, looking inside mesmerized by the dark, leather seats with the lateral stitching, split-folding rear seats, moon roof, and 18-inch wheels.

The price tag was $58,000. AZ could afford it. He was ready to pay cash for it. He sat in the driver's seat, and it was all him, a baller and shot-caller. The car was eye-catching.

"You care to take it for a test-drive?"

"Nah, I trust it."

"So, is this the perfect upgrade for you or not?"

AZ didn't reply. His focus was on the dashboard and the sound system. He sat behind the steering wheel and mulled it over. He then turned and looked at the dealer and said, "I'll take it."

"Great. I'll get started on the paperwork."

"Yeah, I'll take it," AZ repeated to himself, nodding his head and feeling like a king in the sleek Benz.

After the paperwork, with the dealer knowing how to make magic happen with showing proof of income and other things, AZ rolled off the car lot in his brand-new Benz. In fact, it matched the Benz that B Scientific drove around town in. His Yukon was beat up and outdated, and he needed a car that spoke for him.

AZ rolled down the car windows, put a CD in and had Jay Z's "Big Pimpin'" blaring inside the car. He nodded his head to the track and drove toward East New York feeling like a new man. He smoked a cigarette and caught his reflection in the rearview mirror. "You are on your way," he said to himself.

AZ planned on giving Aoki the Yukon. She needed the transportation. He decided to call her and surprise her. The truck was going to be an extra bonus for being his 'bitch'.

Yes, life was good. His relationship with Connor was

better than ever. In fact, he planned on seeing his lover this weekend to spend some quality time with him. They had been talking every day.

AZ maneuvered his new ride down Linden Boulevard and pulled into one of the parking lots of the Pink Houses. Heavy Pop and a few others lingered in the parking lot, throwing back liquor and bullshitting.

AZ's sleek C63 AMG caught immediate attention. He slowed his ride near the gang and honked his horn.

Heavy Pop couldn't believe it. He walked toward the driver's window and peered inside. "Damn, AZ! You went all out with this one."

"You like it, Heavy Pop?"

"Yo, you might as well stamp 'NYPD come get me' on the back windshield," Heavy Pop remarked.

"What you mean?"

Heavy Pop shook his head. "I mean, it's nice. What happened to the truck?"

"I'm giving it to Aoki."

"Oh."

The men that Heavy Pop was chilling with surrounded the car and praised AZ's new ride.

"Yo, this you, my nigga?"

"Damn, AZ! You comin' up. Shit is nice."

"This Benz is hot!"

"Yo, you gonna take me for a ride?"

AZ ate up the flattery. But while they were complimenting him, Heavy Pop stood near the door with a concerned look.

"Yo, AZ, let me holla at you for a minute, in private," he said, staring at the local goons surrounding the car.

They all knew to step away and let the two men talk alone. Heavy Pop climbed into the passenger seat, and the two went for a ride.

"I thought this wasn't you. You steadily preached about keeping things simple, keeping a low profile, not wearing ice, and suddenly you go out and buy a sixty-thousand-dollar car."

"You don't like the car?" AZ asked.

"I like it, but don't you think it's too soon to buy something like this?"

"This dealer, he cool peoples, dealt with our kind before and knew how to maneuver around the paperwork. Everything looks clean; it ain't gonna come back to haunt me."

"At least the truck was used and we made it legit by paying installments, you know, to keep the trouble away from us."

"I understand, but this is legit too."

They continued driving, jumping onto the Belt Parkway, heading toward Coney Island.

Heavy Pop lit a cigarette, exhaled, and said to his friend, "You still thinking about the future, right?"

"Of course, that ain't change."

Then Heavy Pop said, "I know you heard about Peanut. He and four others shot dead. Did you have something to do wit' that?"

"What?"

"I'm sayin', I know we took a loss wit' that kilo, and then he ends up dead. If you did it, then you did what you needed to do."

"Listen, the man just got what he deserves."

"You contracting out killers?"

"I'm just tryin' to keep us alive and afloat in this game, Heavy Pop. You feel me? We can't afford to have anyone run over us or cut us short on business."

Heavy Pop nodded. "I understand."

"I thought Peanut was cool. But he turned out to be an asshole. But you know what? The word is out not to fuck wit' us."

"Yeah, but let's not buy into the stereotype, AZ. We promised ourselves that we wouldn't be too flashy, that we wouldn't attract any unwanted attention. That we were going to be cautious and do this right, and so far, we've been doin' it right."

"You think I'm slipping, Heavy Pop?"

"Nah, but let's not get used to walking on ice."

Heavy Pop didn't want to switch it up. He was making money and continued to drive around in his used Charger and stack his money for a rainy day. He was smart and always cautious. Though he didn't admit it to AZ, he felt that his friend was buying into the stereotype of being a drug dealer—flashy woman on his arm and now he had a flashy car. He and Aoki had been friends for years, so why get into relationship with her now? He didn't understand it. He began to not understand his best friend and business partner at all.

TWENTY-TWO

Aoki strutted out of the Best Buy at the Gateway Center carrying a few shopping bags of electronics and walked to her Yukon feeling proud. It was the best gift she'd ever received. AZ was the best fake boyfriend she'd ever had. He was giving her the best, and she felt that she deserved the best.

Looking fantastic in her bohemian-style strapless printed dress and a pair of wedge heels, Aoki was eye candy in the parking lot. She looked young, fresh and trendy. It was another beautiful summer day with the 4th of July right around the corner. Aoki had plans with her girls to spend the day on the beach. They wanted to catch some sun and enjoy the water.

She got inside her Yukon and settled in, and as she was about to back out of the parking spot, a black Mercedes-Benz came to an abrupt stop behind her, preventing her from exiting the parking spot.

She reached down and gripped her pistol, at the same time peering through her rearview mirror. She had made enemies, and she was ready to shoot first and protect her life.

Her nerves cooled down when she noticed it was B Scientific getting out of his car. She was still alert, but was grateful it was him.

He walked her way and she finally noticed he had a slight limp. It was sexy. He was handsome in a pair of cargo shorts and a white V-neck T-shirt, highlighting his slim, muscular physique, and a pair of bright, white Nikes. His dark skin glimmered in the sun, and his goatee was trimmed meticulously.

"Ya got me blocked," Aoki complained.

He stood by her window. "You in a rush to leave?"

"Me got a busy day."

"Can I get a few minutes of your time then?"

"What, ya following me?"

He chuckled. "Nah, just feel that it's fate that I ran into you like this."

"Ya know I'm a busy girl."

"That's good."

She looked him up and down then looked into his eyes, and it looked like he wasn't taking no for an answer. Aoki didn't mind. She put her truck back into park and surrendered her time to him.

"Where's your man?"

"Him busy."

"Busy, huh?"

"Yes, busy."

"So he won't mind if I take you to get something to eat?"

Aoki hesitated to answer him. She didn't know whether to say yes or no.

"I can see you fretting about it a little, but you don't have to worry. AZ and I are cool, and I'm harmless. All I'm asking is you and I get something to eat at this place I know. It's a cool spot, and I know you'll like it."

"Ya and me?"

"Yes."

"Alone?"

"Like I said I'm harmless."

She sighed. "Okay. Me go."

"You can stay parked and ride with me," he suggested.

Aoki killed the ignition and stepped out of her truck, but not before securing her pistol in her handbag.

B Scientific hopped into his Benz, and she got inside. Aoki hoped she was making the right choice. As B Scientific drove into the city, their conversation was flowing. He was a very intelligent man and spoke about everything from science to history.

They went to a place called Gerber Group's the Roof, an indoor/outdoor place overlooking Central Park. It was the city's hottest spot. They sat outside in the sun and dined on shrimp Alfredo and salad. The mid-afternoon sun was a ball of fire in the sky, blazing brightly, reminding everyone how hot the summer could get.

Aoki was overwhelmed by the posh, stylish ambience. She felt she didn't fit in. She felt that the people could see right through her and was able to tell she was a hood rat.

B Scientific noticed her discomfort and said, "Just relax, gorgeous. They're not worried about you."

"Dis ah different fi me," she said.

"Different is good."

She took a sip of wine and focused on B Scientific. He was able to make her relax and smile. It was like he took her hand and was leading her to a place where the upper class could be intimidating for a gangstress like her.

"Has AZ ever taken you to someplace nice like this?"

"No."

"Why not?"

"Him just too busy."

"He can't be too busy to wine and dine a beautiful woman like you."

"Well, him just is."

"If you don't mind me asking, how long have you been seeing him?"

"We been friends forever."

"I didn't ask how long y'all been friends, but in a relationship."

"Long enough. Him takes care of me."

"I can respect that," he replied.

Two hours later, they were enjoying dessert and cocktails. Aoki didn't think she could smile or actually laugh with anyone besides AZ or even Emilio. But B Scientific was filled with humor and great conversation.

Aoki kept saying to him that her relationship with AZ was perfect, but he didn't believe that. If it was perfect, she wouldn't have accepted his invitation. B Scientific had a woman. Her name was Brandi, and if he ever found out she went out to eat with another man, he would flip out. There was something about Aoki's relationship he wasn't buying.

For now, B Scientific was the perfect gentleman. He didn't push up too hard on Aoki. It was merely casual talk and getting to know each other. If things developed deeply with him and Aoki, then he was ready to make his move, and if it needed to be done, then he was ready to murder AZ if the man stood in his way when it came to what he wanted.

❧

"Me went out ta eat with B Scientific," Aoki told AZ, giving him the heads-up.

"Say what?" he asked. "When was this?"

"Da other day."

"How did y'all meet? Whoa! I mean, h-he came at you," AZ stammered.

"We ran into each other at de shopping center."

"And he asked you out?"

She nodded.

"And you accepted?"

She nodded.

"Wow!"

"Ya mad at me?"

"I'm just taken aback by the sudden news, that's all."

Aoki didn't want AZ to find out through the grapevine that they went out. So she thought it was best to tell him as they sat in his new Benz and talked. Aoki loved the car. She felt AZ deserved it. Maybe in a few months, she could upgrade like him. She was ready to work hard for hers.

AZ sat in silence for a moment, reflecting on the news he'd just heard. Why was B Scientific pushing up on his woman? He couldn't help it, or explain why, but he felt a pang of jealousy inside of him. Why Aoki? He didn't like it; it didn't feel right to him. He looked at Aoki and pretended to be cool with it, but he wasn't.

"What ya tinkin' about?" she asked him.

He sighed. He decided to come out straight with it. "Look, you can't be chillin' wit' him like that."

"Why not?" she asked, confused, knowing he was gay and knowing their "relationship" was for show only.

"Because it won't look cool, and that can start some unnecessary beef with him. Think about it, Aoki—if niggas start seeing my girl fuckin' wit' the next dude, what you think is gonna happen? They gonna expect me to retaliate, because you're mines. How it gonna play out that you're my bitch, but you're fuckin' around wit' B Scientific? It can get nasty."

Aoki understood where he was coming from. "It was just dinner."

"But for a nigga like him, it could mean much more—giving that nigga an opening to come through."

"Fine."

Aoki promised she wouldn't see him again.

⁂

Less than a week later, AZ purchased a brownstone in downtown Brooklyn and invited Aoki to move in with him. He told her that it was the natural progression if they were really an item. There wasn't any way his girl should be living in poverty, especially in that run-down house in the ghetto.

Aoki felt somewhat slighted by his comment. She saw that house differently. Yeah, it came with some heavy shit, from the abuse to the drug use, but she grew up there. It was her home. That place had the potential to be someplace nice, as she gradually put her money into it for renovations to try and make it comfy and cozy.

However, she did like the new area. Downtown Brooklyn had a special vibe to it. The brownstone was luxurious from wall to wall with the exposed bricks on the walls, 11-foot ceilings, open kitchen plan, and fireplace-equipped family room that opened on a private garden at the rear. And it had central air. Coming from East New York, the place was paradise for Aoki.

Aoki agreed to stay over a couple of nights a week to make things look more legit between them. She also planned on saving close to fifty thousand dollars to renovate her home and make it lux. She had goals, and she was determined to make them happen.

Meanwhile, AZ tried to tell himself that he was simply protecting his investment by getting the apartment and inviting Aoki to stay over. In the pit of his stomach he was aware that things were becoming more complicated. He didn't want any trouble with B Scientific, knowing that once the man set his eyes on something, he had to have it. The last thing AZ wanted was to go to war with B Scientific. He wasn't equipped to fight a legend like him. So it was best to try and keep Aoki away from the hood—out of sight, out of mind.

After moving in together, AZ and Aoki spent every day talking and relaxing in their new home. Aoki had access to all the latest amenities, including a 90-inch TV and a high-end stereo system. Aoki also didn't have any problems walking around in her panties and bra, or leaving the bathroom door open when she took showers. She always walked around comfortable in her own skin. In her mind AZ and she were good friends, and he was gay, so he wasn't looking at her anyway.

TWENTY-THREE

He *don't call, he don't pick up*, Connor complained to himself. He was angry and upset. He missed his boo. It'd been two weeks since he'd last seen AZ, and two weeks since they'd made hot, passionate love. Connor was determined to see what had AZ's attention, because it sure wasn't him. He hopped into his Lexus, jumped on the Long Island Expressway, and hurried toward Brooklyn.

Connor continuously tried reaching AZ via cell phone, but his calls went straight to voice mail. He fussed and tossed his phone. "It better not be someone else."

He arrived into Brooklyn and drove around Canarsie, trying to remember where AZ lived. AZ had brought him to his place in Canarsie twice, and both times he cherished the memories. It took him an hour, but he finally found the location. He parked on 91st Street and got out of his Lexus, gazing at the front entrance to AZ's home.

Connor marched up the stairway onto the porch and rang the doorbell and then knocked gruffly. Connor didn't care about the neighbors as he shouted, "AZ, open the door. I know you're not trying to ignore me!"

Connor had no idea that AZ didn't lay his head at this address anymore. He hadn't been there in weeks. AZ never told him about the Downtown Brooklyn brownstone.

He repeatedly dialed the cell phone, but still no answer. He decided to leave an unpleasant voice mail.

Connor barked into the phone, "AZ, I'm at your front door and I'm not leaving until I see you. Why are you ignoring my phone calls, huh? You don't miss me? Well, I miss you. I haven't seen or heard from you in two weeks. The last time I remember, you fucked the shit outta me, and it was good, and then you promised to spend more time with me. Then you fuckin' go MIA. Nigga, what is up with that, huh? Are you fuckin' someone else? Better not, because I love you! But I need you to call me, AZ, because it's really important. I'm not leaving your front door until you do. Do you understand me? I hope so. Good-bye and I love you."

Connor then sat on porch, lit a cigarette, crossed his legs, and waited impatiently, determined to find out what was going on with his lover.

A half-hour later, there was still no AZ or call back from him. Connor decided to call and leave another harsh voice mail.

"AZ, you know what, you are starting to piss me off! Here I am calling you and calling you and you want to ignore me. Nigga, I don't like to be fuckin' ignored! Where are you, and why aren't you calling me back? This isn't cute. Call me back! If you don't, then I'm going to drive around Brooklyn looking for you, calling you out, letting everyone know that we fucked and you are my lover!"

He hung up and scowled. It was getting late. But Connor was determined to stay put until he heard from AZ.

Fifteen minutes later, his cell phone rang. It was AZ calling back.

"Yo, what the fuck is wrong wit' you, Connor?"

"What? AZ, you have the audacity to ask that when you don't call or come by in two weeks? I'm worried about you. Where are you?"

"I'm not home. I'm out."

"Out? Out with who?"

"You don't need to worry about that."

"What do you mean? Am I your boyfriend or not? You fucking someone else, AZ, huh? Be honest with me."

"No, I'm not fuckin' anyone else."

"Then why the secrets, huh? Why keep me in the dark? Why haven't you come by, huh?"

"I told you, I've been busy."

"You busy, all right—busy cheating on me. But I'm at your house, and I'm going to stay here until I see you. And, believe me, if you keep me waiting too long, then I'm gonna start raising hell and let your neighbors know that you're in the closet."

AZ released a frustrated sigh. He was sick of Connor's threats and mood swings. One minute he was cool, the next he was a jealous, controlling bitch.

"I'll be there in ten minutes," said AZ.

"I thought so," Connor said.

Fifteen minutes later, AZ pulled up to his place with Aoki seated in the passenger seat.

Connor perked up when he noticed AZ's new ride, but then he frowned when he set his eyes on Aoki. Before AZ could step out of his truck, Connor was marching off the porch and shouting, "Who is that fuckin' bitch? Huh?"

"Yo, Connor, you need to relax," AZ said.

"Nigga, do not fuckin' tell me to relax! Who is that bitch? I thought you wasn't fuckin' anyone else. I don't care if it's pussy or dick, she needs to fuckin' go!" Connor shouted, his hands flying around in the air.

Aoki looked his way and smirked. She didn't feel threatened by him at all. *So that's him*, she thought. She looked at AZ, and then she looked at Connor—total opposites. She wanted to laugh in the boy's face. *Fuckin' batty bwoy*. Connor was more feminine than Aoki and her friends put together.

"She's just a friend," AZ tried to explain.

But Connor didn't want to listen. "You expect me to believe that bitch is just a friend?"

"Bitch!"

"Yes, bitch!" Connor repeated, pointing at her.

"AZ, ya need to check ya friend," Aoki said coolly.

"Connor, you need to chill out."

"I love you, and you're cheating on me with that skinny beanpole?"

AZ had heard enough of his insults. He was close to punching him in the face. He shouted, "I told you that we ain't fuckin', nigga! How many times do I gotta tell you that?"

"I don't believe you."

Aoki sat in the car and let AZ handle his own problem. His sex life was no concern to her. She watched as AZ forced Connor into the house while she remained outside. She had problems of her own, from Polo, Emilio, and B Scientific, who had been calling her phone for several days now. They had been conversing, and she was breaking her promise to AZ. There was something about B Scientific that had her intrigued, making it hard for her to stay away.

TWENTY-FOUR

The mood was set, and Brandi was ready to please her man. She got on her knees and positioned her naked frame between his legs, grabbing the dick, stroking it nicely, and then lowering her full, luscious lips to wrap around his thick, black, throbbing dick. She placed the mushroom tip in her mouth and toyed with it with her tongue. She wanted to take her time with the dick. She wanted to suck his dick so good, he wouldn't be able to think about another woman. Lately, her man had been growing distant from her. She could feel it. He hadn't been home but in the streets, proclaiming it was business, but she knew he was out there with his whores.

She sucked his dick while he was slouched on the couch, butt naked, texting on his phone while his girl's head bobbed up and down, working all his private areas skillfully, from cupping his balls to deep-throating the one-eyed monster.

B Scientific moaned lightly, though his attention seemed someplace else. He had been having problems with his girl at home, and couldn't keep his mind off Aoki.

As Brandi sucked her man's dick, B Scientific gripped the back of her head, entangling his hand into her long, black hair, and pushed her head farther into his lap. He almost made her choke on his big dick, but she was persistent to take in every inch of him and have him come.

"I want you to come in my mouth," Brandi said, working his dick in her hand and her mouth like a porn star.

He sat back and watched his girl work her lips to his dick, her lips milking the come from his balls. Brandi was the best, and she was willing to do anything to keep her relationship strong and zestful. Whatever B Scientific wanted from her, from anal to an hour-long blowjob, she was down.

"I'm gonna come," B Scientific announced.

"Go ahead, baby. Come for me," she said, sucking his dick and jerking him off simultaneously.

It didn't take long for B Scientific to explode inside Brandi's mouth. His sperm shot out like a geyser, and she took all of his semen down her throat and swallowed his load like it was dinner. He felt his dick twitch with the last spurts of his seed into her mouth. Brandi continued to suck and lick the last of it from his dick. B Scientific looked down at her, and she stared up at him, hoping he was satisfied completely.

After his nut, he stood up, put on his jeans and shirt, and marched out the door to make a phone call, leaving Brandi behind looking dumbfounded.

Brandi jumped to her feet and followed her man out the door, not caring that she was naked. She stepped outside to find her man seated in his Range Rover parked in the driveway, talking to someone. Her heart ached with jealousy.

Brandi tried to please her man twenty four/seven. She cooked and cleaned. Her one downfall was he wanted to have kids, but Brandi had always been skeptical. She took birth control. She wanted to be a model and get into fashion, one day open her own fashion boutique either in Brooklyn or the city. B Scientific had promised to help her with her career. He'd promised to invest into her, but that was years ago, and she found herself being stuck in limbo with her career and her relationship.

She marched toward the Range Rover naked and tapped on the window, catching his attention.

B Scientific turned and frowned. He curtailed his conversation with whomever and rolled down the window.

Brandi was ready to leap through the window and snatch his phone. "Who was that?" she barked.

"Brandi, that's business," he said.

"So you gotta step outside and sit in your truck to talk about business?"

"You know me. It's business, and you need to shut up about this," he said with a stern look. "You know I'm a busy man. You know I got money in the street that needs to be collected. You think I want you all in my business? You see this truck? It's my fuckin' office."

She pouted and then pivoted and walked away.

When Brandi was back in the house, B Scientific jumped back on his cell phone and dialed the number again.

When she answered, he said, "So, where were we?"

"Ya were tryin' to get wit' me," Aoki said.

"I was, right. I definitely want to see you again. I can't stop thinking about you, Aoki. So when and where?"

"Ya tell me."

"Tomorrow. I'll come get you. Just let me know where you want me to pick you up from."

"Okay, tomorrow me will call you."

"You do that, baby girl."

B Scientific hung up and smiled. He was excited about seeing her again.

B Scientific had flawless black skin and deep, stirring eyes. His physique was strong like a bull, and his swag made her want to get to know him better, both physically and mentally. She fixed her eyes on B Scientific as he pulled his shirt over his head and exposed his rock-hard abs. There was no denying it. He had the body of a god. She wanted to touch him everywhere, but there was time for that. In fact, they had all the time in the world.

B Scientific had gotten them a suite at the Marriott in the city, with a king-size bed and a large overstuffed sofa in an adjacent room. The suite was fitted with a marble bath featuring a deep soaker tub, a large flat-screen TV, and twenty-four-hour room service.

It'd been months since Aoki had sex. She was excited about this evening.

He stepped to her, eyeing her sexy body as she stood in front of him in her panties and bra.

Before he could wrap his arms around her, she said to him, "You know me love AZ. He's me childhood sweetheart, and me not leaving him, B Scientific. Not for anyt'ing or anyone."

"Cool. Because I don't plan on leaving Brandi. However, tonight you belong to me, Aoki, and AZ and Brandi don't have to find out about us. Let's just enjoy each other."

They kissed each other fervently, and his hands groped her body. Aoki took his hard flesh into her manicured hand and stroked his penis, which felt like a steel pipe protruding from her small fist.

B Scientific shoved his tongue deeper down her throat, and their bodies pressed together heatedly as she jerked him off and felt him throbbing like a heartbeat.

He scooped Aoki into his masculine arms, and she straddled him. He tossed her onto the bed and dove between her open legs, tearing off her panties and sinking his face into her pussy. He tunneled his long tongue inside of her, causing her to squirm and moan. He tasted her clit and massaged her vagina walls.

Aoki's legs quivered as she bit down on her bottom lip, her body washed with stimulating pleasure. B Scientific became a beast while eating her pussy out, causing a wave of pleasure to sweep over her body.

He tore open a Magnum condom, rolled it back onto his thick, long length and positioned himself between Aoki's spread legs and slowly started sinking his dick into her liquid heat, which was dripping with excitement. She wrapped her legs around him. Their kisses were erotic and passionate.

He stroked gently inside of her. They fucked position after position, and the last position was the one with Aoki riding his big dick as she straddled his body with her thighs pressed tightly against his sides. B Scientific had his hands full with the curves of her backside. She grinded against him, leaning forward with her hands pressed against his chest and felt his erection bringing her closer to an orgasm.

"I'm gonna come!" she cried out. She held on tight with his dick firmly inside of her, thrusting, and it made her feel like she was floating on air.

She suddenly felt her breath leave her lungs as she came suddenly, her body quivering on top of B Scientific's, her fingernails digging into him for support. She screamed out in passion and was literally breathless.

He got his too, and they both collapsed against each other, looking pleased and wanting to start off round two soon.

Several hours later, Aoki got dressed while B Scientific lay in bed watching her every movement. He wanted her to stay longer, but she had to go back home to AZ.

It had been a pleasurable and memorable night. They'd fucked for hours, matching each other with stamina, and Aoki had multiple orgasms. The dick was good. His dick was *so* good.

When Aoki was fully dressed, B Scientific removed himself from the bed naked, his flaccid penis still looking impressive as he walked toward her. He wrapped his arms around her and pulled her into a hug.

Just being against his hard, strong flesh made Aoki want to undress again and fuck some more. But she didn't want to spoil him.

"Call me when you get home, okay? I want to make sure you're safe."

"Me will."

He kissed her forehead and then her lips. Then she pulled herself away from his naked flesh and made her exit. The grin she carried was so wide it stretched from ear to ear.

꧁

They met two days later in another ritzy hotel in the city and fucked each other's brains out. Then, a week later, the same thing. Aoki couldn't get enough of B Scientific, and he couldn't get enough of her.

꧁

"Ooooh shit! I'm gonna come, baby," Emilio cried out.

Aoki continued to grind her hips into him, riding his dick, pleasing him fully.

Emilio gripped her hips and started to make faces, her legs clamped around him and her pussy locked tight, contracting. She leaned forward and kissed his neck.

"Oh shit, girl! Oh shit! You feel so fuckin' good!" he cried out.

Aoki started breathing faster. She was about to come too. Aoki started to speed up. Emilio spanked her ass and it felt like his dick was inside her stomach.

"Fuck me!" she yelled. "Fuck me, baby!"

They both soon reached the point of no return.

Emilio grasped Aoki's sweaty hips and conveyed his soul as they exploded together and then collapsed beside each other, breathless.

The next half hour was strictly pillow talk. It was the summer, and business was always slow in the summer. Students were back home with family, and his customers had dwindled down to maybe a half a dozen, so Emilio spent most of his time working part-time in the city or in Brooklyn keeping Aoki company. She didn't mind. She managed to juggle both men and was great at it.

TWENTY-FIVE

They were soaking themselves deeply in the street life with their kills, but at the end of the day, Aoki, Rihanna, and Tisa were still young girls at heart. They still liked teenage things—boys, clothes, hip-hop, and *106 & Park* on BET. They still laughed and had their silly antics. They had crushes and dreams.

Tisa and Rihanna were smoking weed, and Aoki was smoking her cigarette. They all were chilling in Rihanna's living room watching *Love & Hip Hop: New York*. It was one of their favorite shows. New York was their favorite, because it was their home, and Atlanta was their second favorite. But *Love & Hip Hop: Hollywood*, they felt, was corny and wack.

"Yo, I can't stand that bitch Erica," Tisa said. "I swear, if she was doin' that bullshit around here, that bitch woulda been cut."

"I know, right?" Rihanna agreed.

"Fake-ass bitch!" Tisa said.

They were glued to the newest episode. The two of them had reconciled with each other, putting the Staten Island incident behind them.

"Now, Yandy, she looks like she's a cool bitch," Rihanna said.

"I know. But why she fuckin' wit' a bird nigga like Mendeecees. He looks like a cornball. You know I heard that he had a small dick."

They laughed.

Aoki sat there with a lot on her mind, from B Scientific to Emilio.

Tisa asked, "You okay, Aoki?"

"Me fine," she said.

"What's on your mind?" Rihanna asked.

Aoki looked at them both and said, "If me tell ya someting, can ya keep it ah secret?"

Rihanna and Tisa glanced at each other and then looked back at Aoki. It had to be something juicy.

Rihanna said, "Yeah, you know you can trust us, Aoki. Shit, we kept one secret for how many years now?" she added, referring to the dead bodies still concealed in her backyard.

"You got drama?" Tisa asked.

"No drama."

"Then what is it?"

"Okay. I'm fuckin' B Scientific."

"Whoa! What?" Tisa said, taken aback by the news.

"What happened to AZ?" Rihanna asked.

"Him still around."

"So ya cheatin' on him?"

Aoki, not wanting to expose AZ's secret, simply said, "It's complicated."

"What's complicated about it?" Tisa said. "I thought y'all were childhood sweethearts and finally decided to make things official."

"How'd you get wit' B Scientific, girl?" Rihanna asked.

Aoki sighed. She expected the questions from her friends. She started dishing the details on how good his dick was.

Tisa felt some type of way. Why did she have to have AZ and B Scientific too? Why were two of the finest men in Brooklyn chasing her?

Aoki continued talking about B Scientific. She was glowing when discussing him. Her friends could see the contentment all in her face.

"Me tink he's in love wit' me."

Unbeknownst to them, Gena was eavesdropping from the kitchen, listening to every word Aoki was saying about her relationship with B Scientific. Hearing that, she marched into the room, suddenly making her presence known. "B Scientific has a bitch already, so how is he in love wit' you?"

It was stunning to see Gena take up for a woman that she didn't know. Aoki was caught off guard. She knew about Brandi, but she didn't care. Nor did she think telling her friends about B Scientific was going to lead to this. She also planned on telling them about Emilio, however Gena's interruption had stopped all further disclosures.

"Him don't love her," she stated.

"What makes you think that, Aoki? Huh? What? You think because you givin' him some pussy that he supposed to leave his woman?" Gena said gruffly, with an intense stare.

"Ma, chill," Rihanna said.

"Nah, fuck that! Who this bitch think she is anyway, tryin' to break up someone's happy home? Aoki, don't you already got a man, from my understanding? Ain't you fuckin' wit' AZ? Huh? You is a dumb bitch to fuck up a good thing. But you know what, I guess that's what stupid sluts do."

"Ma, what is wrong wit' you?" Rihanna shouted.

"Ain't shit wrong wit' me! And mind ya fuckin' business, Ri-Ri!"

Aoki scowled at Gena. She was tempted to pull out her pocketknife and plunge it into Gena's neck. She saw the jealousy in Gena's eyes. That bitch didn't know who she was fucking with.

Rihanna saw the tension and drama escalating in the room and tried to calm things down. She shouted to her mother, "*You* need to stay out of people's business!"

"Fuck that bitch!" Gena glared at Aoki.

"Ya know what," Aoki spat, standing abruptly and glaring back at Gena, itching to really hurt her.

"What, bitch? What the fuck you gonna do, Aoki?" Gena shouted, egging Aoki on.

Tisa sat and stayed out of the drama. She agreed with her mother all the way, but she wasn't about to let Aoki know that.

Rihanna found herself in between her best friend and her mother, desperately trying to keep the peace in the room. Tisa wasn't doing a damn thing but sitting there looking amused.

"Ri-Ri, check ya mudda before me hurt her!"

"Ma, just chill!" Rihanna screamed.

"Ya know what, me gone. Me don't need dis shit," Aoki said, pivoting away from Gena and Rihanna and leaving the apartment suddenly. If she didn't, she was going to end up killing Gena.

After Aoki left, Gena looked at her daughters and proclaimed, "I don't want y'all hanging out wit' that bitch anymore. She's a slut and a fuckin' whore. I'm telling y'all, that bitch is bad news."

"And what that makes me, Ma? Huh? Because I damn sure fucked a lot more niggas than her. And you have the audacity to talk!"

"She's right, Ri-Ri," Tisa said, backing up Gena's words.

"What? Are you serious, Tisa?"

"I'm saying, why Aoki got to have it all, huh? We always have her back, protecting her secrets and doin' what she says. What about us, huh?"

Rihanna couldn't believe it. She figured that they both were jealous of Aoki, but she didn't understand why her mother was going after Aoki for no damn reason. It didn't make any sense to her.

Rather than continue this fruitless argument, Rihanna stormed into her room and slammed her door shut.

"Slam another door around here and see if I don't put my foot square up your ass!" Gena screamed.

TWENTY-SIX

Multiple police sirens blared through the streets of Brownsville. A young girl was shot in the head at point-blank range at the corner of Rockaway Avenue and Dumont. Her body was face down out in front of Wah Yung Chinese takeout place. It wasn't a robbery, just a brazen killing. A hooded stranger hastily approached the beautiful, young girl as she stepped out of the Chinese food place and shot her dead—one shot to the head and several to her body.

Cop cars and homicide detectives flooded the scene trying to question witnesses and survey the area. They didn't have the woman's identity yet. She was well dressed and pretty.

The streets were talking, saying it was finally payback for Greasy Dee's murder. It'd been months since the incident, but now that Polo was home and healthy again, revenge was inevitable. The streets were saying that Greasy Dee and Polo had been set up by three pretty, well-dressed bitches. One of them was dark skinned with long, black hair and looked like a baby doll.

Two homicide cops, Detective Williams and Surdak crouched near the dead body and examined the victim with their latex gloves. They took in everything about her. She was sprawled face down on the concrete, her blood pooling underneath her, turning the sidewalk into a crimson stain. She was clean cut, and she had no visible tattoos.

"Who was she?" Detective Surdak asked.

The first cop to respond to the shooting shrugged. "Don't know. Witnesses say she was leaving the place, and a man approached and shot her multiple times. First shot was to her head."

"This was a revenge killing for something," Detective Williams said. "Our pretty face must have upset someone around here."

Without any ID, the cops didn't have much to go on. The locals didn't know who she was. Either she wasn't from the area, or she wasn't well known.

They continued to investigate the crime scene. Detective Williams knew he needed to reach out to one of his snitches to find out what was going on. He thought about Polo, who had been out of the hospital for weeks. His gut instincts told him he had something to do with the young woman's death.

The coroner came and took the body off the corner. The looky-loos were whispering and gossiping to each other deep behind the yellow crime scene tape. But they refused to talk to the police.

Detective Williams looked at their faces from a distance. He knew someone knew something.

❧

A week later, another homicide happened in the stairwell of the Howard Houses on Mother Gaston Boulevard. The victim had been shot multiple times inside the fifth-floor stairwell. Sink's body lay bloody, slumped in the dim light, a half-dozen cops surrounding him, including Detectives Williams and Surdak.

It was all connected somehow, Detective Williams told himself. It was all connected to Polo.

❧

Aoki heard the news about Theresa's and Sink's murders. The streets were talking, saying Theresa and Aoki resembled each other greatly. Aoki was no fool. Sink and Theresa knew each other. She lived in the same building, but she was a quiet girl in college. She always minded her business and kept to herself. Aoki knew it was Polo striking back. He'd mistakenly murdered the wrong girl. Now it was her time to retaliate before it was too late.

Polo had been showing his face again in Brooklyn, making his presence known. He had gotten his weight up physically, and he and his crew were on the hunt. It was no secret that Polo had been cruising around Brooklyn looking for the girls who'd tried to kill him. He put money on the table for anyone who had intel on their whereabouts.

Aoki couldn't wait any longer. She made it a priority to go after Polo. It was now or never. She met up with her crew and gave them the rundown about the murders and Polo. And, of course, they were worried, especially Tisa.

Aoki was willing to pay for information, anything that could lead her to Polo. She offered two large, courtesy of AZ. It didn't take long before someone took the bait and approached her with reliable information about him.

"He likes to hang out at this strip club in the Bronx called Limelight with this stripper named Dawn," a male associate of Polo told her.

She paid him his money. Everyone had a price, and loyalty was only a word.

Aoki was ready to use the information. She and her crew drove to the Bronx and observed the place on the sly.

The source was accurate—it didn't take them long to spot Polo exiting the strip club with a shapely black woman with long, golden locks. They climbed into a Lexus and drove away.

Aoki followed them cautiously, determined to finish this. She followed them into the city, driving through Harlem. They ended up on the east side of town on Madison Avenue. Aoki watched Dawn and Polo walk into a busy restaurant, where patrons dined inside and outside on the sidewalk on a balmy, summer night.

She watched the area, observed the crowd, and knew it was now or never. They had the element of surprise in their favor. If they didn't do it tonight, then Aoki had no idea when they would get a chance again.

Polo and Dawn were seated at a round table outside, eating a meal, talking. Polo looked like a different person with his female friend. He probably thought he was safe a few blocks away from Central Park in the city with his stripper girlfriend.

"Let's do dis," Aoki said to her friends.

They all donned different color wigs and dark shades. Coolly, they exited the stolen car they were in and calmly walked in Polo's direction. Tisa was very nervous, but she was determined to stand by her friends' side this time. No running away. Being in the city where there was traffic, people, cops patrolling and most likely surveillance cameras all around was risky, but they didn't care. They believed their disguises were good enough to conceal their true identities.

Aoki just didn't give a fuck; she wanted the job done.

Aoki set her eyes on Polo, his back turned to the danger approaching as he engaged Dawn in conversation. Aoki took a deep breath. She shrewdly pulled out a sharpened icepick and held it stealthily in her fist. Her heart pumped faster, and her rage was turned up. This time she wasn't about to fail.

Tisa and Rihanna were right behind her, looking like china dolls in their baby doll dresses and the short, Chinese cut wigs.

Before anyone could suspect anything, Aoki slammed the icepick into the back of Polo's neck abruptly and began to stab him repeatedly, almost prison yard-style. He never saw it coming.

Dawn, traumatized by the attack, screamed. The patrons suddenly flung into panic and chaos.

Aoki stabbed Polo to death while people fled away screaming, falling over chairs, plates smashing to the ground, and folks tripping over each other trying to escape the sudden carnage.

Dawn was a witness, so she had to be taken care of.

Rihanna quickly raised the 9mm to her chest and fired multiple times, as she fell backwards from her chair almost slow-mo style and dropped dead on the ground.

Aoki was absolutely sure that Polo was dead this time as his body lay on the ground next to his last meal.

The girls tried to get lost with the crowd fleeing. They kept their heads low and craftily removed their wigs and glasses, tossing them into the bag Tisa was carrying, and hurried away from the murders. They cut down a side block to avoid the surveillance cameras, trying to limit their footage on video.

They reached the stolen car parked only a block away and jumped inside.

Aoki sped away and exhaled with relief. "We burn everything," she said about the wigs and glasses, "and the car too."

⚜

From 92nd Street to 93rd Street, Madison Avenue was shut down completely as police cars and dozens of cops flooded the area. Two dead bodies lay in front of the chic eatery, overturned tables and chairs scattered on the sidewalk, personal items left behind as customers desperately tried to flee the area.

Both bodies were covered with white sheets. Homicide inspected the crime scene painstakingly and started taking down witness statements. They couldn't believe someone was brazen enough to murder two people in cold blood at a popular eatery in the city.

When the detectives questioned a middle-aged man who saw the whole thing unfold, all he could say was, "They almost looked like dolls, man. Fragile dolls."

The detective taking his statement was confused. "Dolls?"

"Yes," the man said, "there was three of them, all dressed in short dresses, something young kids would wear, with cropped haircuts and that straight bang the Asian women wear. And shades. They were so tiny, fragile . . . looked like dolls, baby-faced girls. One, I mean, she just stabbed this man in his neck like it was nothing. The second girl shot his girlfriend in cold blood. I've never seen anything like it," he said to the detective, shock and grief written all over his face.

Almost all of the witnesses said the same thing—three ladies, young and beautiful, dressed nicely and most likely wearing wigs, looking like dolls.

The next day, the front page of the *Daily News* read: "Killer Dolls at Large." Then the article went into details about the brazen murder on Madison Avenue and there was a fuzzy, grainy still shot inserted into the newspaper taken from a camera in the restaurant of Aoki, Tisa, and Rihanna, heads hung low.

TWENTY-SEVEN

AZ was in awe. He couldn't believe that Aoki was bold enough to murder someone in the city. He'd read about it in the papers, and it was all over the news. AZ was nervous for his friend, but at the same time he was equally nervous for himself. Getting this type of attention could cause heat from the local authorities.

Now that the original hit had finally been concluded, Aoki came up with a brainstorm. She had a taste for blood and profit. She wanted to make some money. In private, she had a word with AZ. She wanted to be hired out and be able to do murders for other drug dealers and his acquaintances. She strongly felt that her peoples were ready.

At first, AZ didn't comprehend it or recommend it. She would be putting herself and her friends at serious risk. She explained to him that she was willing to take that chance. The risk was worth the reward.

It was crazy. But she had always been crazy.

AZ promised to take care of her. If she needed money, it wasn't a problem. But Aoki didn't want anyone taking care of her. Her mother relied on a man to take care of her and look where it got her. She and her crew wanted to stand on their own feet and make things happen for themselves.

Reluctantly, AZ said to her, "Okay, I'll put the word out on the streets, see what I can do for y'all."

NYC wasn't ready for "the killer dolls."

❧

Emilio caressed Aoki's body and made love with his hands, touching her body like it was the most delicate flower. He definitely knew how to hold a woman and have sex with her. His strokes inside of her were long and deep, as her pussy lips were spread as an invitation to him, and he was extra hard.

First, they made love in the missionary position, inside her bedroom. She climbed on top of him and brought her pussy down on his hard dick, her juices flowing freely.

He squeezed her tits together and enjoyed the ride she was giving him. Both of them cooed, feeling extra special. The way her pussy felt when she rode him had Emilio's dick feeling like it was out of control.

Aoki rode him gently, taking her time with his dick, enjoying his tender touch. She made eye contact with Emilio and moaned. She pressed her hands against his chest, and he grabbed her ass tight and groaned from the muscles inside of her milking him.

He continued to play with her nipples as her juices coated him. "I'm gonna come!"

Aoki continued to work his dick until they both came. She collapsed on top of him, both spent.

❧

Over time, Aoki had become a little slut to him and B Scientific. Both men had different characteristics that she liked and enjoyed. B Scientific was powerful and imposing, while Emilio was refreshing and intelligent. B Scientific had a woman, though, and Emilio was single and wanted her for life.

Emilio wasn't shy to admit that he saw a future with Aoki. He had fallen in love with her. He treated her special and always put her first. He always came by her place and helped her with small repairs in the house, being a jack-of-all-trades.

Whenever he inquired about her past or background, she told him the same story she told everyone else: Her mother had moved back to Japan, and her father was lost in the streets on drugs, and she had a hard life growing up.

❧

Aoki woke up to the sunlight shining in her face. It was early morning, and Emilio wasn't by her side. She knew he had spent the night. She lifted herself from the bed and gazed around the bedroom. His shoes were still on the floor.

She donned a robe and left the bedroom. She walked downstairs and noticed the door to the backyard was open. She walked outside to find Emilio standing by the tin barrels in her yard.

She asked nervously, "Emilio, what ya ah doin' out here?"

"Aoki, why do you have these two barrels in your backyard? I mean, they are an eyesore. Why don't you just get rid of them? What's in them?"

"Dem ah none of ya business!" she barked.

"I mean, I can help you get rid of them."

"Look ya don't need to fret 'bout me backyard, ya understand?"

Emilio was taken aback by her harsh tone. "I didn't mean to offend you."

"Ya just don't need to touch dem. Me gon' have dem move when me ready, ya understand?"

"Yeah, I understand. I'm sorry."

"Ya don't need to be sorry—just come inside an' suck me pussy."

He smiled. "I can do that."

Aoki took him by the hand and led him back into the house, where they made love some more, ate breakfast, and talked all morning.

TWENTY-EIGHT

No "work" made Aoki a very normal person. So she decided to play when she wasn't murdering people. B Scientific had gotten them another ritzy hotel room in Manhattan, where they spent hours fucking their brains out and enjoying room service and cable TV.

After they'd had sex, B Scientific started to complain about Brandi, dropping hints to her that they should make it official.

"If you tell AZ, I'll tell Brandi," he said to her.

Aoki wanted for them to simply stick with the program—having an affair, having fun with each other, and going back home to their significant others.

B Scientific was relentless. The more she refused to let go of AZ, the more he wanted her. He was used to women doing everything in their power to get him and be his number one, but Aoki was doing everything in her power to stay number two, his side-chick. B Scientific hated it.

B Scientific walked around the room naked; the only thing clasped to him was a beautiful diamond rosary he always wore under his shirts. Aoki had noticed it a few times. It was the most exquisite piece of jewelry she'd ever seen.

She decided to ask him about it. "Why do ya always wear dat?"

He looked at her and said, "You like this?"

"It's beautiful. Ya never take it off?"

"I can't," he said. "This is special to me. It belonged to my brother. He was killed last year."

"Me sorry to hear 'bout that."

"Yeah, I made them Baltimore niggas pay severely, though. They fucked with the wrong family. I remember having this feeling right before he was murdered, like something was about to happen. I went to my jeweler and had him make this rosary for him. Then I took it to the church and had it blessed by a priest. But it didn't save his life. So now I wear this to remind me how dangerous the game can get, how ugly it is out there. You can't get caught slipping. Every time I look at it, it reminds me of my brother," he said, looking nostalgic.

The room fell silent.

B Scientific unclamped the rosary from around his neck. "I want you to wear it," he said.

Aoki was shocked. "No, me can't."

"Nah, I want you to wear it, not have it."

"Why?"

He sighed. "Because, every time I look at it, it reminds me of my brother, so I want you to wear it, so every time you look at it, it will remind you of me."

Halfheartedly, she accepted the gift.

B Scientific clamped it around her neck. "It looks great on you, sexy."

❧

With Polo out of the picture, AZ's had no beef and no worries. He was making money. He had his respect. The streets were talking, once again linking him to Polo's demise. Word around the way and through Brooklyn was: Don't fuck with AZ.

His relationship with Connor was rocky. Since that day when he'd showed up at AZ's place unannounced and stirred up drama, AZ decided to call things off.

A week later, he found himself back in Connor's arms again, but it didn't feel the same.

❧

AZ and Heavy Pop drove through the Holland Tunnel on their way to Oscar's waterfront condo in Union, New Jersey.

When they finally arrived there, Oscar greeted them with a handshake and a smile. "Fellows, nice seeing y'all again," he said.

"We came bearing gifts," AZ said.

AZ had come with a briefcase filled with Oscar's cut from AZ's growing business in the streets. Product was great, and profits were soaring through the roof.

AZ opened the suitcase filled with cash, totaling in the hundreds of thousands.

Oscar smiled. "I knew I liked something about you."

They sat down and talked.

AZ needed a re-up. He was moving twenty to thirty kilos a month, and almost more in marijuana sales. Business was definitely good for the duo. AZ wanted to keep it like that. But he also had another business proposition for Oscar.

AZ threw back the glass of scotch in his hand and said to Oscar, "Can we talk in private?"

Oscar nodded. "Anything for you, my friend."

"Yo, Heavy, excuse us for a minute."

Heavy Pop was confused. Why did AZ have to talk to their connect in private? Usually they spoke openly about everything.

Oscar gestured for them to talk on the terrace. AZ and Oscar stood up from their chairs, and AZ followed Oscar outside, while Heavy Pop remained in the room with the bodyguard and the bar.

Outside on the terrace, Oscar closed the glass door for added privacy.

AZ stared at the city's skyline from afar. It was a beautiful, bright day, and a picturesque sight. Who wouldn't want to live like this?

"What's up?" Oscar asked.

"I have a minor business proposition for you outside of what we have going on."

"I'm listening."

"In this business, we gonna always carry enemies, and they gonna always need dealing with, so my proposition is that if you ever have a problem that you want outside help on, I can offer you a quick solution."

"A quick solution, huh?"

"Yeah. I have a crew of women who can handle your dirty work."

"Women?" Oscar raised his eyebrow. "Who sends a woman to do a man's work?"

"Oscar, don't underestimate them. They're professional, and they will get the job done. I've used them myself on a few jobs, and it worked out fine, no problems. And think about it—You hire them, and it will be less heat on your organization—no ties back to you at all."

Oscar pondered it, a look of reluctance on his face.

"Have you listened to the news recently?" AZ asked.

"I have."

"You heard about the Killer Dolls?"

He grinned. "Yeah. It was a risky hit, still no clues, no suspects, only a grainy video."

"Do I have your attention now?"

"That was you?"

AZ nodded, looking smug. He went on to say, "It will be twenty thousand a contract."

"I'll see, my friend. I'll see."

The men walked back into the room.

Heavy Pop was working on his second drink. AZ had something else going on, and it didn't feel right. He felt left out, but he didn't express his feelings right away.

"You ready?" AZ asked his friend.

Heavy Pop replied quietly, "Waiting on you."

They headed toward the door. When they got on the elevator and descended, Heavy Pop asked, "So, what was all that about? The meeting on the terrace?"

AZ looked at his friend and simply replied, "Business, that's all, Heavy Pop, business."

"And when did you start excluding me from business?"

AZ sighed. "You really don't wanna know."

Heavy Pop shook his head and didn't push the issue. Whatever AZ was up to, he was hoping it didn't come back to bite them in the ass and ruin everything they'd worked so hard to build.

TWENTY-NINE

B Scientific, his breathing a bit ragged, groaned as Gena sucked and stroked his big dick. With her firm grip around it, she made him grow harder in seconds. She wanted all of his cock inside her mouth. She was on her knees tasting him, loving him completely, trying to outdo every bitch he'd ever been with.

Her head rapidly bobbed back and forth, swallowing the dick whole, while playing with his balls. Then she took his balls into her mouth and sucked and chewed on them while jerking him off.

"I want you," she said. "I want you inside of me. I want you to fuck me."

B Scientific didn't respond to her cry for sex. He wanted a blowjob, nothing more, nothing less. Gena had been begging for his dick for over an hour now, but it was going to be on his time. He wasn't rushing to fuck her. If he'd had his choice, he would have been with Aoki, but she wasn't answering his calls that night. B Scientific got a motel room in Queens for himself and Gena, something average and nothing fancy. She wasn't special to him, just a jump off.

Gena loved the sensation of having his dick grow huge inside her mouth and the taste of his ejaculation. She knew how to open wide and relax her throat.

She continued to bob her head back and forth, throwing the penis down her throat. B Scientific moaned and watched his manhood disappear into her gaping mouth like magic.

B Scientific groaned as she continued to take him deep in her mouth.

Gena had him nice and wet, sliding her mouth up and down on his throbbing, rock-hard erection that looked like a missile about to launch. She then pulled back to lick him from the balls up to the head, covering his sensitive area with her entire mouth, before doing it again.

She grinned up at him. "I wanna fuck, baby. I want you to take this pussy."

B Scientific made Gena get up off her knees and curved her over the dresser, her legs spread into an upside down *V*. Her pussy was so wet, juice was dripping down her legs. He made sure to strap up, throwing on the Magnum condom. The last thing he wanted was to get this bitch pregnant. Or any bitch. Except Brandi and, maybe, Aoki. He knew they would have some pretty kids.

He slammed himself inside of Gena, and she groaned with the sudden jolt of pleasure. He gripped her hips and roughly pounded her with his big dick, her pussy pulsing nonstop around his cock. Gena's groans turned to screams, the dick from the back taking her out of this world.

B Scientific thrust into her, treating her like the nasty, dick-craving ghetto bitch she was, pulling her hair and smacking her ass, and she loved it.

A strong orgasm struck Gena like lightning, and she let out a wail of ecstasy. Her entire body quivered from the pleasure as she rode out the orgasm.

They chilled for a moment and fucked again. He got his nut, and she got hers again.

It was like that for hours until he fell asleep. He didn't mean to stay, but she took a lot out of him.

While B Scientific slept, Gena noticed he wasn't wearing his rosary. She couldn't help but think, either he'd lost it, or Brandi was rocking it.

Gena frowned as a wave of jealousy washed over her. She couldn't believe he was fucking Aoki too. She expected to share him with Brandi, not anyone else. She'd put in the work, doing her best to make B Scientific believe that she could be his, but Aoki was fucking things up.

Gena started going through his phone, and she retrieved Brandi's number, which was all she needed.

❧

Back at home, Gena didn't waste any time implementing her plan. After buying herself a burner phone, she texted Brandi: You need to leave my man alone. He doesn't love you anymore. He likes my pussy better, just ask him yourself.

A reply came back minutes later: Who the fuck is this?

Gena texted back: Bitch, you don't know? Ask around, my name is Aoki.

Fᴜᴄᴋ ʏᴏᴜ Aᴏᴋɪ! ʏᴏᴜ ᴛʜɪɴᴋ ʏᴏᴜ ᴄᴀɴ ᴄᴏᴍᴇ ᴀᴛ ᴍᴇ ᴀɴᴅ ᴍʏ ᴍᴀɴ?

I ᴀʟʀᴇᴀᴅʏ ᴅɪᴅ, ᴄᴜᴢ ᴜʀ ɴɪɢɢᴀ ʟᴜᴠs ᴍᴇ, & ᴀɴʏᴡᴀʏ, ʙɪᴛᴄʜ ʜᴏᴡ ᴅᴏ ᴍʏ ᴘᴜssʏ ᴛᴀsᴛᴇ?

Bɪᴛᴄʜ, ᴡʜᴇɴ I ꜰɪɴᴅ ᴜ, I'ᴍ ɢᴏɴɴᴀ ꜰᴜᴄᴋ ᴜ ᴜᴘ!

Dᴏ ɪᴛ ᴛʜᴇɴ, ʙɪᴛᴄʜ, I'ᴍ ʜᴇʀᴇ!

Gena smiled at her deviousness. The fuse was lit. Now all she had to do was sit back and watch the fireworks.

B Scientific ducked from a flying object thrown at him just as he came through his front door.

"You fuckin' asshole! I hate you!"

B Scientific wasn't home one minute and the drama had already started. He glared at Brandi, who had her cell phone in one hand and one of his pistols in the other.

"Brandi, what the fuck is your problem? Yo, baby, put the gun down."

"Who the fuck is Aoki?" she barked.

B Scientific was shocked that she knew that name. *How did she find out about her?* His face alone gave her the confirmation.

"Who told you about her?"

"The bitch came to my fuckin' door."

B Scientific knew it was bullshit. He'd already told Aoki that she could have him if she wanted him. He scowled. "I don't believe that shit. You're lyin', bitch!"

"Oh, now I'm a fuckin' bitch?" She raised the pistol and pointed it at him. "You forgot who got the fuckin' gun."

B Scientific didn't even flinch. He glared at her, and the intensity in his eyes could cut the entire room in half.

"Who is she?" Brandi screamed.

"She ain't none of your business," he replied coldly.

"Oh, she ain't none of my business, huh?"

B Scientific stepped toward Brandi, who was in tears and still had the gun trained on him. He was calling her bluff, knowing she didn't have the balls to shoot him.

He quickly snatched the gun from her hand and punched her so hard, she went flying backwards and hit the floor. "You stupid fuckin' bitch! Don't you ever pull a gun on me in my own home!" he shouted heatedly.

This was the first time he'd ever struck her over a bitch. In the past, if she even mentioned another bitch's name and hinted to leave him, then B Scientific would practically be on his knees begging her to stay, and the next day, he would purchase an expensive gift for her.

Evidently that was the past. He was a fierce drug dealer now. He was respected and feared. He had everything from money to pussy, but the one thing he wanted was kids. And Brandi never gave him any.

Brandi picked herself from off the floor, lip bleeding. She was shaken by the blow. He now had the gun, but he wasn't going to use it.

"You need to remember who the fuck I am," he said through gritted teeth.

She looked at him, standing frozen, her eyes showing more concern than terror. Was her time as reigning queen almost up? For years B Scientific begged her to have his baby, but she refused, always saying she wasn't ready. She always went the extra measures not to get pregnant. And the one time she got pregnant, she had an abortion.

All types of concerns and fears ran through Brandi's mind. *Is Aoki pregnant?*

Truthfully, after B Scientific's brother had been murdered, Brandi felt that he would suffer the same fate one day. She didn't want to raise any baby or babies alone; that would have brought her stock down. Besides, B Scientific had never hinted at marrying her.

"Do you love her?" she asked.

Still frowning and upset, he looked at Brandi and spat, "Bitch, go clean yourself up and get the fuck out my face!" He turned and walked away, exiting his home.

An hour later, after drying away her umpteenth tear and sulking in her bedroom, Brandi texted Aoki: MY MAN DON'T WANT U HO. HE SAID UR UGLY & UR PUSSY STANK.

Gena texted Brandi a picture of Aoki she'd gotten from Rihanna's iPhone, with the words: BITCH, DO I LOOK UGLY 2 U, DON'T GET IT TWISTED. UR NIGGA IS LOVIN' ME & LOVIN' THE GOOD WET PUSSY THAT I GIVE HIM ALL THE TIME. UR TIME IS UP!

When Brandi saw the picture of Aoki, her mouth fell open. She was crushed, hurt, and furious. It was going down. She was ready for war.

Gena knew it was a win-win situation for her. If B Scientific didn't cut off Aoki, he would no longer trust her for breaking his code. At the very least, she'd created some friction between Brandi and B Scientific. The only thing she felt she had to do was sit back and be patient, and soon, the man would coming running into her hands, knowing she was the right bitch for him. Besides, she was the mature one, right?

For days, Gena, pretending to be Aoki, battled with Brandi via text messages, heating up the pot more and more until it was about to boil over. She warned Brandi to stay away from Brooklyn, baiting her. Finally, she texted: I'M ON VAN SICLEN AVE EVERY DAY, COME SEE ME BITCH IF U WANNA GET IT POPPING!

THIRTY

Scientific brought his Range Rover to a sudden stop at the park on Stanley Avenue. He spotted Aoki sitting on the benches with a few girls. He had been looking for her. He leaned near the passenger window, his elbow pressed against the console. "Aoki! Let me holla at you for a minute."

He immediately caught her attention along with everyone else's. Everyone knew that when B Scientific called your name, then you better see what he wanted.

Aoki stood up and removed herself from the group. She coolly walked toward his truck, smiling at him. She climbed into his Range Rover, saying to him, "Hey, baby," and he quickly drove off, giving her the cold shoulder.

"Ah . . . everything okay?" she asked.

"No, it's not okay."

He stopped and parked a few blocks away. Then he turned and said, "What the fuck is wrong with you? You got the audacity to text my lady with some bullshit!"

Aoki had no idea what he was talking about. The perplexed look on her face didn't register to him yet.

"What ya ah talk 'bout?"

"I'm talking about the texts you sent to Brandi."

"Me ain't sent no texts to nobody. What foolishness ya ah talk?"

"You sure you ain't tell anyone about us?"

"Me sure." Aoki kept very hard eye contact with him, never mentioning she had told Rihanna and Tisa.

B Scientific looked in her eyes and saw something that made him believe her. Aoki had always been straight up with him. "It just a misunderstanding then, that's all," he said.

His mood changed swiftly, and next thing Aoki knew, he was all over her, kissing on her neck, complimenting her, and happy to see that she was wearing the rosary.

"I missed you," he said.

"Me miss ya too."

B Scientific was ready to take Aoki into the city and get a hotel room, but she couldn't, explaining that she had to meet with AZ later on.

He grimaced when she mentioned his name. "You can't cancel on him?"

"Me can't. Someting important."

"Like how important, business or pleasure?"

"Him ah still me boyfriend, B Scientific."

"Don't fuckin' remind me," he returned dryly.

"Ya don't need to be jealous. Ya can have me soon."

"I want to have you now, but if not, then tomorrow definitely, no excuses."

She smiled.

He kissed her again and drove her back to the park. Aoki got out of his Range Rover and sighed heavily. As he drove away, the girls on the bench were staring at her, ready to get into her business, but she wasn't going to tell them anything. Her affair with B Scientific wasn't for any gossip. She tucked his diamond rosary into her shirt and returned to her friends.

"What de fuck y'all lookin' at?" she said.

"You, girl," one of the girls said. "B Scientific pickin' you up like that, what was that all about?"

"None a y'all business, an' me don't want me business out dere," she said and left it at that.

She didn't want AZ to find out about the affair with B Scientific, knowing there could be repercussions. The only time she wore the rosary was when she was out the house and around B Scientific. Otherwise, she always took if off and placed it into her purse. That evening, she was fortunate to have it on.

❧

Aoki did tell AZ about Emilio one day.

"He's a nice guy. He's cool and he treats me nice. He helps with repairs around the house, and we can talk about anything," she had said to AZ about him.

AZ pretended to be happy for her, but he couldn't explain his discomfort and possessiveness. Was he was falling in love with her?

THIRTY-ONE

A Z had gotten the call from Oscar. He wanted to use the girls for a hit he needed done right away. He also wanted to meet them personally.

AZ was ambivalent about the job, knowing it would propel Aoki and her crew into the majors because, if Oscar needed someone killed, then it was probably a major player in the game. He was hoping Aoki and her crew were ready for this, because he didn't want to see anything happen to her.

He made the call to Aoki, feeling somewhat apprehensive.

"Hello," she answered.

"Aoki, I have some work for you," he said, getting to the point.

"Ya do?" she said, sounding excited.

"Yes, but not over the phone. I need to meet you in person today."

"Me there."

Several hours later, Aoki was riding with AZ in his Benz on their way to meet Oscar at a discreet location. It was dusk and cool, and there was a full moon. Riding in silence, they drove through the Holland Tunnel, came out into New Jersey and ended up in the parking lot of Liberty State Park, opposite Liberty Island and Ellis Island. The area was quiet and sparse with people and cars.

Oscar was already waiting, his black Bentley idling opposite where AZ had parked. Three silhouettes showed inside his car.

AZ and Aoki stepped out to meet with Oscar, who climbed out of his Bentley alone. He set his eyes on Aoki. From where he stood, she was beautiful under the glow of the moonlight. Her eyes were fixed on him intensely.

"You must be Aoki. I'm Oscar." He extended his hand to her, which she accepted. "You are a very beautiful woman, I might add."

"Thank you," she said.

"AZ tells me you can help me out with a favor."

She nodded.

"Good. Let's go for a walk and talk," Oscar suggested.

AZ stood close by. The trio went walking deeper into the park via pathway, moving farther away from their cars. Their only company was the open area, a playground, the illuminated NYC skyline across the Hudson, and a lit-up Jersey City from a distance.

Oscar moved with confidence and coolness. He occasionally made eye contact with Aoki, who was cautious and quiet, but ready to hear him out.

"Who ya want killed?" she asked.

Oscar looked at her and said, "My father."

Aoki didn't draw back from the news, nor was she shocked, but the look on AZ's eyes said it all. He remained quiet, though. He let the two of them talk.

Oscar added, "The old man doesn't want to retire. Therefore, I'm going to have to make him retire. We've been at odds with each other for years, and now my patience has reached its end. It can't look like anyone in my organization had anything to do with it. He's a powerful man, so the hit has to be subtle and fast. I have an open window for you, Aoki, and it will be the only open window you'll have. If you miss it, then there will be no other chances, and the bloodshed that follows will be on you."

They walked a few more feet and stopped on a long bridge, where there was a body of calm water on both sides. It was a tranquil and scenic place where couples could entangle themselves on the benches and enjoy a small taste of the sea, where a few sailboats drifted in the water.

Oscar gazed at the still Hudson waters and continued with, "He will be in town for a few days for my wedding. I know for a fact that on a certain day, he'll be at a certain massage parlor because it's his favorite. Let's just say that my father likes 'happy endings.' I will arrange for you and your girls, Aoki, to be there on the day of my father's arrival. But from there, everything will be on you. I will frame my stepmother for his murder. She had always been tired of his cheating ways, so it will give her the motive."

Oscar reached into his pocket, removed a small item, and placed it in Aoki's hand. It was a diamond teardrop earring.

"I want you to leave that earring at the scene, with the body. It belongs to my stepmother. Also, no guns. Only knives," he said, not knowing she preferred knives.

Aoki nodded, listening to the details carefully. AZ played the background; it was no longer his world. He was only a guest, listening in silence and praying the entire thing played out well.

"Each time my father and stepmother got into an argument, she would always reach for a knife, threatening to kill him. This time, she will have made good on her threats. It will take the heat away from everyone, and she will be blamed. Also, he has bodyguards, and they are very protective of him. So it won't be easy. Can you do it?"

Aoki nodded, sure of herself.

Oscar nodded and smiled. He reached into his suit jacket and pulled out a brown envelope with $5,000, an advance on the job. Aoki accepted the payment, and the deal was sealed.

They walked back to their cars. Aoki felt assured to implement the hit on Oscar's father. He'd already made the arrangements; she just had to move in with stealth and violence. It would be her most difficult kill, but she had to prove herself.

AZ and Aoki were seated in his C63 AMG. He looked at her with concern and asked, "You sure you ready for this?"

She nodded. "Yes."

He took a deep breath. The fire in Aoki's eyes said it all. She thirsted for this opportunity. AZ felt like he had created a monster. He didn't know she was born that way.

THIRTY-TWO

Aoki told her crew about their next hit. Juan Aponté was a well-connected cartel figure from South America. Rihanna's and Tisa's hearts were pumping with trepidation. The risks were great, and failure meant death. However the twenty-thousand-dollar payment was very rewarding.

"This is fuckin' wit' the cartel, Aoki," Tisa expressed with concern.

"And if we do it right, it won't link back to us."

Rihanna asked, "And how are we supposed to do it right?"

Aoki went into details. She explained how his son already had everything set up. They weren't alone in this. He was backing them fully. Juan was in town for only three days for Oscar's wedding, and it had to be done before the wedding ceremony.

"Talk about family feud," Rihanna said.

Aoki put a thousand dollars in their hands to give them a taste of the cash that was coming their way when the job was done.

KILLER DOLLS

The massage parlor in Chinatown was quaint and comfortable and located on a narrow street, one block from Canal Street. The area was flushed with tourism and Chinese businesses. The girls were already planted inside as masseuses when Juan showed up. Oscar had paid the owner of the parlor to specifically assign Aoki to his father.

Aoki stood in the small room clad in a short, colorful kimono, her long, black hair looking sensuous. She was calm and collected. Nothing strange stood out about her. She looked like one of the regular girls at the parlor. Everything was ready inside the room. Her weapon of choice was hidden inconspicuously not far from her reach. The only thing missing was the target.

Soon, there were a quick few knocks at the door.

"Come in," Aoki said.

Juan walked in. Aoki hooked her eyes on him and smiled. He was very handsome and tall. He was in his early sixties and moved with confidence like he owned the place. He was wearing a charcoal gray Armani suit, black wing tips, and had salt-and- pepper hair that matched his grayish goatee, and his diamond Rolex glimmered around his wrist.

Juan's three bodyguards came in and did a quick sweep of the room, which was clean. One then gave Aoki a quick pat down to make sure she didn't have any weapons on her person. Truth be told, the bodyguards were more lax at the massage parlor. The girls were hardly a threat. After feeling confident that their boss was safe, the bodyguards went to the front reception area of the parlor and stood conspicuously, making their presence known.

Juan had his privacy with Aoki. He looked at her, and his eyes spoke loudly, saying that he liked what he saw. He approached with an intense appetite to eat her up sexually. She pretended to be shy and pushed him away.

"Undress," she told him, trying not to say much, hiding her accent.

He started to peel away his fancy suit. When he was shirtless and down to his underwear, his bulge showing in his drawers, he winked at Aoki. "Not bad for a man my age."

Indeed, his appearance was impressive, but she wasn't there to admire his body.

Juan got up on the massage table and lay face down, and Aoki stood over him.

"Where are you from?" he asked.

She told him that she was part Japanese, and part Honduran. He ate it up because he was part Colombian and part Honduran. The atmosphere was right, and Juan immediately warmed up to her.

Aoki oiled her hands and gently started to massage his shoulders and neck. She gradually worked her massages from the shoulders to his back, and rubbed down his thighs.

She felt his body go limp; he was fully relaxed. Rihanna and Tisa cracked the door to the room and Aoki nodded. Both girls quietly slid into the closet, as backup, and waited.

Juan continued moaning. He was thoroughly pleased at how the tiny woman worked her small hands, kneading his tense muscles and melting all this aches away.

He finally turned over, and his erection was staring at her very boldly. "I definitely need a happy ending after that massage," he said.

"I see," she said.

Patiently, Rihanna and Tisa hid in the small closet inside the room. They kept quiet and watched everything. The entire plan had to be executed perfectly, since his armed bodyguards were strategically placed up front. If they heard any trouble, commotion, or yells of distress, they wouldn't hesitate to charge inside the room and use deadly force against the threat.

Aoki was ready to give him his happy ending. Her hands were oiled and warm. She removed the towel, and his penis was fat and pink, looking like a raw sausage. She wrapped her fingers around his erection firmly, and moved her fist up and down his cock in a slow, steady motion as his penis began to steadily grow. She mixed up her speed and pressure as his arousal became more intense.

Juan groaned and closed his eyes.

Aoki had one fist wrapped around his cock, while the other hand cupped and caressed his balls. She then handled his member with both hands working with precision. One hand scaled down his erection, followed by the other.

As he neared ejaculation, Aoki subtly tried to reach for her weapon, the sharp six-inch hunting knife taped underneath the massage table. She quickly tried to free it from its confinement with one hand, while the other jerked his dick. But she ran into a complication. Her hands were too slippery from the oil, and she couldn't grip the knife the way she needed to.

She stopped her action and Juan opened his eyes. "Why did you stop?" he asked.

"I need to wash my hands," she said, concealing her accent the best she could.

"Wash your hands?" He looked at her like she was crazy. The oil is what made the happy ending so happy.

"No, just continue. Make me come!"

Aoki didn't have a choice. She didn't want to look too suspicious. As she jerked his dick again, she looked her friends' way and pleaded with her eyes for their help.

As she engaged in the hand-job, Rihanna slowly removed herself from the hiding space and helped Aoki remove the blade that was strapped tightly underneath the massage table.

Rihanna gripped the knife, and Aoki nodded for her to execute the contract.

Juan's eyes were still closed as Aoki's hand-job, coupled with the pleasant music chiming in the background put him into a deep sexual trance.

The girls locked eyes and spoke to each other in silence. It was now or never.

Quickly, Aoki gagged Juan's mouth with a long piece of cloth, preventing him from screaming while Rihanna slammed the large knife into his chest. Juan squirmed violently and struggled with his captors, but it was a short-lived struggle as the blade pierced his heart.

For good measure, Rihanna stabbed him again, assuring his death. Juan's body lay lifeless on the table, his blood dripping to the floor like a leaky faucet. He was dead, but the girls still weren't out of the frying pan yet.

Aoki placed the diamond teardrop earring in Juan's hand, and Rihanna and Tisa quickly left the room, and exited the building through the back exit, taking the bloody knife and a bag with Aoki's clothes with them. Aoki left the room too, but only to get a cup of hot tea, to play out the plan entirely.

Now came the hard part—convincing the bodyguards that she wasn't part of their boss' murder. Aoki took a deep breath, ready to put on an award-winning performance.

She dropped the tea and screamed suddenly. Within seconds, all three of Juan's bodyguards came bursting into the room with their guns out, ready to react. Seeing their boss dead on the massage table sent them into a twisted rage.

"What the fuck happened?" one of the men shouted. "Who did this?"

They quickly tried to tend to Juan's body, while Aoki stood there in tears, looking horrified. They glared at her with an intensity that could collapse a city, so Aoki knew she had to quickly explain.

"A woman, she ran out . . . I went to get some tea, and she killed him. She just stabbed him and killed him," she said, once again, disguising her Jamaican accent.

The second guard shouted, "What woman? Where?"

Aoki pointed toward the back exit. She was trembling, looking very afraid and in shock.

One of the bodyguards ran out of the room, gun in hand, to search for this mystery woman.

Another bodyguard found the diamond earring clutched in Juan's hand.

"She just killed him," Aoki repeated, looking like she was about to have a panic attack.

One guard grabbed her arm with a crushing grip. He locked onto her like handcuffs. "You're coming with us!"

"What?" *This isn't how Oscar said it would go down.*

Two goons roughly escorted her out the backdoor toward a black Escalade like she was a prisoner, while the third bodyguard remained with the body and made phone calls. He stayed behind to watch the body and clean up the mess, and pay the people at the parlor some hush money.

While Aoki was being shoved into the backseat of the Escalade, she desperately searched for Rihanna and Tisa to help her, but they were nowhere around. She pleaded with the men, but they weren't listening to her cries of innocence.

Oscar had told her that, once they found his wife's earring, they wouldn't harm her. However, Aoki found herself being whisked away to some unknown location.

Rihanna and Tisa watched frantically as the two bodyguards manhandled Aoki and threw her into the backseat of the Escalade. They didn't know what to do.

The vehicle took off, and they had no way of following it. They tried to hail a cab, but by the time one finally stopped, the Escalade was long gone.

"What the fuck we gonna do?" Tisa cried out. "Where did they take her?"

"Like I fuckin' know, Tisa. Shit, shut the fuck up and let me think!"

Tisa paced back and forth, her heart beating a thousand times a minute. They were stuck and looking stupid, holding a bag with a bloody knife, and Aoki's clothes.

"We gotta get outta here, go back to Brooklyn," Rihanna said.

"And leave Aoki?"

"We don't even know where they're taking her."

Tisa was losing it. "I knew this was gonna be bad. I knew it!"

"We gotta go. We gotta call AZ," Rihanna said.

The girls hurried out of Chinatown via the subway and headed back to Brooklyn. They rode the train in silence, their minds spinning wildly about Aoki's whereabouts and safety.

Tisa leaked a few tears, thinking the worst. Aoki had nothing on her, not even her cell phone, so trying to call her was pointless.

THIRTY-THREE

The black Escalade came to a screeching stop in front of the Eventi Hotel on 6th Avenue. Both men urgently exited the vehicle and pulled a half-dressed Aoki from the backseat and roughly ushered her inside the swanky location. They swiftly moved through the lobby, which was bustling with employees and guests. The hotel was preparing itself for a large wedding in a few hours—Oscar's wedding.

The goons weren't too subtle when they shoved her inside the elevator and pushed for the top floor. The elevator quickly ascended. Aoki stood behind them as they guarded her, like two large pillars. She wasn't escaping anywhere.

She was sweating and nervous, her mind racing, knowing this could be the end. She clenched her fists and was desperate to fight the men, but it would be a losing battle. She wasn't a skilled assassin. She wasn't like Fox in the movie *Wanted*. Aoki wished she had the type of skills to beat these two men to a bloody pulp and make her escape.

The doors opened to the penthouse suite, and they dragged her off the elevator and toward the son's suite. Every square inch of the top floor offered a sweeping view of the city. They shoved Aoki to the floor, and she landed on her side. Both men glared at her heavily. She felt like she had been double-crossed.

"We will get to the bottom of this," one of them said.

Aoki could only wait and see what was in store for her.

Before long, Oscar walked into the room dressed handsomely in a white and black tuxedo and black bowtie. He was about to get married in two hours. He approached Aoki like the two had never met. He glared at her.

One of the men uttered, "Your father is dead!"

"What?" he uttered, looking shocked.

"She was there."

Oscar glared at Aoki. "What happened?"

"Some woman, I don't know . . . she killed him! She stabbed him!"

Her tears seemed real, and so did her story and innocence.

"We found this at the scene," the guard said, handing Oscar the diamond teardrop earring.

He glanced at it and immediately said, "It belongs to my stepmother. Bring her to me. I'll take care of her."

Both men nodded and hurried out of the room, leaving Oscar alone with Aoki. Once the doors shut and they were in private, Oscar's hard frown transformed into a smile. "Job well done."

Aoki lifted to her feet and exclaimed, "What ah dis?"

"I see you can hide your accent very well. Nicely done. My apologies, though, for their mistreatment of you. They only took the necessary measures as they were trained to do."

Aoki didn't know what to think. She believed that she was a dead woman and they had double-crossed her. But Oscar's words were a relief to her.

"I have to admit, I did underestimate you and your crew," he said.

"Ya shouldn't have."

"Obviously."

He walked over to the minibar and poured himself a drink. He downed his liquor. He gazed at Aoki with a deadpan look. He then handed her the rest of the payment she was owed.

"I put a little bonus in there for you," he said.

Aoki was pleased. "What now?" she asked.

"What now? I get married now and live my life, and you live yours. I have some extra clothes for you to change into, and I'll have one of my men drive you home."

Aoki couldn't wait to get back to Brooklyn. It was one hell of an episode for her. Oscar had one of his personal security goons escort Aoki through the back of the hotel, using the service elevators, and she got into an idling Lincoln parked right outside.

While being driven home, she realized she would never do a hit like that again—too many risks for herself and her crew, leaving them open and vulnerable.

*

Tisa and Rihanna found themselves back in Brooklyn still filled with worry. It had been four hours and still no sign of Aoki. Rihanna lit a cigarette and paced back and forth inside her bedroom, wishing AZ would call her back. She'd left several voice messages on his phone, but she hadn't heard from him.

"The only thing we can do is wait," she said.

Tisa sat at the foot of her bed and was going through the bag of clothing that contained all of Aoki's things. While rummaging, she came across a diamond rosary. It definitely belonged to Aoki. It was precious.

Rihanna's back was to Tisa as she smoked her Newport and gazed out the project window.

Tisa clutched the jewelry and wondered what if Aoki was dead, what if she wasn't coming back. The jewelry piece had to be a gift from one of her lovers.

As she was inspecting it, Gena burst into the room.

Tisa quickly hid the rosary underneath the mountain of pillows on Rihanna's bed. She didn't want anyone to see it.

"What's goin' on wit' y'all?" Gena asked, looking at Tisa suspiciously.

"Nothin', Ma. We okay," Tisa said.

"You sure?"

"Yes!" Rihanna replied with an attitude.

Gena pivoted and walked out of the room, but she decided to eavesdrop from the hallway.

The girls were sloppy. Rihanna didn't shut her door completely, leaving it ajar.

Rihanna stood near Tisa and said, "AZ's gonna call back; he has to."

"What if he don't?"

"He needs to know about Aoki."

They discussed their dilemma briefly, and then Tisa gave Rihanna the bag of clothes. "We need to get rid of them," she said.

"We need to wait."

"Why?"

"Because, we need to wait for Aoki," Rihanna repeated.

"But what if something happened to her? What if she's dead, Ri-Ri?"

"She's not dead. She'll be back around. I know it," she replied, trying to convince herself.

"What if she got caught and snitched on us?"

"Aoki ain't no snitch, Tisa," Rihanna returned quickly.

Tisa blew air out of her mouth, trying to think rationally. Rihanna refused to move without any direction from Aoki or AZ. Nor did she think Aoki's clothing needed to be dumped, saying it was just blood on a shirt. Tisa had to remind her sister about DNA and forensics—it was easy for blood to be traced and transferred. Aoki wouldn't care about some dumb clothes; she would want all evidence burned. They'd done it before, so now wasn't the time to veer from that routine.

Gena unexpectedly burst into the bedroom again. "What's goin' on in here? What are y'all up to?"

"I told you, Ma—nothing!" Rihanna shouted.

The two started to argue.

Tisa stood up and snatched the bag of clothes and promptly left the bedroom. There was too much going on. She wanted to retrieve the jewelry piece, but Rihanna's room was too hectic.

Rihanna stomped out of her bedroom, yelling at her mother, "Fuck it! I'm out!"

They both left the apartment.

Tisa figured she would go back to retrieve the rosary later. No one knew where she'd placed it, so she wasn't worried about anyone finding it.

❧

Unbeknownst to Tisa, Gena had peeked exactly at the right time and saw her hiding something under the pillows. She'd charged into her daughter's room and started an argument on purpose, knowing her daughter would sooner leave than fight with her.

Once the girls were gone, Gena went back into Rihanna's bedroom and looked under the pillows. She found the rosary. She didn't know what her daughters were into, what trouble they were in, or where Aoki was, but the diamond rosary was heaven-sent in her eyes.

And then she realized who it belonged to. "That fuckin' bitch!" she uttered in disbelief. She was hurt and upset knowing B Scientific had given the rosary to Aoki.

She held back her tears of hurt and decided to teach everyone a lesson and get paid while doing so.

She left the apartment and marched down to the nearest pawnshop with the rosary. When the owner told her that she needed ID to pawn anything, Gena started to wild out and got ghetto inside the pawnshop. She came up with an excuse that she'd lost her wallet and everything else inside.

The pawnshop owner inspected the diamond rosary thoroughly. He was impressed. It was worth quite a hefty penny. He definitely wanted it, but he needed some identification from Gena. "It's the rules," he told her.

"Then you can bend your fuckin' rules," Gena snapped. "You own this place, nigga."

The man sighed, staring at the jewelry piece. He then said, "I'm gonna need your name and address then."

"Not a problem. My name is Aoki Ross," she said, and she proceeded to give him Aoki's address.

"How much do you want for it?"

"Thirty thousand," Gena said with a straight face.

He laughed at her. "C'mon, let's be serious now," he said. "I'll give you thirty five hundred for it."

"That's not even close to what it's worth."

He looked her directly in her eyes, "Come back with proof of how much you paid for it and maybe we could negotiate a higher price."

Gena quickly accepted the offer. "Okay, I'll take it."

The owner pulled out a wad of cash and counted out $3,500 in front of Gena, and she took the cash and left the store, knowing Aoki was about to be in some deep, deep shit with B Scientific for losing that chain.

"Fuck that bitch!"

THIRTY-FOUR

The Lincoln car dropped Aoki off in front of her home twenty thousand dollars richer. Oscar had added an extra five large to her bundle. She hurried inside, took a needed shower, and changed clothes. She had no cell phone to contact her friends, and her Yukon was parked in the parking lot at the Pink Houses. She called a cab to take her there, knowing her friends were worried about her.

Aoki climbed out of the cab on Loring Avenue. The moment she climbed out of the cab and headed toward the projects, she ran into Rihanna and Tisa.

Simultaneously, they screamed out, "Aoki!" They ran and hugged her.

"What happened?" Rihanna asked.

"It's a crazy story."

"Tell us, how'd you get away?" Tisa said.

"I didn't."

They both were confused by her statement. Aoki was ready to explain to them everything that happened, but she didn't want to talk out in the open. They decided to go back to her place to talk.

An hour later, Aoki explained to them everything that had happened. She also told them in all honesty that Oscar had given them an extra five grand. She decided to give the girls six grand apiece, and keep eight for herself, which was still netting Rihanna and Tisa more money than the original cut.

Tisa had a problem with the payment arrangement, saying, "I thought we were equal in this."

Aoki and Rihanna were taken aback by her remark.

Rihanna shot back, "Equal? This comin' from someone who's yet to kill someone."

"She's right. Ya want fair, Tisa, then ya do ya part in de bloodshed." Aoki stared at her friend stoically. Aoki didn't take the lion's share because she continually got her hands bloody. Nor because she wanted to floss. She simply wanted to renovate her home with the money.

Tisa knew not to argue with her. She remained quiet.

"Me thought so."

Tisa sat on the couch and moped.

Aoki had no time for foolishness. She needed to make moves. She turned to Rihanna and said, "Me need me clothes. Where dem?"

"Your clothes?" Rihanna said, looking befuddled.

"Yes, Ri-Ri, me clothes."

"Tisa got rid of them."

Aoki shouted at Tisa. "What? What made ya get rid of dem?"

"I thought we had to, Aoki. They had blood on it. We couldn't take the chance."

"Me God! Ya know what ya done to me, Tisa?" Aoki exclaimed, panicking.

"Aoki, they were just clothes."

"Nuh, they weren't just clothes. Me had someting very important in me pockets, Tisa. Ya didn't check?" Aoki sighed with a deep frustration.

"No, I didn't check anything," Tisa lied.

"Ya so foolish!"

"Maybe it got left back at the massage parlor," Tisa said.

"Where ya dump me clothes?"

"At the dumpster by our building," Tisa said.

"Let's go!"

"Go where?"

"To de dumpster."

They hurried back to the Pink Houses. Tisa showed Aoki the dumpster where she'd tossed the bag. The dumpster was filled with trash, and it reeked. But Aoki didn't care. She dove right into it and started searching for the bag. She tore into bag after bag, each smelling worse than the other.

Ten minutes later, she came across the bag her clothing and knife was in. She frantically tore it open and went digging through her pockets. No rosary! How couldn't it be there? Could it have dropped? Could someone have taken it? How could a diamond rosary just disappear? She tossed the bag out of the dumpster and decided to take everything with her, to burn it all.

Aoki looked at her friends. "Ya two sure y'all didn't see nuthin'? Huh? Don't fuckin' lie to me." She was ready to attack them. She needed to find that piece.

"Aoki, I swear to you, I didn't find anything in that bag," Rihanna said timidly.

"Me too."

Aoki felt like her chest was about to cave in, like she couldn't breathe. How could she be so stupid? She was smelly, exhausted and frustrated. She pivoted and walked away from her friends, almost looking defeated. She just needed to get away. She needed someone to talk to.

"Aoki, where you going?" Rihanna called out. "Whatever it is you're lookin' for, we'll find it."

"Yeah, Aoki, it's gonna be okay."

Aoki climbed into her truck and drove away. As she drove, her tears started to trickle. She quickly wiped them away from her face. She had to remain strong. She always had been strong. She couldn't falter now and look weak in front of everybody. But today had been a trying day for her, and now she had lost B Scientific's rosary, a sentimental piece of jewelry.

What was she going to do?

Aoki found her way to the brownstone she shared with AZ in downtown Brooklyn. She had a key and let herself inside. The rooms were dark, but she heard movement upstairs and the shower running.

She slowly peeled away her clothing and left them wherever, leaving a trail from the entrance. As she approached the bathroom, she took off her panties and bra and walked into the bathroom. She could see AZ's silhouette behind the glass door. She startled him by sliding the door back and joining him in the shower.

"Aoki, what the fuck!" he uttered. "What's goin' on?"

Aoki threw herself at him, wrapping her arms around him and pressing her lips against his.

AZ was floored, but he didn't resist. Incredulously, he felt excited. He felt something strong sexually.

Aoki didn't care if he was gay; she just wanted to be with him for that night.

He kissed her back, and their mouths hungrily devoured each other. Aoki was entwined with him as the water cascaded down on their naked flesh. She could feel his erection growing against her, and he was super-hard.

"I want you," she said to him.

They continued kissing fervently.

She touched his chest then reached down and grabbed his manhood with her fingers. He was thick and big. She started to work him smoothly, stroking him back and forth, drawing a pleasing moan from his lips.

She found herself on her knees and slowly taking his dick into her mouth. She latched onto the tip and swirled her tongue around it.

"Oh shit! Ooooh!"

Her mouth wrapped around his dick and tightened. She had him growing harder and harder, her head bobbing back and forth as the water cascaded down on them. It went on like that for several minutes.

They took their sex into the bedroom, where Aoki instantly straddled him. He was hard for her as she slowly sank her body down onto his, taking him deep inside her. She started to move her hips up and down. Her pussy pulsated like it was trying to pull his dick farther into her.

They fucked on his bed, rolling around, enjoying position after position.

While they were sexing, AZ's cell phone rang, but they both ignored it. As they bumped and grinded, they accidentally knocked his cell phone onto the bed. Aoki's ass cheek rubbed against it, inadvertently answering the incoming call.

"Hello," Connor answered. "AZ? Hello?"

"Ooh, fuck me, AZ, fuck me!" Aoki cried out.

"Oh God! I love you."

AZ and Aoki didn't know Connor was listening and could hear the moaning and groaning.

Connor listened intently, crushed and betrayed.

Aoki's pussy continued to suck AZ's dick in like a vacuum as he took her missionary-style. He was cooing, squirming between her legs. He groaned, gripping the bed sheets tightly and soon exploded inside of her, shuddering. "Oh my God!" he uttered. "Shit! Shit!"

Aoki came too and quivered beneath him with delight.

Aoki lay nestled in his arms.

"I'm in love with you," AZ said, out of the blue. Aoki was the only woman that could truly arouse him.

"I love you too."

"No, I'm in love with you, Aoki. I always have been. So, where do we go from here?"

"I don't know," she said faintly.

She loved him, but she wasn't in love with him. He was gay. He had Connor. They were great friends, but it was only a moment between them. She just wanted an escape, and he was it. They talked some more and she told him all about the Juan hit, the bodyguards, and Oscar. AZ shook his head in disbelief. How could someone so tiny withstand so much?

Early the next morning, before dawn, Aoki freed herself from AZ's gentle, sleeping grasp, got dressed, and left suddenly, like a thief in the night, leaving him asleep in the room.

AZ woke up the next morning to find Aoki gone. He looked all throughout the house for her, but there was no sign of her. He sighed, wishing she'd stayed. He went back into the bedroom and sat on the king size. He thought about Aoki and wondered why the sudden attack on him in the shower. Was it a one-time thing?

He took a deep breath and noticed his cell phone on the floor. He picked it up and saw the calls from Connor, but was shocked to see that one was received late last night. He shrugged off the mystery. It was about that time. He couldn't do it any longer. He couldn't do Connor anymore. Their relationship had grown tiresome. He dialed his number and waited for him to answer.

"What do you want, AZ?" Connor answered.

"Hey, we need to talk

"Seriously?"

"Yes. But I want to see you in person. I'll be over there in about two hours."

"Whatever," Connor said indifferently.

AZ hung up and prepared himself for the trip to Long Island. He was ready to move on.

Three hours later, he was parking in front of Connor's home. He stepped out of his Benz and approached the back door with determination to tell him once and for all that they were through. No more casual sex and no more up-and-down with their feelings for each other. Their turbulent relationship had to end.

AZ knocked on the backdoor roughly and waited.

"Who?" Connor said.

"You know who. Open the door."

Connor swung the door open and glared at AZ. He was clad in a long robe and looked a bit disheveled.

AZ thought he had been drinking. He shook his head and asked, "You okay?"

"No, I'm not okay."

"Well, look, I came here to talk," AZ said civilly.

"You not coming inside?"

"No!"

"I can't get a kiss from you, saying hello?" Connor said.

Connor leaned toward AZ, ready to press his lips against his, but AZ backed away.

"I didn't come here for that."

"Then what did you come here for?"

"Like I said, just to talk."

"So I can't get a kiss from you?"

"No, Connor."

"Why not?" Connor asked, looking upset.

"Because you and me, we're done. I can't see you anymore, Connor. We should go our separate ways. I mean, you're going to Yale in the fall—"

"What the fuck that supposed to mean, AZ? Don't you love me?"

"We just come from two different worlds."

"You dumping me because of that bitch, huh? Is that it, AZ? You fuckin' that whore? What's her name, Aoki?"

"Watch your mouth, Connor."

"No, fuck you and that bitch! After all we been through and you do this to me."

"I'm not fuckin' her."

"Fuck you, AZ! Fuck you!" he screamed. "I loved you! I still love you!"

Connor was livid and brokenhearted. The tears started to trickle from his eyes, and he felt disgusted and used.

"I just wanted to tell you face to face; felt it was respectful."

"Respectful?" Connor chuckled. "Seriously, you drove all this way to tell me respectfully? You sure you didn't come for something else, huh? Some dick, nigga, or a blowjob?"

"I owed you that, at least," he said coolly.

"Fuck you! I was tired of your shit anyway, nigga! You ain't shit, AZ. Go run to that fuckin' whore! Go run and be with that bitch and when you catch AIDS, I hope you rot in hell, motherfucker!"

AZ turned and walked away.

Connor screamed out, "You know what, nigga? Maybe I should go to Brooklyn and tell everyone that you're a gay and cowardly liar! Maybe they need to know the real AZ! Maybe everyone needs to know how you like it up the ass, how you like taking it from the back more than pitching."

AZ, his face in a strong scowl, spun back around and charged toward Connor. He grabbed him by his robe and slammed him against the house. He was in his face like his own breath and exclaimed through gritted teeth, "Nigga, you think you fuckin' know me, you don't! You don't know who you're fuckin' messin' with, Connor. So I advise you to shut your mouth and move on with your life. If you don't, I swear to you, I can really hurt you, or even worse. And there won't be Yale in the fall. You don't know my world, but if you want to, I promise you'll regret it."

AZ released his strong grip from around Connor and stepped back, leaving him shaken and wide-eyed. He had never seen this part of AZ.

The only thing Connor could say was, "You changed."

"Get the fuck out my face and don't call me anymore!" AZ sternly replied.

Connor burst into tears and hurried inside.

AZ marched back to his ride. He shut his door and lit a cigarette. He was done with Connor. If word got out about him being gay, then he would kill him. Period.

Connor was right. He had changed.

THIRTY-FIVE

Tisa knew she fucked up. The rosary was missing. But how? She started to worry. Who could have taken it? She thought it could have been Rihanna, but they'd been together since she hid the jewelry under her pillows. It had to be Gena. She was the only one. Tisa couldn't beef about it, because then she would have to admit that she'd stolen it. She was upset and disappointed, because pawning that chain could have been a major payday for her.

For almost a week, Tisa walked around with a major bitch attitude. She tried not to run into Aoki, feeling somewhat guilty for stealing her chain.

The phone call came early that morning. B Scientific was calling. Aoki didn't know what to do or what to tell him about his missing rosary.

"I wanna see you," he said.

Aoki took a deep breath. "Today?"

"Tonight. I got a special place for us. I miss you, Aoki. I miss everything about you. I can't wait to see you."

She agreed to meet him.

Several hours later, he met her in the city. She climbed into his Range Rover, and his lips and hands were all over her right away.

B Scientific slid his hand under her skirt, ready to fondle her goodies and grab himself a handful of pussy. "You make me so damn hard, Aoki. You are an addictive person."

Aoki wanted him too, but she was worried. The rosary she lost was on her mind at all times. She knew she couldn't keep giving him excuses why she didn't have it on her and why she couldn't see him. He would figure it out sooner or later. She had two options, to either tell him the bad news or replace the rosary with a new one. Her one big dilemma— she couldn't afford the $80,000 price tag she was sure it cost.

He picked up on her distance. "What's wrong, baby? You okay?"

"I'm fine."

"Then what it is? You don't wanna fuck?"

She smiled. "Of course."

"So why you actin' funny?"

"It just been ah long week."

"I know. It's been a long week for the both of us."

He started to kiss her neck, cupping her tits and taking in her sweet scent. But then he leaned back into the seat, looking at Aoki oddly. "Yo, where's my rosary? Why isn't it around your neck?"

Aoki played it off and acted surprised that she wasn't wearing it. "Me must have left it at de house," she said.

"Oh, you left it home?"

"Yes. Me was in a rush to come see ya."

B Scientific looked at her and wanted to believe her story. "So, it's at your house right now?"

She nodded.

B Scientific started to think it was a mistake entrusting her with something that held so much sentimental value.

Aoki, wanting to take his mind off the piece, threw a naughty smile his way. Then she unzipped his pants, twisting her body at the waist and squaring her shoulders toward him, leaned into his lap, took his erection into her mouth, and sucked him off.

"Oh shit, ma. It's like that!"

⁂

Brandi constantly blew up B Scientific's cell phone, but he wasn't answering. She couldn't stand the thought of her man being with that bitch named Aoki. Once again, he had stayed out all night. She couldn't sleep or find peace at all while her man wasn't home.

She got on her phone and called a few friends, expressing her beef and concerns to them, feeling that B Scientific had found love somewhere else. They tried to console her, but Brandi wasn't consolable. She wanted to rant and rave. She wanted to beat a bitch ass. She wanted to kill a bitch.

B Scientific walked into his home at six in the morning. Brandi was up and waiting for him. He went into the bathroom to undress and wash up.

The minute he started taking off his clothes, Brandi aggressively charged into the bathroom screaming, "Where the fuck was you all night? Was you wit' that fuckin' bitch? And where is your fuckin' rosary? I haven't seen it around your neck. Did you give it to that fuckin' bitch?"

Before B Scientific couldn't get a word or two out, Brandi slapped and punched him a few times, her frustration finally pouring out. "I fuckin' hate you!" she screamed. "I hate you and that fuckin' bitch!"

B Scientific's backhand came quickly and fiercely and sent Brandi flying, stumbling backwards out of the bathroom. She found herself on the floor with a bloody lip.

"You dumb, stupid bitch!" he shouted.

The assault didn't deter Brandi's mouth. She glared up at B Scientific and screamed, "I hope you and that fuckin' bitch die! Kill yourself, nigga!"

B Scientific struck her again, punching her in the face and almost knocking her out. She tried to fight him, but he beat her severely.

"Stay in your place, bitch!" he shouted, before leaving again.

B Scientific stormed out of his home and quickly dialed Aoki's number. He was through with Brandi, and he wanted Aoki to get rid of AZ.

When she picked up, he told her he wanted to see her again, but she turned him down because something important had come up. He decided to settle and called Gena, who jumped at the opportunity to be with him.

Gena rose up from the motel bed and a sweaty B Scientific. The dick had been good to her again. She'd come like a geyser, and he'd made her body shake like a 5.0 earthquake. She'd also thoroughly pleased him from head to toe. Now it was their intermission before things started to heat up again.

She sat up and lit a cigarette. B Scientific was awake, but he was resting. He stared blankly at the ceiling, leaving no personal interaction for Gena. She took a few pulls from the Newport and blew out smoke. She glanced at him and wanted to converse. She wanted a relationship with him, but he continued to make things very clear to her—she was a jump-off, a bird bitch that was only good for sex.

She started to feel some kind of way. She wanted his attention on something that mattered to her, but he lay there looking uninterested in anything she had to say or what was going on in her life. She pretended to be worried about something, but he didn't address her sadness. She took a few more pulls from her cigarette.

"I'm worried about my daughters and her friend," she said. "Things are so fucked up, B Scientific."

He stayed quiet. It was like after the sex, he wasn't even there.

She turned to face him, and then she boldly asked, "I hate to ask you for this, but can I borrow five thousand dollars?"

He turned and frowned at her. The intensity written across his face made the cigarette shake in Gena's hand. "You asking me for money when you know we don't even get down like that?" he growled.

Quickly, she responded, "It's not for me. I'm just trying to help out one of my daughter's friends. Aoki, you know her?"

B Scientific perked up. "Who?"

"Aoki, she needs it."

"Why you askin' to borrow money in her name?"

"She's a friend to my daughters, and she's been through a lot. I care greatly for my daughters and their peoples. Aoki always had a hard life, growing up poor and having two crackhead parents that abandoned her two years ago. Now she's losing her home and might be put out on the streets. I hear she owes the bank some money, unpaid taxes or somethin'. I think, eighty-five hundred dollars. She has some of it but she needs to come up with the remaining five thousand dollars soon."

"And you're the angel willing to help her so quickly," he replied coolly.

"She's like one of my daughters, B Scientific. I love her just the same. But Aoki's a very resourceful girl. I think she came up with thirty-five hundred already. I think she pawned some chain. But she's still short."

B Scientific went from cool to furious in 0.1 seconds. He jumped out of bed and screamed at Gena. "Get out! Get the fuck out!"

"But, baby—"

"Get the fuck out!"

He threw a deadly look at her that made her mute whatever she was about to say.

"That fuckin' bitch!" He thrust his fist into the wall and made a hole the size of a basketball.

Gena hurriedly got dressed and ran out the room like it was on fire.

B Scientific snatched up his cell phone and dialed Aoki's number, but her phone was turned off.

THIRTY-SIX

AZ couldn't stop thinking about that night with Aoki. It meant a lot to him. He wanted some more of it. He didn't want Aoki to be with anyone else. Connor was officially out of his life, and he didn't want to be gay anymore. He wanted Aoki by his side and no one else.

He continually dialed her cell phone, but it was going straight to voice mail. He decided to stop by her place and surprise her. He wanted to take her out to dinner and treat her to a very special evening.

He parked and got out of his Benz. It was another glorious and sunny summer day. The block was green with leaves and flowers, and it felt great to be alive. He walked toward the front door with a huge, golden smile and knocked a few times.

AZ waited. He wanted to surprise her with gifts, by taking her on another shopping spree, knowing she would love it. He knocked again, wondering what was taking her so long to answer.

And then it opened, and AZ caught the surprise of his lifetime.

Emilio answered her door in his boxers.

AZ frowned, and he sharply asked, "Where's Aoki? And why are you here?"

Emilio smiled. "She's in the kitchen."

AZ looked at him like he was crazy. He barged right past Emilio and marched toward the kitchen.

Aoki was in the kitchen in her panties and bra, munching on breakfast Emilio had cooked.

"Yo, what the fuck—you got this nigga living here now?" AZ looked like his puppy had died.

Emilio walked into the kitchen.

"Emilio, can ya wait outside while me have ah talk wit' AZ," Aoki said kindly.

"Not a problem," he replied, quickly stepping out of the kitchen.

"So, you with him now? You love him?" AZ asked.

"AZ, we ah just friends, and I'm nah in love wit' ya."

"So what do you call the other night, when we had sex?"

"It was ah mistake."

"A mistake? Seriously?"

"Ya gay."

"I ain't wit' him anymore. I want you."

"But ya like ah brother to me."

"A brother?" AZ chuckled in disbelief. "You have my heart, Aoki. You always did. I love you, and I care for you."

"And me grateful, always will be, but we can never work," she said nonchalantly.

He sighed heavily. "You think we won't work, is that what you're telling me? After everything I did for you, the secrets I kept for years so you won't go to jail, from your parents, the ones you still have dead in them containers in the backyard—which is insane! I gave you food and clothes, I always protected you, helped you out. I did those things because I always loved you, Aoki. And you betrayed me."

"Me betrayed ya? How dat, AZ?" Aoki retorted. She was furious that he would even go there with her parents.

Most times Aoki forgot her parents were even dead. But now that AZ was hitting below the belt, she felt it was time to strike back.

"Me could never take ya seriously, ya hear? Cuz ya a batty bwoy," she came back. "And don't forget, AZ, we both have secrets. Me go down, ya go down."

AZ grimaced. He had nothing else to say to her. He turned away from her and walked out crushed, angry, and confused.

Emilio came back into the kitchen with a concerned look in his face. He stared at Aoki and asked, "Is everything okay?"

"Me fine," she responded, looking pensive at the kitchen table.

Emilio had his concerns too. AZ was his connect. He would need a re-up when the fall semester came. Would AZ forgive and forget and continue their business relationship, or would he take that he was fucking Aoki personally and not deal with him anymore?

Two days later, Emilio spent his weekend with Aoki, helping her do repairs around the house. That Saturday, the HVAC company came by to replace the system. It was costly, but it was worth it. Aoki finally had enough money to put in a heating and air conditioning system. She and Emilio regularly went back and forth to Home Depot for supplies. Emilio was building a deck in her backyard.

She started to spend more and more of her time with him. He was the one. He was almost perfect. He had nothing to do with her world of chaos and murders. He was her escape. She didn't have to fear him or question his sexuality, since he was 100% straight, a handsome heterosexual male. He didn't have the baggage that B Scientific had, and it wasn't about sex with him.

She continued to ignore calls from B Scientific, AZ, and Connor, who was leaving voice messages on her phone, saying that he hated her, and that he was going to stomp her head into the ground, and that she better watch her back. Sometimes he would call from different numbers, or a private number, and she would hang up on him.

But he was pushing her buttons. There was only so much she was going to take from him and his threats.

She decided to keep a low profile for a while and chill at home, making it better. She just wanted a normal weekend with Emilio. He was the one she saw a future with. He was going to be somebody in life.

THIRTY-SEVEN

Gena continued to taunt Brandi with several text messages to her phone.

U STUPID BITCH, UR MAN OVER HERE NOW SUCKIN' ON MY PUSSY & I'M LOVIN' IT. THINK ABOUT ME, BITCH! THINK ABOUT ME & UR MAN FUCKIN' OUR BRAINS OUT. HIS DICK IS SO GOOD. I MIGHT JUST GET PREGNANT BY HIM. I KNOW U AIN'T GOT ANY KIDS, BUT SOON I'LL HAVE HIS. WHAT YOU THINK ABOUT THAT BITCH? I GOT UR MAN, BITCH, AND I'M LOVIN' IT. FUCK U!

She was on overdrive with her scheme to ruin Aoki's and Brandi's lives. With B Scientific and Brandi furious at Aoki, she felt like a mastermind and wanted to pat herself on the back for a job well done.

❧

Brandi read the text messages with tears in her eyes and a strong desire to do something about Aoki. She couldn't take the taunting anymore. She couldn't take her becoming pregnant by the man she loved. Even though he hurt her bad, physically and mentally, it was hard to let him go.

"Fuck this bitch!" she exclaimed.

Brandi got on her phone and made some phone calls. She reached out to Michelle and Joquia—her closet friend and her first cousin, who both had a reputation for violence.

Michelle was in her late twenties and once had ties to the Bloods, but now she was a single mother of two children, trying to live a normal life. She still wasn't shy about beefing and brawling if she needed to.

Joquia was Brandi's first cousin on her mother's side. She was fresh home from prison for committing check fraud and was close friends with Brandi. If Brandi had problems, then she had problems.

Both women didn't hesitate to meet with Brandi and drive to Brooklyn to finally meet and confront Aoki. They wanted to fuck that bitch up so bad.

They drove around Brooklyn in Brandi's jeep for hours, searching and asking around for Aoki. They parked on the block near Van Siclen, asking around, but there was still no sign of her. Most people said that they hadn't seen her around in a couple of days.

Brandi didn't want to give up. She wanted to spend all night hunting the bitch down, even if she had to set up camp on the street. But she also knew that B Scientific would probably beat her down in front of her peoples if he caught her in the neighborhood searching for Aoki.

Hours later, Aoki still wasn't around. It was time to give up and go home.

Brandi felt defeated. She was upset. She was so tired and stressed, she was losing weight and not looking like herself.

Michelle tried to comfort her, and Joquia was ready to come back the next day and start the search all over again.

Brandi jumped on the Brooklyn Bridge and headed back home. She smoked a cigarette and couldn't take her mind off of her problems. She drove in an angry trance. She was itching to find Aoki. She wanted to teach that bitch a lesson so badly that her pussy was wet.

Joquia said, "We gonna find that bitch, Brandi. Tomorrow, watch—I don't care if we gotta kick in every door in East New York and wild the fuck out."

"We wit' you," Michelle said.

Brandi smiled somewhat. It felt great to have true friends. She was determined to end this battle of texts and her boyfriend's infidelity. She sighed and continued driving.

Just thinking about those texts sent to her phone, including one saying, SUCK ON MY PUSSY BITCH, and another of B Scientific sleeping nude in a cheesy motel room made her so angry, she forgot to brake and accidentally slammed into the car in front of her.

"Aw fuck!"

Brandi shook her head in disbelief. "Everyone okay?" she asked. *Why me?* She was so stressed out, she wasn't watching where she was going.

No one in the jeep suffered any true injuries. It was a fender-bender, both vehicles suffering slight damage.

The Hispanic driver and his wife emerged from their car ready to confront Brandi for her negligence.

Just then Michelle curved over, wincing from sharp pains in her side and gripping the headrest. "I need to go to the hospital. I think I might be pregnant."

Both Brandi and Joquia blurted out simultaneously, "You're what?"

⁂

Michelle found out at the hospital that she had a miscarriage and that they were going to admit her overnight for observation. She cried a little bit.

Brandi had quickly said, "I want you to use my name, Michelle."

Confused, Michelle replied, "Why?"

"Trust me, I got the perfect plan to finally get this bitch and make her pay for fuckin' wit' me," Brandi replied.

Michelle agreed to go along with the idea. She gave them Brandi's name as her name, and they admitted her into the hospital. Brandi shut off her phone and stayed with her friend for the entire ordeal. She didn't plan on going home anytime soon.

The next afternoon, Brandi and Michelle left the hospital with her discharge papers. Brandi asked Michelle to have her back, and to pretend as if Brandi was the one who'd had the miscarriage.

Michelle was giving Brandi a hard time, so she decided to bribe her best friend with two grand and the promise of another two grand at the end of the week. Michelle went with it. She gave Brandi the discharge papers, along with the hospital bracelet with Brandi's full name on it.

⁂

Before he made his way home to Brandi, B Scientific decided to make a quick stop at the pawnshop Gena had told him about. He planned on apologizing and making it up to her. Things with Aoki weren't turning out the way he'd expected.

He parked on the street and climbed out of his Range Rover. He marched into the pawnshop hoping everything Gena said was untrue. He stared at the young female working the counter and looked around the place. They had everything from TVs and laptops, to jewelry and guns.

"Hello," she said. "Can I help you with something?"

"Yeah, you can, I'm looking for a chain, a diamond rosary that was pawned here a few days ago."

"Do you have a pawn ticket?"

"Nah, I don't."

"Well, I'm sorry, sir, but I cannot give out that kind of information unless you are the holder."

"You see, this thing that was pawned, it didn't belong to the person that pawned it in the first place. It belonged to me."

"Still, without a ticket and your identification, there isn't much I can do, sir. It's the rules here."

He frowned. *Fuck y'all rules!*

She repeatedly glanced over her shoulder, looking at the owner.

B Scientific suddenly got it. He leaned closer to the young woman and whispered, "Look, I got five hundred dollars just for some information." He pulled out a wad of hundreds, showing her that he was good for the money.

The girl smiled. "I take lunch at one o clock. What is the name of the person who could have pawned this jewelry?"

"Aoki."

"Do you know her last name?"

He thought about it. "I don't."

"Okay, I still might be able to find it. One o'clock then. I'll meet you."

An hour later, the young girl met B Scientific at the pizza place around the corner. She sat, he stood. She said, "There was a diamond rosary pawned at the shop a couple of days ago by an Aoki Ross. She received thirty-five hundred for it."

B Scientific wanted to snap Aoki in half.

The girl continued to tell him Aoki's address.

"Look, can I just give you the cash on it and take it?"

"I'm sorry, I can't do that. It's against our policy. I'll get in trouble. I'll lose my job."

B Scientific was boiling hot. It was like reliving how he felt when he'd heard his brother was murdered.

The girl added, "My boss, he really like that piece though. He's hoping she doesn't come back to retrieve it. It's locked away in the vault."

B Scientific pulled out his cash and peeled off five hundred-dollar bills and gave it to the girl, and she left. He lingered in the place, determined to hunt Aoki down, beat the shit out of her, and then drag her to the pawnshop to retrieve his jewelry. But he wasn't sure whether he should kill her or not.

THIRTY-EIGHT

Aoki's home and the deck Emilio was building in the backyard were coming along just fine. Her place was feeling livable again. The sun was beaming as the two lovers took time out in the kitchen to down a cold glass of homemade lemonade and talk. Emilio was shirtless and sweaty. He had been working hard. He had the golden touch when it came to repairs and building.

It was late in the afternoon. Emilio wanted to touch up the joists that strengthened the deck, which ran parallel to the house. The deck was looking magnificent. He was out of deck stain and needed Aoki to run to Home Depot again.

She was willing. She gathered her things, kissed Emilio, and before she left out the door, Emilio called out her name. She turned, thinking maybe he needed something else.

"I love you."

She stood still and smiled. It was so refreshing hearing it, and even more refreshing saying it. "I love you too."

She left with the biggest Kool-Aid smile across her face.

Two hours later, she returned home, only to find Emilio wasn't around. She called out his name and went room to room looking for him, but he was gone. It felt like he'd vanished suddenly. His tools weren't in the backyard, and he didn't complete anything else.

"Emilio!" she called out.

No answer.

Aoki started to worry. *Where did he go? What could have happened to him?* She had a gut feeling that something wasn't right. She lingered in the kitchen and saw a note left for her on the kitchen table. How did she not see it before? She picked it up. It was from Emilio. She started to read it, and the more she read, the deeper her heart sank into the bowels of her stomach. Her tears trickled down her face and she couldn't believe it:

```
    Aoki, I can't believe the woman
I fell in love with has two dead
bodies in her backyard. Curiosity
had gotten the better of me and I'm
appalled. That is some sick shit.
Why? I don't even think I want to
know why. I left and I will not be
coming back to see you anymore.
Don't call me or come by, ever, or
else.
```

Or else?

Aoki called his cell phone. She was worried about many things. He could go to the cops. He wouldn't come back to her. He now knew her dark secret. She was upset with herself too for being so careless.

Her call went straight to voice mail. She decided to leave him a message.

"Listen, ya had nuh reason to violate me business, dat didn't concern ya, but I'm warning ya—shut ya mouth or me will go to the NYU and inform them of ya illegal business on de campus, ya understand? Me mek sure ya lose ya scholarship—Don't fuck wid me."

She ended the call, but immediately she started to feel guilty. He had been nothing but good to her. Things were going so good between them.

She wanted to call him back and apologize, but her pride wouldn't allow it. It was his fault. Why did he have to look and be curious? He should have minded his business.

Ten minutes after she left that message, Emilio called back.

Aoki refused to answer.

He called again, and she didn't answer. She sent all his calls to her voice mail.

Days ago, she'd had three men vying for her attention. Now she had none.

THIRTY-NINE

B Scientific walked through his front door and into a dark home. He felt his day couldn't get any worse. The place was silent and still. He came to apologize with his gifts, but he felt she had finally left him, sick of his shit. Brandi had been there for him when he had nothing, when he was just getting his reputation and respect. B Scientific felt in the wrong for everything. He would always make it up to her, no matter how bad things got with them.

He called out, "Brandi!" but got no answer.

He walked into the bedroom to find her sulking on their bed, looking a hot mess, her eyes flooded with tears. She was crying in the dark. He felt she was angling for pity.

"What is wrong with you?"

Brandi slowly picked herself up from the bed, her eyes red from crying, her hair disheveled, looking like she was ready to commit suicide.

"You wanna know what is wrong wit' me, then ask your bitch."

B Scientific wasn't in the mood for her bullshit. "You ain't gotta worry about her anymore."

"How can you stand there and defend her? How can you fuckin' stand there and love that bitch when she took away something so precious from us?" she barked.

"What are you talking about, Brandi?"

"I was pregnant, and she killed our baby!" Brandi exclaimed.

"What?"

"I left you numerous voice messages after it happened, but you don't call me back. You don't come home. I just got out of the hospital. I had a miscarriage, B, and it's all because of that bitch, Aoki."

B Scientific was confused. "Hospital? After what happened?"

"Aoki and some bitches came to our home, to our front door, and they attacked me. They disrespected your home. They took away our baby!" she exclaimed.

He was wide-eyed with shock. Aoki wouldn't do anything so foolish. How did she even know where he lived? He didn't get any messages from Brandi, and she had never said she was pregnant. Was she trying to get him to react violently toward his mistress? B Scientific was ready to stomp a mudhole in her ass for lying to him. Screaming about a baby and miscarriage was nothing to play with.

Brandi tossed some papers at him, and they fell to the floor.

B Scientific picked them up, scanned over them quickly, and saw the name of the hospital. It clearly showed they were discharge papers. Then he noticed the hospital bracelet around her wrist.

"I didn't know I was pregnant until that day, B Scientific. I didn't know," she cried out, dropping to her knees, her tears falling like raindrops.

B Scientific couldn't hide his pain. He was flooded with emotions. Aoki had done enough—first the rosary and now the miscarriage.

"Baby, I'm gonna fuckin' fix this," he said, contempt in his voice.

He snatched open the closet door, went inside and got two large guns—Desert Eagle .50 cal.—and he stormed out of the house.

Brandi she smiled devilishly as she sat on the floor. "Fuck wit' me, bitch, you die!"

※

AZ was on Stanley Avenue politicking with his peoples. He was posted against his Benz and drinking E&J, trying to drink his worries away. He wanted to try and forget about Aoki. She had hurt him a lot. He just wanted to focus on his business and continue to get money.

Heavy Pop was by his side. The two were enjoying the sunny summer afternoon with plans of going to the strip club later that night. They had money to burn and some time to waste.

"You good, my nigga?" Heavy Pop asked.

"Yeah, I'm good." AZ took a sip of liquor and checked for messages on his phone. Nothing.

Local niggas were joking around, smoking a blunt and talking shit. Alvarez, one of their friends, was sharing his most recent sexual escapade with the group, going into details about some bitch he'd fucked the night before.

"Yo, that bitch pussy was so big," he said, "I almost fell down the rabbit hole. You feel me? Yo, I'm fuckin' this bitch from the back, and the bitch got some wet pussy, but—"

"Nigga, you just got a small dick," one of his friends quipped, creating strong laughter among everyone.

AZ laughed. He took another swig as he observed the black Range Rover coming their way. It had to be B Scientific. They hadn't seen each other around lately, both busy with their own worlds.

AZ locked eyes on the vehicle, coming their way slowly. He could see B Scientific seated in the passenger seat with the windows down. It looked like he was going to stop and maybe have a few words with AZ.

AZ managed to smile. If he wanted Aoki, then he could have the bitch. He was done with her.

As the Range Rover crawled closer their way, AZ was ready to greet him with respect and kindness. Then he noticed the harrowing look on B Scientific's face and his right arm extended from the passenger window with a Desert Eagle attached to it.

AZ was caught completely off guard. What he heard was, "This is from Aoki."

What B Scientific said was, "This is for Aoki," and then he opened rapid fire on the unsuspecting group. *Boom! Boom! Boom! Boom! Boom! Boom! Boom!*

The gunfire sent everyone scattering in different directions.

AZ hit the ground swiftly and took cover behind his Benz. The .50 cal. put large holes in his side door and shattered his glass. He could feel the shots whizzing by him. "What the fuck!" he muttered, scared shitless.

Then just like that, the gunfire ended, and B Scientific was gone.

AZ caught a glimpse of the Range Rover turning the corner erratically, leaving hell behind. He picked himself up from the ground.

It seemed like everyone was okay, but then he got the shock of his life when he saw Heavy Pop on the ground bleeding badly, shot twice in the chest and side.

"Heavy!" AZ shouted, hurrying to his friend's aid. He dropped down near his fallen friend and scooped him into his arms. "Yo, you gonna be all right, Heavy Pop. You gonna be okay. Just stay wit' me. Someone call nine-one-one!" he screamed out.

Heavy Pop was eventually rushed to the hospital. It was unclear to everyone if he was going to live or die.

AZ couldn't believe it. Did Aoki place a hit out on him? Did she get B Scientific to do her dirty work? Did she fuck him too? He was furious. He didn't know what to believe. But he knew one thing for sure. It was on.

EPILOGUE

After Aoki had calmed herself down, she frantically tried to get in contact with Emilio, but he wasn't taking any of her phone calls, nor was he anywhere to be found. She went looking for him at NYU, but she couldn't find him. It was after midnight when she finally made it back to her place.

Her phone had been ringing nonstop all day; B Scientific, AZ, Connor, but no Emilio. She parked her ride and was on the phone with Rihanna. She was stricken with grief and sadness when she heard the news about Heavy Pop. He was in critical condition at Brookdale Hospital, and AZ and B Scientific were at war with each other.

"They sayin' the target was AZ," Rihanna said to her.

"Why?"

"I don't know. But shit 'bout to heat up around here, Aoki, fo' real."

Aoki had already told B Scientific that she wasn't leaving AZ for him, and no one knew about their recent differences. The hood still thought they were together as a couple. Why would B Scientific want AZ dead? She felt it had to be a drug beef.

Then she thought about something else, something that made her sick to her stomach. She was in a quandary. Aoki was sure AZ would hire her and her crew to kill B Scientific. Which was something she couldn't do, no matter how much money he offered her.

She also couldn't let B Scientific murder AZ. She wasn't about to stand for that. Yes, she and AZ weren't talking, and they'd had some harsh words between them, but he was still her friend. She wasn't about to let anything happen to him.

While on the phone with Rihanna, Aoki had the urge to call AZ and hear from the horse's mouth what was going on between him and B Scientific.

"Ri-Ri, me gonna call ya back. I'm gon' call AZ."

"Okay, do that and give me a call back."

Aoki was dialing AZ's number as she approached her home. When she got out of the car, something caught her attention—a shadow in the alleyway near her home.

A dark figure looming behind her exclaimed, "Yo, you like to play games, bitch?"

Aoki turned in the direction of the voice and found herself staring down the barrel of a pistol. Before she could react or speak, she heard intense gunfire.

Pop! Pop! Pop!

Aoki dropped to the pavement. When she opened her eyes, she saw AZ gasping for air.

She cried out, "W-w-why?"

FOLLOW
NISA SANTIAGO

FACEBOOK.COM/NISASANTIAGO

INSTAGRAM.COM/NISA_SANTIAGO

TWITTER.COM/NISA_SANTIAGO

MAFIO$O

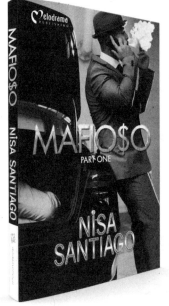

Ambitions as a Mobster

Scott West and his wife Layla have an infatuation with the Mafioso way of life. Armed with what they've learned, they assemble their own family based on the careers of the most successful mobsters and are now in charge of a powerful crime family. Their six children—Meyer, Bugsy, Lucky, Bonnie, Clyde, and Gotti—are all being groomed to manage the family business.

Al Capone's legacy taught Scott to run his drug empire upon fear, helping him prosper as a daunting opponent. When challenged by Deuce, the daring Baltimore crime boss, Scott has to play the game for real as they clash in a mob-style power struggle. When the smoke clears, only one will have a seat at the head of the table.

The enthralling new series by Nisa Santiago